# THE GUARDIAN'S HEART

## LOST SOULS BOOK ONE

# GABRIEL LEA

# DISCOVER WHERE IT ALL BEGAN...

## Download Book zero for free.

Visit www.gabriellea-author.com. You'll also get an official illustrated copy of The Soul Guardian's Code, plus a replica of the original monograph of all known go-lite powers and their properties. Or if you just want to hang out and chat, you can find me on Instagram, Goodreads, Facebook or Pinterest. Gabriel x

No soul will ever be alone.
No voice will go unheard.
I am a guardian of souls,
a light in the darkness, and
I will watch over them.

The Soul Guardian's vow

# A HARSH AND BEAUTIFUL TRUTH

I have seen human suffering in all of its spawning variations and there are as many expressions as there are stars crowding the sky. Just as a star is born of dust and debris, suffering is born from the debris of your longing. It swirls in your mind, gains momentum from rage, collides with your fears and blazes to life. I've gazed upon many 'stars', so to speak, tiny pricks of light struggling to be seen through infinite black. They might all appear the same from a distance, but viewed closely, are as varied and unique as a fingerprint. Some rage white hot and blue; others simmer a slow, pale yellow; others a deep, lonely red, but all eventually collapse and burn out in the end. When your suffering is spent and dull dust and ash are all that remain, only then can you understand that you never really lost anything at all, but gained something infinitely brighter – compassion.

# ONE

The clock ticked relentlessly on my dresser. I'd been lying awake listening to it for so long that I'd begun to imagine it was scolding me. *Tsk ... Tsk... Tsk ... Tsk ... Tsk !* I shook my head and forced my eyes open even wider. There was no way I was going to let a clock, a heartless collection of moving metal cogs, bully me into sleeping before I was ready. I needed to savour a few more moments of peace before I drifted off to sleep. I knew I'd have to give in eventually and close my eyes  but I wasn't ready to face what would happen when I did, not quite yet. Besides, was it really so terrible of me to keep them waiting, just this once, after spending the last two hundred and fourteen nights helping to save them? *Two-hundred-and-fourteen-nights, two-hundred-and-fourteen-Souls. Yes, I'd been keeping count.*

I rolled over to hug the spare pillow on my bed and gazed out the open window as an owl sent its call into the night, slicing the stillness in two. A yellow moon was hanging from the belly of a black cloud like a ripe, golden fruit, dangling from an unreachable bough. I purposely avoided looking at the time on my judgemental, persnickety clock but I knew how late it was because the scent of midnight jewels were wafting through my window. The minute, white flowers only opened for a few short hours after midnight, their waxy petals reflecting the moonlight and making them gleam like gemstones. Unlike me, I doubted Christian or Sky were lying awake right now. They seemed to take Soul Guardian duty in their stride.

I really did want to help all those poor, lost human Souls. Not just because it was my duty, but because I saw what they went through and I wanted to bring as much hope and comfort to them as I could. But, I also wished that every once in a while, I could take just one night off and remember what it was like to have pleasant dreams. I longed to sleep soundly and dream of blissful things, or not dream of anything at all, but that was a glorious luxury that had ceased the day I became a Soul Guardian and took my vows. My sleep-scape belonged to struggling humans now. Instead of blissful dreams, their myriad minds with their pain, insecurity and disillusionment had become my night-time companions. Every night they cried out for assistance or long forgotten answers or just an end to it all.

Humans were so terribly complicated. Much more than I had ever imagined they would be. When it came to the functioning of their hearts and minds they were almost the antithesis of go-lites, but I supposed that if they were like us, they wouldn't need our help in the first place.

As my father had once told me without prejudice or judgement, 'Humans know so little of what they carry inside.' The day he looked into my eyes and uttered that wisdom, I had barely an inkling of how deep the truth of it ran. I had just taken my vows along with twenty-seven others before the Council of Elders. We had all stood beneath the cut crystal ceiling of Ophanim Dome, decked out in our white ceremonial robes, while pearlescent light poured through from above lighting the chamber. Our voices, bright and hopeful, had resonated through the crystal dome like the clinking of glasses. We were all in our twentieth year, we had come of age and it was time for our Soul Guardian duties to begin.

After the ceremony, my father had wrapped me in an all-encompassing embrace and gazed upon me with such loving pride, I'd felt like Panacea's greatest treasure. But, I am not unique and I am not special. I am not a god or an angel, I'm just an ordinary girl, and like every other go-lite on our planet I'd been in training for Soul Guardianship since birth. His hand had felt so warm on my shoulder as he gifted me those all important words. His hazel eyes had glistened, warring between sadness and hope, and darting through memories of things that could never be unseen. I hadn't understood that look then. Now, it was a different story.

It had been six months since the ceremony - *two hundred and fourteen nights to be exact* - and I knew that with practice and patience the Source would grant me the wisdom to thrive as a Soul Guardian. I just wasn't quite there yet which was why I was tossing and turning in my bed, chasing away sleep, because it was the only way I could avoid the inevitable for a little while longer.

I sat up in bed, plumping my pillow for the hundredth time and flopped back down. I should have been asleep hours ago. I had potions class at *magistrument* tomorrow and, as usual, Master Heilus would be expecting great things from me. My mother had been his star pupil in her day and he said that no other since had shown such 'adroit aptitude for the concoction of elixirs. Until now,' he had added with a wink, his bushy eyebrows wagging. *Now, if only I could rustle up an adroit aptitude for making myself go to sleep!*

Unable to put it off any longer, I closed my eyes and prepared myself, as I'd been taught. It didn't take them long. Within seconds, an endless cue of struggling human Souls appeared. Wisps of broken voices and hazy, cracked images swirled through my mind's eye. There were so many. It really was as though they'd been waiting for me to close my eyes. A small boy was cowering in a corner with trembling hands, trying to shield his head from a bloody fist. I saw a man listening to a doctor tell him he had roughly four months to live. A woman was wailing and rocking in the dirt. She was clutching something in a torn, dirty rag. It was her dead baby. More and more people crowded into my mind, their sad scenes blooming and blurring in horror and confusion.

I drew in a sharp breath. I could feel my sense of peace starting to slip so I sent a silent prayer to the One Source to give me the strength to do my duty. The answering warmth was immediate, sedating. It flowed around me and through me, allowing the fragmented pictures of so many humans to sift through my subconscious like soft powder. I sighed with relief and gratitude and nestled further into my pillow. I felt light, weightless, a single feather set adrift in the endless expanse of the universe, knowing that I would float in my sleep to whichever Soul on Earth needed me the most. Now that I was filled with the strength of the One Source, I could watch it all with peaceful detachment and wait to be shown which of these Souls I would be soothing tonight. I breathed slowly and evenly, waiting to feel a *pull* toward the one I could serve best.

Through the melee of sadness and struggle I noticed a strange pinprick of light far off in the distance. It shone steadily, its pale beam reaching out to me like a still beacon cutting through the chaos. *Curious.* I'd never seen anything like it before but I could feel the *pull* that I'd been waiting to sense so I trusted my instincts and drifted forward. I followed its thread, wondering what it was and what it meant as I moved through the wash of Souls. I floated on the black ether of my sleep-scape as the snapshots into their lives dissipated around me like smoke, until there was nothing except the lone light glowing through still black.

In all the endless hours of training for Soul Guardianship, I had never heard of anything like this happening. Connecting with a human was usually a straightforward process. The Soul Guardian would drift off to sleep, glimpses of suffering Souls would appear in their mind's eye and the Source would guide them to a Soul to help. So where did all the Souls go and what in the Source's name was this light?

I squinted, trying to make out who or what was at the end of that beam as I drifted nearer. Then I heard a low hum, a single, vibrating note that went through my entire body. It was becoming louder and more intense and suddenly an image flashed in my mind: a pair of tortured, pale green eyes. I gasped and froze. Those eyes were eerily familiar, yet I couldn't place them. I hung there, staring into their depths. They held so much pain that it felt like a numbing physical weight and I shivered as though someone had walked over my grave. I hovered there, transfixed, trying to understand what was happening when a shocking pain twisted through my heart. I let out a pained and frightened yelp and recoiled. The sheer intensity of it stole my breath away and catapulted me backwards through the blackness.

I clutched at my chest, breathing hard. The calm connection I had felt with the Source was completely gone. Without it, I felt vulnerable, exposed. I could feel the emotion of fear starting to take control. I had to get my connection to Source back. I had to balance and focus. *Fear is nothing but an energy,* I told myself. *It is only as strong as the power I give it.*

Before I had a chance to balance myself and reconnect, I was yanked forward again. It felt like being pulled along by a strong current and I didn't know how to make it stop. Instead of slipping effortlessly through the silken blackness to the person in need, I felt like I was caught in a riptide being sucked out to sea! Icy pins pricked at my skin and my body began rattling with cold. A weight was pressing around me as though I was immersed in water, yet my hair and clothes felt dry. I frantically searched all around me but saw only soft, black ether and straight ahead, the beam of light. I did the only thing I could do and focussed my attention there.

I was no longer sliding smoothly through infinite space, my body was rocking and tossing on an increasing, invisible swell. I tried to steady my nerves and make calm sense of what was happening and came up blank. I was convinced I could smell the salt and taste the brine. The cold sting of it whipped at my face. Persistent waves rose and fell, tossing me like a cork on their torrid surface. I could feel it but I couldn't see any of it, I could only see black. I drew in a shaky breath. All I could do was trust that I was protected and that no harm would come to me. It was much easier said than done.

I could hear the waves now, roaring and squalling. They climbed higher and higher, reaching out for heaven and then shattering down in a thunderous mess, spewing salt and spray. I heard a guttural roar building in the distance. It rumbled closer, like a wild animal rapidly closing on its cornered prey. The immense wall of water lunged, and its jaws came down around my helpless form. It drove me under with furious force and the roar was immediately extinguished. I tumbled repeatedly through the echo of the roar from above, not knowing which way was up or down, wafting through the thick, fluid sounds of submersion.

I desperately tried to right myself, looking for the beam of light to guide me. Fear was sounding an alarm in my mind and telling me to kick to the surface. My body finally stopped tumbling and I found the light. As soon as I did, that piercing gaze overtook my mind again. As I reconnected with the intensity of those eyes, there was nothing I could do but surrender to them. I stared into their bottomless depths like I was looking into a watery grave. They were beautiful... mesmerizing. Their hypnotic pull drew me closer like a silent song and I sailed on like a ghost bound to its past.

A spellbinding peace washed over me as I drifted closer. My limbs floated in slow motion through the softness, then without warning, the green deep sucked me down fast like it was swallowing a bullet, obliterating the warm cradle of euphoria that had enveloped me a moment ago. The speed made a blur of me. My insides felt like they'd been left behind and I could barely see a thing through the rush of water. I had never been drawn to a human this way before or with such urgent force. I shot along the slipstream towards my target and after what seemed mere seconds, stuttered to a halting stop inside a dim, dusty room. I sucked in a great lung-full of air even though I was never underwater at all. My body swayed, dizzy from the intensity of speed. The roar of water had vanished, the crush of it; gone. I was perfectly dry despite having almost drowned in an invisible sea and the light that had brought me here had vanished. *Had I imagined all of that?*

I looked up to see a lank figure lying motionless on a sagging couch. I could still feel the overwhelming pull towards this Soul. He smarted back tears as they welled up like tidal waves to envelop the two soft, green worlds residing in his perfect face. Although I was right in front of him now, I knew he couldn't see me. The veil between worlds made that impossible but I'd often encountered human Souls that could sense my presence even if they didn't have the proof of seeing me with their own eyes. They knew us as a soft voice in their heads, like the whisper of a butterfly's wings; or a flush of lightness that lifts their wounded hearts; or a silent breath that cocoons them in stillness, stopping time and bringing peace, if only for a little while.

I listened intently trying to hear the source of this human's wordless pain. There was only silence, as though a great wall had quickly been erected to hold back the tide with practiced precision and careful purpose. I waited patiently, just as I had been taught, for his questions. He had only to ask for my help and I would give it freely. The silence was never a good sign. I'd come to recognize it as the quiet resignation that often spelled defeat. I could feel the burden on his shoulders, the effort and struggle of this dense world weighing him down. I looked to the light inside his Soul. It was burning very low; a melancholy glow where a blinding radiance should have been. I was here to ensure it didn't go out. My wish was to see every human Soul blazing so brilliantly, that they could no longer deny or fail to see how magnificent they truly were.

Everything was very still. He was very still. The room bore no air of turmoil, just that quiet resignation. It was small, modestly furnished, with pale mint walls and dusty polished boards that had lost their lustre long ago. His tall frame was splayed on a threadbare couch with one foot carelessly thrown onto the wooden coffee table. It was a litter of magazines; the subscription kind from Greenpeace, WSPA and the like. From the far wall, a television flickered mutely. No doubt the journalist on the screen was relaying Earth's latest atrocities. This world was nothing like mine, and yet, it had the potential to be.

My home town, Citrine, was truly beautiful. Through every meandering lane, there was evidence of the artist's hand, from the street sculptures wearing mantles of moss, to the crystal mosaics set into walls, to the ancient symbols pressed into sidewalks. There was colour everywhere. Life sprang from every crevice. Between stout cottages and tall terraces, prolific greenery spilled from vertical garden walls like the lush tresses of Mother Nature herself. It was a city dreamt up by sages and visionaries, and born on the backs and belief of the people. In my world there was a flowing circle of respect that bonded all things. For us, it was as natural and instinctive as drawing breath.

An exasperated sigh escaped the boy's lips as he shifted restlessly on the couch. I watched a whirlpool of thoughts spiral in his mind. I glimpsed a horror house of memories from his childhood; the mounting bills he couldn't pay; an empty bed where his lover had once lay, her face, her laugh, her beautiful smile. The thoughts pierced like knives – every single one. *Just ask and I can help you,* I whispered to him. Nothing coherent came back, just fragmented memories that repeated in his mind and served no purpose other than to wound him further.

His eyes were closed and I wondered if he was about to fall asleep. If he did, it would certainly make things easier for me. A sleeping mind was an open mind. If he was asleep, I could easily slip in and lend him guidance through his dreams. *How lucky humans were to be allowed to dream.*

His breathing was metered through clenched teeth. The muscles were held taut in his neck and stubble shadowed his jawline making it look sharply angular. I traced the line to the centre of his chin and up to the curve of his lower lip. Its pale, softness seemed out of place. His complexion reflected a lifetime in the sun: rich and olive. Those hypnotic green eyes were now shuttered behind relaxed eyelids and a mess of sandy, tousled hair hung limply over one deep line that was carved vertically between his eyebrows. As I mapped every angle and curve, something was gnawing at me. It wasn't just his eyes that were familiar, *everything* about him was, but at the same time unknowable, like trying to cling to a fading dream at daybreak.

As I waited silently, I sorted through dim recollections of the hundreds of human Souls I had encountered in my work so far, trying to place him. There were so many people, so many stories. I don't know how long I'd been staring at his face when the afternoon sun leaked between the shady trees outside and poured through the grotty window. The dirt clinging to the glass created patterns of light that danced across his features and glinted off the hidden tawny streaks in his hair. He inhaled deeply and surrendered a sigh. His voice was a monotone whisper addressed to the peeling paint on the ceiling. "I don't want to be here anymore. I don't belong." He was decided, resigned. There wasn't any hint of self-pity in his words. He could just as well have been ordering a cup of coffee – *black, no sugar.* I'd heard similar declarations from many human Souls before, but they always sprang from deep wells of pain and were spoken in times of utter despair. His just sounded like the simple truth and I found myself being drawn even closer to him.

Usually, human emotions were felt as a tugging at the fringes of your heart. We felt compassion for the human condition, not the emotions themselves. We could feel them and understand them, but we never held onto them. A Soul's emotions belonged to them and them alone. Nor did we get caught up in the webs that emotions wove. So why was I finding it so hard to let this boy's emotions go?

I took in a deep, cleansing breath to steady my focus and regain my composure. This entire encounter had rattled me. I wondered if it was normal to be affected this way sometimes? Perhaps the plight of some Souls required more energy than others to remain impartial? Granted, I was still new at this but I'd been in training since birth. The Elders certainly wouldn't have appointed me if I wasn't ready. I reminded myself to breathe and recited the Guardians' Code of Conduct in my head. I was up to rule four – a Guardian sees only light in the heart of every Soul and helps them to remember, recognise and bring forth that light – when he spoke again.

"Why do I have to be here? What's the point? This is a shitty world. I don't understand it and no-one understands me."

My reply came with absolute certainty. "You're here because you chose it." My voice was clear and even. He would hear me as neither male or female, no distinguishing features, just a voice; smooth and calm in his mind.

"Ha! Why would anyone choose this?" he bellowed, rising from the couch. "People are cruel, selfish and crazy! I feel like an alien... I feel alone." His voice cracked on the last word and faded to a whisper.

My reply was immediate. "How will you ever recognise true joy unless you've first experienced true sorrow? Light cannot exist without shadow."

Focussing my intent on his immediate surroundings, I willed warm energy to flow around him. The air glittered with a thousand tiny sparks that gravitated to his side and then swirled and encircled him from head to toe. The tiny points of light vibrated a pure angelic note. They hung in the air momentarily and dispersed into a fine gold mist that seeped into his skin and brought life to the air he breathed. His features softened as the despair drained from his body and the light returned to his eyes. He stood in the centre of the silent room and I watched his chest rise and fall with a bit more ease.

A rustling sound caught his attention at the open window. A beautiful bird with rainbow feathers had alighted on the sill. It looked almost the same as a sapient bird from home. They were clever little things. They knew how to weave the sturdiest of nests to weather any storm and protect from any enemy. They tended the nest over the course of their lifetime, repairing as needed and making it stronger. If it had been built wisely enough and treated with care, it would still be hatching eggs for generations to come.

Now, this clever little bird, whose name I did not know, was boldly perched on the sill, staring at the boy as though it wanted to be invited in... had even expected it. The boy was frozen in place, not wanting to frighten off his visitor. They merely looked at one another for a minute, maybe two, but neither one moved. Eventually, an accepting smile twitched at the boy's lips and he faded from my view as the window into his world closed and the veil came down.

# TWO

I woke up with a sharp gasp and sprang upright in my bed. I sat and blinked a few times, trying to clear my head, then slumped back down, confused by what had happened and wondering if I'd succeeded in helping him. *What a bizarre encounter!* I had absolutely no idea what to make of it. My view into his world had cut off abruptly so I didn't know if I'd managed to do any good at all.

I needed a shower. I tried to swing my legs over the side of the bed, only to wind up face down on the floor with my legs securely tangled in the sheets. I must have been really thrashing around last night. *Ah, that's right... 'drowning'.* I flopped there for a second, laughing, then reached down to untangle my cottony shackles. I dragged my weary body upright and plodded to the bathroom. I felt weighted down somehow and a little off-balance. Maybe I was getting sick.

The pale creature staring back at me in the star shaped mirror only confirmed my suspicion. My hair was just as tangled as my sheets had been so I took to it with the brush and spun it up into a loose knot on the top of my head. I splashed cold water on my face, pausing to feel the clear rivers trickle off the end of my nose and chin and snuggled my damp face into the towel's soft loops. It smelt like sunshine from hanging on the clothesline a day too long.

♡ ♡ ♡

"Good morning, Lilly! Sleep well?" Sky chirped, as I was drawn to the kitchen by delicious wafts of freshly brewed coffee.

"I think so," I yawned. Sky's early morning cheer was as reliable as the sunrise. Having moved from cold, snowy Endua just four short years ago, Sky had discovered that a day can actually mean more than five hours of sunlight. Consequently, she never took a single ray for granted and made sure she was awake to catch every one. She was an incredibly cheery morning person – something I had managed to adapt to over time.

"You look a bit... wrung out," she observed.

"Well, we can't all be morning people, can we?" I raised an eyebrow and slumped into the chair.

Her returning smile widened as she swept across the kitchen and spun back setting a plate of fresh fruit on the table. She slipped into the chair opposite me.

"Eat up," she encouraged.

"But I want coffee… and chocolate… is there any chocolate cake left?"

"No, there isn't," she released an exasperated sigh, "because you already ate it all. *This,* however, is fresh from Bertie's farm this morning." She gave the plate a determined shove towards me.

Sky was forever fussing about my diet. I saw nothing wrong with eating cake upon waking. What were muffins, if not little cakes masquerading as breakfast? They had eggs and butter and milk – perfectly respectable. "You've been out already?" I shouldn't have been surprised. "What time is it?" I asked, feeling a bit disoriented.

"Lilly, it's 10am," she raised an eyebrow. "I looked in on you before I left for class at seven, but you were out like a light. Should I have woken you?"

"Oh." I'd not realised how late I'd slept. I'd completely missed potions class. Master Helius would not be amused. The green-eyed boy's beautiful face flashed into my mind. "No, no, I'm glad you didn't wake me," I reassured her. "You're right though, I do feel a bit zapped of energy. I think I'll just go to afternoon class today."

She placed her elbow on the table and propped her gamine face on her hand. Sky was tall and lissome with skin like a china doll and huge eyes of glassy blue, dripping with impossibly long lashes. Her dead straight, black hair framed her face in a sharp pixie cut and was so glossy it threw rainbows in the sun. "Rough night?" she asked surveying my dishevelled state.

"It was actually," I rubbed at my tired eyes, "new and… unusual." It was the only way I could describe nearly being drowned by a human Soul in an invisible ocean.

"Well," she shrugged, "we're still very new little Guardians in training. I'm sure it becomes easier… eventually."

Everyone said the first year of Soul Guardianship was the hardest. I wasn't sure I would ever completely understand humans. Our world, Panacea, was free of the bonds of suffering that plagued Earth. That world was a million light years away, and yet, each night Soul Guardians all over Panacea invited the surreal and abstruse into the intimate space of their dreams to uphold the oaths they had made. They didn't see it as a chore or a burden, it was just the way of our world. They did it gladly because in truth, every earthbound Soul suffers… more than anyone ever sees or knows… and more than they want to admit. Suffering is an inescapable part of what it means to be human; a common thread that binds Souls together.

Lately I'd been wishing that humans could see me when I whispered words of wisdom or comfort into their minds. If they knew that go-lites watched over them and had done so since Earth's inception, it would alleviate so much of their pain just to know someone cared. So why couldn't they see us? Why did they have to take it on faith that help was out there? Especially when it seemed to me that humans didn't believe in much of anything anymore. How could they be expected to believe in us, when at their lowest, they couldn't even believe in themselves?

"Maybe you should go up to the crystal pools and soak for a while," she waved at me with her free hand while nibbling on a wedge of lyla melon with the other. She somehow made it look graceful. Sky made *everything* look graceful. She had a feline way about her. There was such a precise elegance to her every move that I wondered if she hadn't been a tiger in a previous life… or perhaps a well-loved tabby. Then, of course, there was her obvious resemblance to a cat basking in the sun whenever she was worshipping the rays. Although she was always kind and bright spirited and what others referred to as 'such a lovely person', she could muster some sass when she had to. Sky was nobody's fool. She was intelligent and watchful and quite capable of conjuring a regal, prowling air when it served. She was turning it on me now, as she tapped a fingernail on the table, waiting for my response.

"Hmm, I think I will," I told her. The thought of floating in the healing waters of the mountain pools brought an immediate smile to my face. "Then I have class this afternoon and a three-hour shift at *healaxis* tonight, so I won't be home until late." I wondered if Healer Cray would have me treating patients this evening.

"Wow, big day. Do you need me to do the rest of the shopping then?"

"No, it's fine. I'll go after I've been to the pools."

"All right, I'm off to meditate, so I'll see you later."

"Okay, see you."

She rose fluidly from her seat and paused. "And Lilly, I've hidden the chocolate cookies in a different place, so don't bother trying to find them."

She swept through the glass doors that led to the circular garden we had lovingly planted and tended together. This beautiful and cosy home had been ours since the commencement of our first *magistrument* year, which was similar to Earth's universities. While I toiled away with the study of potions, herbs and energy medicine, Sky was studying elemental magic. She possessed a natural gift for manipulating the elements of fire, water, earth, air and ether. I smiled as I watched her sashay along the uneven stepping stones that meandered their way through tufts of fragrant and medicinal herbs. Fire Leaf for muscular aches and pains; Healer's Hand for accelerated healing of broken bones, soft tissue tears and open wounds; Hichter Balm, Silver Cress, Verlanis Flower and Petchin Root were the most common administrations for viral infections; Orin for clearing the vision, both physically and intuitively. I wished our garden was bigger. I could only grow a minute selection of the thousands of flowers, roots, barks and leaves that formed the basis of the herbal healing arts. As it was, Sky had to fight me for space to plant the rainbow of flowers she was unable to grow in dreary Endua.

The outer border of the garden was a tangle of magnolias, wisteria and creeping vines of night blooming jasmine. A tall, natural fence of thick bamboo encircled it, affording complete privacy. Sky had positioned herself in the centre of the soft, circular lawn that formed the heart of the garden. Her lithe body was arranged cross-legged on the meditation cushion I'd bought for her last birthday. It was an ornate patchwork of bright, bold colours embroidered with lustrous thread. Each square depicted teachings and symbols of go-lite philosophies and our way of life.

I was so privileged to be born on Panacea, to live in a world where all life is respected as precious and equal to our own. We took only what we needed from the land, wasting nothing and polluting little. Destructive human inventions like plastic and nuclear weapons were foreign and unnecessary to us. I thought of the green-eyed boy and imagined how amazed he would be by my world. I had seen how he cared about the thoughtless way humans treated their world and the creatures in it. I had felt how he struggled to fit in. I imagined how excited he would be to see homes and vehicles powered by the sun, the wind and the rain, to see a world whose people considered themselves honoured guests, loath to place unrealistic demands on their host.

Panacea was everything that Earth had the potential to be and go-lites had an integral part to play in helping humans realise that. I wondered if the human Souls on Earth would ever realise that if they continue to bleed their host dry, she would forcefully remove them for good? I sighed and finished my brunch in silence, trying not to think of this or any other challenges the humans on Earth were there to learn through and overcome.

I popped a lush, purple berry into my mouth and it exploded between my teeth dripping thick, perfumed syrup onto my tongue. It was so delicious it made me laugh! It was like a happiness bomb! How could one tiny berry hold so much joy? I imagined launching a berry bomb assault on Earth – a worldwide air raid where countless billions of berries were dropped in a hail of purple as people ran around, dancing and laughing, covered in exploded, purple berry goo. I sighed. If only it were that simple.

♡ ♡ ♡

It would take me around twenty minutes to drive to the crystal springs, I could soak for an hour, and I'd still have time to finish the shopping before class this afternoon. I turned left at the end of my street to cut across town, which was the quickest route.

My city, Citrine, sprang from a purple valley, hedged by paper mountains in three directions. In the fourth, a gateway lay open to the silver sea. Scribbled around the city's edges, an emerald vein of river almost made the shape of a heart. Throughout the city, ornate tin rooftops capped the snug sprawl of houses, all tinged with an antique patina. For miles they stretched in blue and green, looking like a patchwork of floating fields.

From them, copper weathervanes sprouted in a metal menagerie of leaping stags, gargantuan insects, and nature sprites. There were thundering horses, coiling sea serpents, cunning foxes and every other winged, finned and furred creature imaginable, only coming to life at the whim of the wind. The little cottage where Sky and I lived had a whole universe spinning atop it, complete with a host of crooked stars and pressed copper discs for planets that orbited on rickety, well-worn arms. The fascination with weathervanes was not exclusive to Citrine. Visit any town in any country on Panacea and you'd be met with a similar sight. Go-lites believed that you should always mind which way the wind was blowing, lest you be carried off your rightful path and lose your way.

Beneath their menagerie-like roofs, houses were artfully assembled from an eclectic array of weathered wood, sandstone, stained glass and iron lace. All resources were regarded as precious so whenever materials could be recycled, they were. Some houses sat like jewelled boxes, others like up-side-down teacups, all jumbled together, lining cobblestone streets in rows reminiscent of mismatched babushka dolls.

In the centre of it all, Ophanim Dome gleamed; a luminous egg, nested amongst candy coloured emporiums and brindled stone buildings adorned with ancient scrollwork. The Dome was the seat of our High Council, comprising thirty-two Elders and three Grand Masters, and was the beating heart of our city. Our world turned under the power of the sun, wind, and rain, and – the most potent of all energies – love.

I left the city behind and drove along kilometres of winding roads etched into the mountainside. The higher I climbed, the denser the rainforest grew. I stopped my little solar powered car at the entrance to the crystal pools' walking track and cut the engine. It was so quiet here I could almost hear my heartbeat. I gathered my backpack and towel from the back seat and headed for a break in the wall of trees where some of the gnarled trunks had parted into a misshapen doorway.

As I crossed the dense threshold, the warm, white light of day surrendered to cool, abundant green. I paused, breathing in the forest and becoming a part of the silence. I began winding my way along the heavy clay path. It was littered with moist decay and the wonderful smell of rich earth released beneath my feet. Leafy arms and lace-like ferns strayed across the path at every angle. Cool fronds delicately brushed my legs, as I stepped quietly and carefully, not wanting to disturb this perfect stillness.

Bellbirds rang through the trees; the high clarity of their song diminished by distance and lost in the ceaseless growth of a thousand years. The very air was iridescent. It felt like the forest had taken a long, deep breath eons ago and held it, knowing that one breath would sustain it forever. Yet underneath that perfect stillness was life: the occasional flutter of small wings; the hypnotic weaving of a spider in its silver web; the silent march of ants up an ancient trunk; a bush rat scurrying for shelter.

Looking up, the towering canopy was striving for the heavens, the trees' majestic heads appearing to bow in reverence of each others' undeniable beauty. I moved slowly down the aisle of the grand, green cathedral. Soft, spears of light pierced the thinning growth and seeped into the forest floor, casting patterns like stained glass windows. As I reached the path's end and emerged from the sanctuary, the smell of peat and moss that had hung thickly in the air gave way to wild mint on a sunlit breeze. I blinked into the white light of the midday sun, trying to readjust my eyes.

My feet found the smooth, warm river stones that sloped gently to a peaceful shore. They clacked happily together as I teetered to the pool's edge and peered into the still water. The crystal pools were usually quiet at this time of day. I had timed my visit well. In the town below, friends and family would be gathering to share company and a hearty midday meal, followed by a leisurely afternoon rest and meditation. For now, I had this glorious sanctuary all to myself. A mere twenty minutes in these magical waters and I'd feel full of life, completely loved and at peace.

I slowly stretched a solitary toe toward the liquid mirror. As it dipped below the surface, languid ripples loped to the opposite shore, caressing the moss covered stones like they were welcoming old friends. Piled behind them was a tumble of shiny black boulders that formed a waterfall in rainy season, their surfaces polished to a high sheen from the swift and constant flow of water. The rocky creek bed wove its way through the rainforest for miles. Tranquil pools like this one could be found all along its path. This was as far as I wanted to go today, though. I wasn't feeling particularly energetic. I smiled at the thought of humans and their artificial swimming pools and shrugged. It didn't make sense to me. I tossed my clothes aside and dove in.

The cool water felt dense as I plunged deep; a comforting pressure enveloping my entire body. A curious penny turtle eyed me and paddled on by as my hands touched on the stoney bottom and I pushed myself back up, bursting through the surface. I breathed in the wild mint and the joy of the moment. I sighed at the pure bliss of it all and floated on my back; effortlessly buoyant, gazing at the slow moving sky – plump, white clouds tinged with ultramarine edges against endless blue. I lay still as the healing waters cradled and soothed me. Each soft ripple against my skin was a mother's touch. I could feel the haze lifting from my mind and my usually sharp focus returning. I felt myself again; re-energised and peaceful.

"Hey there." A rich, silky voice came from above me somewhere. A voice that had been there for as long as I could remember.

I whirled to see Christian standing barefoot on a boulder high above with his arms folded, grinning cheekily. "Chris, you scared me half to death," I laughed, splashing water at him. "Have you no respect?" I scolded. "This is a place of *private* healing."

"Ah, and I suppose throwing the sacred water at other people is perfectly respectful conduct?" He arched a dark eyebrow over the twinkle in his eye that always spelt mischief. "And as for privacy," he said smoothly, "why would you need that when I already know you better than you know yourself?" All teasing left his face and he just stood there smiling his handsome smile.

"Doesn't matter. I was done anyway." I rolled my eyes but couldn't help returning some of the warmth that Chris so freely radiated. He was my closest friend. We'd grown up together, joined at the hip, wreaking havoc wherever we went. He loved telling Sky of our adventures, even the ones that made my cheeks flame. It didn't matter that I knew just as many embarrassing stories about Christian Palladen because nothing ever seemed to embarrass him. He'd always been so confident and sure of himself. Annoyingly so at times.

Once there had been a splinter lodged in my finger. The four-year-old me had defiantly refused to tell my parents or have it removed, even though Christian said it would get worse if I didn't. Days passed and of course, he was right, it festered. It swelled to the point where I couldn't bear to touch it and I had no choice but to ask Chris to pull it out. He snuck into his mother's drawer, while she and my mother sipped tea, retrieved a pair of tweezers and operated. I remember being frightened but Chris held my hand so lightly, all the while murmuring reassurances in his velvet cadence, that I barely felt a thing. The pressure where the wood had been lodged was instantly relieved. "You made it stop hurting!" I'd declared incredulously, blinking into his big, grey eyes as though he'd exacted a minor miracle. Instead of being smug or saying 'I told you so', he'd just smiled and thoughtfully gazed at his handy work before placing a whisper of a kiss on my wounded fingertip, and... I had let him. Even back then, I knew without question, that Christian would never let anything harm me.

"Pass me my towel?" I smiled as I waded back to the smooth basalt shore. He sprang lightly down the dry falls and draped the towel around my dripping shoulders. It had been heated by the warm rocks and I shivered as the toasty pile hugged my skin. "So you came to check up on me because I missed class this morning?" I surmised with a grin.

"Am I that predictable?" he arched a bemused brow. "What a terrible bore I must be. It seems I'll have to work on my spontaneity and charm before you tire of me completely," he smirked.

"Ha! I think you have an infinite well of charm. Ask Petra Honeywell if you don't believe me. You seemed to have her swooning on the campus lawn yesterday."

"Who, me?" He blinked his thick lashes with indubitable surprise. As per usual, he was completely unaware of the devastating effect he had on the opposite sex.

"You know, Christian, you're such a master of sarcasm that one day someone is actually going to believe you're the pompous ass you play so convincingly."

"Never!" he immediately snapped back into 'ass' mode. "My stunning displays of *ass-ery* and efficacious wit are purely reserved for you," he winked.

"Oh, lucky me. I feel so blessed."

"Anyway, you did miss a great lecture. Master Green was discussing the steady decline of community spirit throughout human history and how it's led to feelings of separation on Earth."

I recalled the green-eyed boy's emotional words, *'People are selfish and cruel. I feel alone.'* A wave of compassion washed over me for his struggle and I stared, unspeaking, into the glassy pool. The next thing I heard was my name.

"Lilly, are you okay?" Chris touched my shoulder.

"I'm fine," I answered, my eyes snapping up to meet his. "Just had a heavy night, that's all."

He studied my face. A dark lock of hair fell into his eyes and he raked it back with long fingers. "Anything I can help with?" he asked carefully.

His frame was shielding me from staring directly into the sun as I squinted up into his face. It formed a halo that glowed about him and he looked like a pinup boy for 'Angel Weekly', if there was such a thing. I stifled a laugh – it was so very fitting. "No, I'm okay," I smiled and chased thoughts of the mysterious boy out of my head. "I think the pools have done their job. Is Master Green doing the same lecture again this afternoon?" I asked, changing the subject.

"Yes, at four. If you're thinking of going I might tag along again. Then maybe we could grab some dinner afterward?"

"Sure, sounds great," I nodded.

"Okay, I'll meet you at quarter to outside the great hall."

"All right. Enjoy your privacy," I laughed as he pecked me on the cheek and turned to dive gracefully into the still water.

I wandered back through the forest at a quicker pace trying to relieve my thoughts of the green-eyed boy. Maybe I should have soaked in the pool a bit longer. His words cycled through my mind, each sentiment a cog in a larger machine. The machine groaned through each cog's revolution, as though straining from work that would never be done. Why was I thinking about any of this? He was one of millions of Souls in need of direction and support. One of hundreds I'd listened to and been with in times of distress. I couldn't recall ever being bombarded with thoughts about any of them. It simply wasn't the go-lite way. We lived in the present, not the past. I'd probably never see him again anyway.

An image flashed into my mind of his set jaw and soft lips. I could see him mouthing the words he'd spoken to me. My chest hurt. I involuntarily shook my head to dislodge the memory from my mind and suddenly found myself standing at my car. I had walked for fifteen minutes, yet I couldn't remember a single step.

# THREE

Sky had dumped a shopping list on top of my backpack before I'd left for the pools. I drove slowly back into town, enjoying the quiet emptiness of the mountain roads. My little car hummed happily as we wound through leafy tunnels of damp green which eventually yielded to serene, open fields. Farmers planting their crops waved as we sailed by. I soaked up the scent of freshly tilled earth showing a rich, shocking red against the pale blue sky. I slowed to let a boy cross the road with his herd of fat, happy goats. They ambled lazily in the afternoon sun, clearly in no hurry. When the last had crossed, the boy grinned at me widely and tipped his head in thanks.

I drove on with the windows down and the warm, summer breeze on my face. I was so blissfully happy I sailed right by the Majeston's coffee plantation. Coffee beans were on the top of my list and the Majestons grew the best coffee around. I did a u-turn and headed up the long, dirt driveway that cut through the coffee trees to their family store, roasting sheds and sizeable home. I parked under a tree to shade my car and made my way up onto the weathered, wooden porch. As I opened the colourful stained glass door, which read 'Majeston's Magic' in mosaic glass, the brass bell jingled happily and the intense aroma of coffee beans slipped an arm around my shoulder and guided me inside. Florence Majeston came bustling toward me with her plump arms stretched wide and a smile to match.

"Lilly, my darling girl! How have you been?" She wrapped me in a sponge cake embrace and pulled back to sweep my hair from my eyes and affectionately pat my cheek. She was almost as wide as she was tall, which wasn't very tall at all, and I remembered that when she hugged me as a child I had been afraid of disappearing into her soft, marshmallow sweetness.

"I'm great, Mrs. Majeston, and how are you? Is Mr. Majeston well?" I enquired.

"Yes dear, the ache in his low back is much better with the liniment you made him so he thanks you for the wonderful remedy and I thank you for the improvement in his mood!" She clamped a plump hand to her lips to suppress her giggles.

"Oh, I'm glad," I smiled.

"So what can we get you today?" She cooed, squeezing herself behind the mahogany counter. The wall behind her was a kaleidoscopic display of stained glass jars housing the various roasts. They rested on glossy wooden shelves extending from floor to ceiling, accessible only by an enormous wooden ladder on castors.

"I would like a quarter sack of cocoa roast and a quarter sack of your famous magic roast please."

"Right you are, dear." In a jiffy, she was ascending the ladder with all the grace of a circus trapeze artist and, with a small push off from a plump finger, was gliding across the shelves to a jar at the far side. The castors squeaked like there was a team of mice inside, running for their lives to propel Florence across the room. "How are your parents? I hear your father is being considered to take over Elder Sparks' role when he transitions." Balanced expertly on her tippy toes, she shovelled the aromatic beans into small hessian sacks and fastened the tops in a flurry of hemp twine.

"Yes, he is," I replied. "Mum and I are so proud of him."

"Such an honour," she bubbled, as she seemingly floated down the ladder rungs, "and a well deserved one. Your father is a wise and wonderful man."

I'd had the honour of meeting Elder Sparks when he was last admitted to *healaxis.* As an esteemed member of the high council, which numbered thirty-two Souls, his role was to support the three Grand Masters in their numerous duties of overseeing the well-being of Panacea. He was an elderly gentleman who had served this world tirelessly and it seemed it was almost time for him to pass from this place, transition, and be reborn on Utopia; the next step in a Soul's evolutionary cycle.

"Tell your father that Morton and I wish him the One Sources' blessings," she bubbled, pushing the coffee sacks towards me.

"I will. What do I owe you?"

"Let's see, I'll have another large jar of Morton's liniment and could you possibly make me a slimming potion dear?" She smoothed her palms over the balloon of her skirt.

"Of course," I smiled. I had expected the request. It was always around summertime that Mrs. Majeston decided it was time to lose weight. My mother had been making her slimming potions for years, but since I had become an Acolyte Healer, the task had fallen to me. My potions weren't going to be any more effective than my mother's unless Florence surrendered the jars of berry drops and cocoa cakes she had stashed all around her house. "Can I bring it by next week?"

"We'll be here!" she giggled and wrapped me in another smothering embrace. She smelt like pink sugar.

♡ ♡ ♡

I turned onto the cobblestone drive that marked the entrance to town and searched for a parking spot in the red laneway behind Milton's Cheesemakers. I could hear noise spilling from the town square as I approached the end of the lane. So many voices blending together was like the buzzing of bees, and the market; their field of wildflowers. Tents bloomed in every colour at dawn, only to close again with the fading sun. Bright flags and banners flapped in the breeze, beckoning shoppers to try their wares. Rows of ripe fruit and vegetables formed rainbows on wooden benches, mountains of freshly baked loaves looked like piles of soft pillows and the catch of the day was arranged on avalanches of ice; silvery scales wet and glistening. Aromas of sweet honeycomb, sizzling meats and fragrant herbs mingled on the air with cheerful musical notes drifting from across the square where a young girl played a bamboo pan pipe. I shuffled my way through the lighthearted crowd adding to my bounty as I went. Card readers dispensed celestial guidance from sagging stools, skillful fingers danced over looms of crisp linen cloth, eager children slowed before brightly frosted cakes that looked like fairy castles and promised to be magic on your lips.

The news of my father's nomination had obviously spread quickly. Warm smiles and hearty congratulations were offered by all I passed on my way through the bustling market square. My dad was loved and respected by all who knew him and I was proud to be his daughter. He was my inspiration and my safe harbour. With all of the praise and well wishes, my shopping took twice as long as it should have and I found myself rushing to get to magistrument on time.

When I arrived, the campus was alive with industrious minds engaged beneath carefree faces. Students were scattered about the lawns in colourful array; waving hearty hellos to passing friends, or immersing themselves in lively discussions, or just sitting in quiet contemplation. Everywhere the bright spark of ingenuity awaited its time of birth. My steps traced the border of the deep obsidian pool that dominated the campus lawn; an enormous jet-black rectangle of polished glass that stretched distantly into an arrow. Below the surface were flashes of undulating colour – fish gliding on tails of silk chiffon, fanning out in brilliant tangerine, turquoise, magenta and sapphire, gracefully weaving around the china white lilies like ballroom dancers in swirling, full skirts.

At the end of the pool, a powerful giant watched over the grounds, roots extending in a supportive net for all who walked on campus and colossal branches providing shelter from the elements. The beloved tree had stood vigil for thousands of years, bending with the seasons and never breaking. The ancient one was a reminder that in order to give freely to others we must nurture ourselves by remaining connected to the Source. Developing strong roots gives us the strength to stretch our branches to the heavens.

I hurried along the grand marble hallway, my footsteps bouncing off the high, vaulted ceiling. I reached the Great Hall just in time and shuffled down a crowded row of seats to a vacant spot. I threw my bag under my seat and was searching the room for Chris when Master Green strode onto the dais. The crowd applauded enthusiastically then settled into reverent silence as Chris slipped into the neighbouring seat. He pecked me lightly on the cheek and gave an excited nod toward Master Green.

"Ritual and myth. Therein lies the key to community spirit and a sense of belonging. The Story Tellers of Panacea are charged with the preservation of our histories and the great wealth of our knowledge. They weave knowledge and lessons into colourful tales that are passed down from generation to generation so that all can grow and prosper. That is the gift of Myth. Ritual - when a plant or animal gives its life to sustain us, go-lites give thanks for its gift with the understanding that the life given is most precious indeed. It has the power to nourish us, to keep us alive. It is through the ritual of thanks that we honour that life force.

"The go-lite way of life was once shared by the humans on earth. It began with the cave men and died with the rise of the modern world 2,000 years ago. The humans have lost their way. They have forgotten the importance of ritual and myth, instead, living vicariously through celebrities, communicating through computers and hoarding material possessions to fill their emptiness. They abuse their planet and each other. They do not live in harmony with all that is, they battle in relative isolation trying to preserve their own lives instead of working together. Where is the sense of community? Where is the harmony? Where is the respect for all life and where will this course take them?"

The green-eyed boy leapt into my mind. I wondered what he would think if he could hear what Master Green was saying about his world? I had a feeling that he would not only understand, but agree. I recalled how helpless and frustrated he'd felt. So this was a part of his struggle. How could he live in a world that doesn't share his understanding? Much later, I felt Chris poking my shoulder.

"Hmmm? What?" I mumbled."

I said, what did you think?" he asked eagerly.

"Yeah, it was great," I replied, trying to snap myself back to the present.

"You don't sound overly excited." He was eyeing me quizzically. "Master Green is hands down my favourite lecturer." Chris animatedly relayed the highlights of the lecture while my mind drifted and picked through the last forty minutes of my thoughts about the green-eyed boy. "Don't you think?" I heard him ask.

I hadn't been listening. "I *think* you are definitely Master Green's number one fan as evidenced by attending the same lecture twice in one day," I smirked. "Perhaps we should make you a fan tee-shirt or something."

"I would probably wear it," he quipped. "I think he's absolutely brilliant." His grey eyes were sparkling. "I know! How about a plain white shirt with a giant green love heart on it?" he smiled triumphantly.

"Hmm… subtle," I nodded at him with exaggerated sarcasm.

He looked bewildered. "Well, yes. I actually thought it *was* subtle. We'd be the only ones who knew what it meant."

I started laughing at the mental image of Christian's broad chest sporting a gigantic, green love heart. I was tempted to have it made for him. Yes, I definitely had to. I poked him in the ribs and took off sprinting through the narrow row of chairs. Chris was right on my heels as predicted. It wasn't fair. His six-foot frame effortlessly took the lecture hall's stairs two at a time. He caught me at the top. I squealed as his right arm swooshed around my ribcage and my feet left the floor. He was holding my body tucked to his right side like I was nothing more than a rolled up newspaper. I continued to squeal and protest, arms waving and legs kicking, but he simply ignored me and kept walking. By the time we were nearly at the restaurant, he decided to put me down. My stomach hurt from laughing so much.

It was such a beautiful evening that Chris had decided we should walk to dinner. The summer air was sultry with only an occasional, teasing breeze. We walked side by side in comfortable silence, guided by the warm, honeyed glow of the street lamps. Perfumed jasmine wafted in heady swirls and hidden crickets sang their hypnotic tune, the rhythmic sound of our feet on the pavement punctuating their twilight chorus. A shimmering silver crescent had been pinned low on an indigo sky and delicate moths took flight on powdery wings, casting shadows that danced in the lamplight. With each step I took, another blessing was counted as the night offered up her beauty to me in an enchanted string of wondrous moments.

"I saw your Dad today," Chris said, breaking the silence.

"Oh really? How was he? I have to go over for a visit soon. I've not seen my parents for a couple of weeks." I pulled my best contrite face.

"Yes, he did happen to mention that once or twice," Chris laughed. "He was good. I congratulated him on his nomination for High Council. He deserves it. Amazing man, your Dad."

"I know," I smiled. "I hope I can make he and mum proud."

"You already do," Chris said with matter-of-fact sincerity.

"I know that but they're my parents – they're biased," I shrugged. "I have more responsibility now with Soul Guardian duties. I don't want to mess it up. I just want to do the best I possibly can." In my mind, I saw myself as a small child. Not because my self-doubt made me feel feeble or wanting, but because I remembered how strong and sure I'd been then, when the world had been a simple, intimate friend who only asked that I be joyful.

I remembered tearing through the tall grass without a clue of what was ahead. I'd been bold, fearless, invincible. Where had that girl gone?

I could feel Chris watching me. "Lilly, your 'best' has always been brilliant. You're a chip off the old block," he bumped my shoulder.

"You're one to talk, Mr. Most Likely to Succeed," I retorted, bumping him back. Chris scoffed like I was talking utter nonsense. "No," I said, "I mean it. You're always so confident, Chris. You're strong and smart and passionate, so sure of everything." It came out in a tumble. It was all true.

Chris had been a Soul Guardian for two years now. He had really been there for Sky and me when we were nervous beginners. Always encouraging us and answering any questions we had. Underneath his thick, black hair was a very clever brain with a photographic memory. I was sure he had a whole library stored up there. He was only a few years older than me but sometimes it felt more like twenty.

I looked over at him when he didn't reply. His steel blue eyes were tipped toward the stars, reflecting their silent watch.

"Thank you." It was the deep, soft croon of his true voice; the way he sounded when he wasn't playing the pompous ass. It was open, mellow, round and soft; like a song you wished wouldn't end. There was a lengthy pause, then he turned to me with his mischievous grin.

"Although… it sounds like someone has a crush. I'm thinking that maybe we need to make *you* a fan tee-shirt," he teased.

"I'd probably wear it," I shot back with blunt honesty. "You know I've always looked up to you."

His joking face softened and he considered me in earnest. He took my hands and stepped in front of me, halting our walk. His hands were warm; mine were always so cold. "Lilly," he sighed, "I wish you would see yourself the way I do. Why is it so easy for you to see the truth and beauty of everything, except when it comes to yourself?" Eyes like sheets of slate bore into me. I didn't know if he was expecting an answer. "You're a brilliant enigma that even you can't explain."

It was hard to accept that someone like Chris would see me as brilliant. Puzzling at times, yes; but brilliant? He was in his final year of study and seemed destined to become a Master Teacher one day or even sit on the Council of Elders. I'd often had the feeling that my father was already grooming him for the role. When his parents had retired and moved to a quieter spot a few years ago, my father was more than happy to 'adopt' him in their absence. And why wouldn't he? Christian was charismatic and a born leader, with a passion for wildlife and interpreting signs in nature. From the time he was a small child it was evident that he could communicate with and understand animals with perfect clarity. Animals would gravitate to him, sensing his attunement, and relax in his presence as though he were one of their own. It was nothing to find him meditating in the company of an owl or silently conversing with a wolf. To him, it was as natural as breathing. He was among a distinguished few who possessed the gift of Translation so strongly.

I looked into his eyes, trying to guess exactly what he saw when he looked at me. Could he hear my thoughts as clearly as a creature with wings or hooves? Were they like a darting deer, a lonely eagle, or a frightened rabbit? We stood silent for a moment and then I saw a familiar flicker of mischief pass over his expression. He let my hands slip from his and shook his head with a pitying sigh. "The reason you've always looked up to me, Lilly," he paused for dramatic effect, "is because you don't have a choice in the matter: you're so tragically and ridiculously short."

We both burst out laughing. I was, in fact, not tragically short. It just appeared that way from Christian's elevated point of view. But I was grateful for the laughter.

♡ ♡ ♡

A superb dinner and lively conversation with Christian had been just what I needed to remove all thoughts of the green-eyed boy from my mind. By the time I arrived at *healaxis,* I was my light, breezy self again. The ancient structure had been modelled in the likeness of a sprawling cathedral from Earth. In the setting sun, the pale sandstone captured the light and ignited the towering spires with fiery pinks and shimmering browns making it look like a glistening crystal castle.

Soft, green lawns rolled up to kiss its foundations and jungle-like gardens, overflowing with medicinal herbs, flowers and trees, crept into every crevice and burst joyfully over the iron lace fences, refusing to be contained. Hidden deep within the altruistic green were natural hot springs ready to welcome weary bodies in need. Their rejuvenating waters bubbled up from crystal caves below; a bed of pure quartz crystal which formed the energetic heart and foundation of our healaxis. The atmosphere hummed with healing and clarity. I almost skipped along the path, humming a tune of my own and bound up the wide sandstone stairs.

Inside, endless amber-lit halls with polished stone floors wound in a hushed labyrinth past rooms for various holistic consultations and treatments. There were crystal therapies, all kinds of energy medicine, hypnosis and past life regression therapies, medical intuitives and specialists in plant medicine and herb lore, to name a few. There was a well-stocked lapidary and an apothecary, hundreds of rooms, all connected to the powerful, pulsing energy of the crystal chamber below.

I launched myself into my work and when there were lulls in the flow of patients, I scouted about for things to keep me occupied, which usually meant formulating potions in the apothecary. I was stooped over the solid quartz bench mixing poultices when I could sense Healer

Cray gliding down the hall. She was so magnanimous that a feeling of lightness always preceded her arrival. A moment later she swept through the door and her radiant smile lit up the room.

"Lilly!" she chimed. Her voice was high and bright like twinkling stars. "I thought I'd find you here," she glittered. She wore a loosely tailored suit the colour of sunshine and a crisp white blouse. Her golden hair was arranged into a ball of silken thread at the nape of her neck and secured with an ornate wooden pin.

"Hi Healer Cray," I beamed back. "Did you need me for something? I'm nearly finished here."

"There's a patient I'd like you to see if you don't mind. Would you like to join us in consult room twenty-four?"

"Yes, I'll be right there. Just let me pack this up," I nodded.

When I entered the consultation room moments later, a lanky teenage boy was sitting wide-eyed on the crystal healing bed. A smattering of russet freckles dusted his nose, matching the colour of his hair. He was squirming as his eyes darted about the room. Failing to find a comfortable spot to rest, they finally settled on his dusty shoes. He was at that awkward stage; on the brink of adulthood and still trying to find his feet.

"Garrick, this is Lilly Flights. She is one of my Acolyte Healers. Would it be all right if she examines you too?" Healer Cray was perched at the desk finishing her clinical notes.

The boy looked up from beneath his thick, rust coloured lashes, nodded uncertainly and slumped into a sigh, reluctantly offering his hand to me. I smiled warmly and approached Garrick to take his hand in mine. With my feet planted firmly on the polished stone floor, I closed my eyes and drew in a deep, cleansing breath. I anchored my energy deep into the earth below and felt a rush of white light surge through my feet, up my legs and climb to my heart. Above me, a second surge of light beamed down from the heavens, entering my crown to meet the first at my heart, as it swelled with a pure and balanced glow. The light steadily grew and radiated outward setting each cell in my body alight like a galaxy of stars. Needlepoints of brilliant light emanated from my hand where Garrick's rested in mine. He flinched slightly as warmth flooded forward, penetrating his palm and scanning his energy field like a laser beam.

I proceeded gently, moving slowly throughout his physical and energetic bodies. His physical body looked okay but it soon became apparent to me that something wasn't right with his energetic body. It was a strange sensation, it felt fragmented in places like there were small tears and holes. I engaged my inner sight and examined the minute cracks up close. I glimpsed movement and strange images within the cracks themselves. What was that? I tried to peer closer but whatever it was, was shifting in and out of focus too quickly to discern what I was seeing.

Garrick fidgeted, detecting my unease and suddenly an image of black, studded iron doors boomed closed before my eyes, shutting me out completely.

I released his hand and looked to Healer Cray for an explanation. She quietly read my expression and told Garrick to rest there while we went to get his mother. Outside in the hall, she asked for my initial findings.

"I'm not sure," I began. "I believe his energetic field is compromised. There were small tears which seem to be filled with something... *foreign;* the beginnings of a physical illness perhaps, although it didn't look like anything I've seen before."

"Hmm, thank you, Lilly," she said thoughtfully. "His mother tells me that his usually sunny disposition has waned of late and that he has been a little withdrawn. She was concerned and brought him in. I'll have to run some further tests to get to the bottom of it. Thank you for your insight." Before I could ask her what she thought it was, she smiled and departed, bestowing loving blessings that seemed to fall from her very being like fragrant blossoms.

# FOUR

## Lilly

I stirred as the smoky shadows came into focus. I felt hot and sticky and there were noises all around me but they were warped and stretched as though my head was wrapped in wet cotton. The scene began to sharpen in my mind's eye and I saw a dim, hazy room, crammed with anonymous, swaying bodies heaving and melding into each other. The air was thick, making it difficult to breathe and the warped and muffled sounds now attacked my ears sharply like someone had turned up the volume. Loud music hacked at the walls and pounded the floor, threatening to explode the scene with each violent beat. The whole room vibrated. My vision snaked its way across the dance floor, around the crushing sweat and dripping heat, where figures groped mindlessly at each other and exchanged careless words and even more careless kisses, the darkness and noise providing the perfect shield against any true intention.

A flash of shocking red satin on the edge of the room grabbed my attention. A girl was draped under the spotlight of the bar, her dress just a whisper of soft, skimming fabric against long, shapely legs ending in razor-sharp, patent heels. Her blood red nails clutched a wine glass and she tossed her sensuous mane with practiced exaggeration and allure. I couldn't see the object of her undivided attention except for two denim-clad knees on a bar stool that she had skillfully wedged her hips between. Her smile was like caramel; rich, oozing and deadly sweet. Her careful eyes were fixed on her prey and refused to release their hold. She lifted one light finger and trailed it suggestively across his bicep, almost purring with satisfaction. "Well, aren't you going to buy me a drink?" she asked from beneath her telescopic false lashes.

"I think you've probably had enough," the guy responded flatly.

"Oh, don't be like that," she crooned. "When was the last time you really let your hair down?"

"Look, Alissa is it? I don't mean to be rude but I've already told you I'm just here with a few friends. It's a boys' night out so..."

She let out a barely discernible huff then recovered herself and shot him a wicked grin. "Okay, but you have no idea what you're missing out on," she sang with a vixen shrug.

"I'm quite sure I don't," he returned, looking

bewildered. With that, she turned on her razor sharp heel and was gone.

The guy swivelled on his stool, back to the bar and I was suddenly face-to-face with the green-eyed boy. *Oh!* The air punched from my lungs as I took in his hollow expression. His eyes were vacant as he slumped on the barstool like a wrung out rag.

"Jay! What the hell man? She was hot!" A burley, brick of a man was charging toward the green-eyed boy throwing his hands up in exasperation.

*Jay, so that's his name.*

"Not interested." Jay cut him off flatly as his friend almost barrelled him over. "I came out to spend time with you guys, not to pick up chicks."

"Nu-uh. That excuse doesn't wash. Do you believe this guy, Ryan?"

Ryan was tall and thin, expensively dressed and quietly spoken in a way that commanded your attention. "Leave him alone, John. I think he can figure out his own life."

"Seriously?" exploded John. "I think he may be blind and it's probably from getting too friendly with his own hand! You need to get laid, man."

"It's none of your fucking business, John! Just lay off okay?" Jay's eyes now burned with a dangerous spark of warning.

"*Geez*, lighten up. This is what I mean." John slammed his drink on the bar losing half of its contents.

"You're wound so tight, you're gonna explode. A bit of harmless fun never killed anyone. How long are you gonna hold a torch for her man?"

Ryan had moved closer to stand in the tense space between them. "Enough." His voice left no room for argument.

John and Jay stared at each other for a moment and I could see the pain radiating from every pore of Jay's body yet he seemed too defeated to be bothered doing anything about it. John huffed, not quite knowing what to do. "Well, are we drinking or not?' he demanded in a bashful sort of way, knowing he'd overstepped the mark.

"Think I'll call it a night," said Jay, already moving for the door. Ignoring his friend's protests, he pushed his way through the vibrating throng and fell out into the chill night air, trying to lose himself in the darkness. He ripped his jacket on, almost violently, and zipped it up to his throat. Punching his hands deep into the pockets, he hunched his head forward and turned in the direction of home. His ears were ringing so loudly that the silence outside was disorienting. His footfalls on the cracked, mouldy pavement sounded distant as he retreated from the club, his friends, the world. His thoughts were a tangle of flowing blonde hair and intense blue eyes that roused desperate longing in one breath and hatred with the next.

I'd read the poems from Earth portraying heartbreak as a thing of violent beauty – an exquisite pain that slowly chips away and alters the bearer into a tragic hero. I didn't understand why humans chose to cling to their suffering like a badge of honour for merely having survived it. As I watched Jay stalking through the gloom, his mind in tatters, I saw nothing beautiful or poetic about heartbreak. There weren't any sentimental words or sweeping, maudlin phrases that could truly express the betrayal or abandonment he felt. It had just hurt, like nothing he'd ever known; an unbearable pain and emptiness that had extinguished anything that was ever bright and good in the world. Now he was a ghost, hovering in the shadows at the edge of his own life.

Across the street, a man cursed savagely as his dog fought against its leash. The eager animal was charging forward, ignoring the noose around its neck. The man's shoulder wrenched painfully, his arm straining in its socket and he cursed long and loud, sinking an angry boot into the dog's side. It yelped in fright and stopped dead in its tracks, shrinking into the cold sidewalk. It was as though the animal was surprised that its owner had turned on it, even though the last time was probably not so long ago. It was the kindness in between beatings that had the poor mutt fooled. Jay wanted to race across the road, to abuse the man, tell him to stop, but he didn't. What good would it do? He knew only too well what it was like to be the dog and that no amount of protesting or explaining can make people kind. He knew the lengths that people will go to to avoid knowing a dog's feelings when they're the ones doing the kicking.

He pictured the girl's face again, bright and golden, her round blue eyes; clear and sparkling. That's what hurt the most – knowing that the one who'd inflicted the pain, likely didn't understand what they'd done and would never want to know. People were good at smashing things and then simply going out and getting a replacement. He sucked in a pained gasp and forcibly cut the thought away as though death had swung its scythe through the memory, turning it to ash.

The splintered steps of his small wooden house groaned beneath his feet. He shuffled listlessly through the door, dumped his keys on the coffee table and threw off his jacket. Moving to the kitchen he fumbled around in the pantry looking for some food to soak up the alcohol haze. Settling on eggs and toast, he stood mechanically at the stove with a spatula in one hand, staring obliviously at the peeling paint on the wall. The eggs sizzled away, the peeling paint remained unmoving and the clock on the wall ticked over to 4am. In just a few short hours the world would begin to stir again.

After downing his meal in uninterested gulps, he threw himself on the couch and kicked off his shoes. He lay there like stone, except for the reflexive clenching and unclenching of his right fist. Probably something he did when he was upset. I watched as the muscles of his forearm tensed and relaxed beneath his brown skin. His hands were rough and calloused, probably from some sort of manual labour. A white tee-shirt moulded over his shoulders and chest and I imagined if I could place my hand there, it would feel warm and solid. The jeans he wore were well loved and tattered, the faded denim slung low, revealing the crescent of his hip and the flat plane of his stomach. My gaze swept the long line of his legs which ended with a pair of large tanned feet; the soles stained a deep, muddy red. My eyes trailed back up his resting body to study his face. A pained smile played on his soft lips as he opened his eyes with a sigh and seemed to look directly at me. At least that's what it felt like. My heart stuttered as pain struck again like a blade. I was locked in place, unmoving, unbreathing. The full force of his gaze slamming me like a wall of water. Then he said the most incredible thing, "How can I survive in a world without conscience?"

I sucked in a sharp breath. I watched all of the ugly, unnecessary tragedy that had dominated Jay's short life, that had left him without hope or faith in humankind: an abusive childhood and his consequent estrangement from all family; the girl he loved with all his heart and her ultimate, gut-wrenching betrayal. I winced as he remembered snippets of the violent beatings from his father and my heart broke for him as he tried and failed to show someone the love that he was never given.

Was it any wonder he was struggling? Here he was, a man divided from what he knew to be good and decent, drowning in the moral inadequacies of the blind and self-consumed. Jay had been browbeaten and exhausted by careless people. People who were so possessed by a malignant self-loathing that it had eaten away at any good that might have once existed inside them and rendered them incapable of the most basic of decencies. He was trying to live with an undeniable contempt for the world in which he found himself, warring with a need to belong somewhere, anywhere.

*Get a grip, Lilly!* I was trying, and failing, to stay impartial as I watched Jay's worst memories. I could feel the depth of his pain and it made me desperately sad and angry at how cruelly he'd been treated. The darkness of his misery was pulling strongly at me and I could feel a pressure beginning to build, threatening to drag me down with him.

I couldn't help him this way. I needed to regain my balance. I inhaled deeply, drawing in more light and relieving the constriction around my heart. I filled myself with the love of the One Source and sent it out to every person who had ever harmed him and then I sent the strength of the Source to Jay. Upon that tired, worn couch lay many broken things. His face contorted in a violent mess of love, bitterness and hopeless confusion until a single tear, overruled by gravity, spilled and exploded against his crumpled chest.

Something urgent stirred in my heart. It wasn't the knifelike pain I'd just felt, this was something warm and vital rearing to life inside. It felt like laughter, pure and elated, soaring into the sun. A thousand dreamy days existing on the edge of a promise. Petals opening like the silent bloom of blood seeping into white linen. It was honey on your tongue while a knife was held to your throat. Hope poisoned by need. It was salt and swelter, raking fingers and wild eyes. It was right here. Alive. Insistent.

Without thinking, I reached for him. The air shimmered. My hand met resistance as flashes like lightning licked at my fingers. I distantly wondered why I wasn't scared, only to find that I couldn't have cared less. A higher need had taken over. Determined, I pushed harder, my hand penetrating the veil like it was piercing nothing more than a sheet of thin plastic. *Is that it? Is that all that separates us from them?* It seemed so insubstantial and anti-climactic. I flexed my fingers, testing them on the other side, blue sparks flying from my fingers. Then without the slightest hesitation or thought of consequences, I stretched my hand toward Jay.

The world seemed to tilt and time warped into languorous motion, almost stopping entirely – a universal pause. Had this moment's grace been provided so I could question what I was doing? As I watched my fingers unfurl in slow motion, reaching with certainty and purpose, did I even have a choice? This was drive and need accompanied by an unexpected pragmatic calm. My Soul knew what it was doing, even if I did not. I let it take the reins and watched as an unspent energy, hovering in wait at the edges of the universe, gravitated to this moment. It was a divine inhalation; vacuuming up starlight and spinning it into the perfect design for life in this moment. It was a single breath, a heartbeat, the space within a fleeting thought, and it was done. The Universe exhaled, breathing it into being.

Pushed by the warm breath back into normal time and space, my palm found Jay's chest and I pressed it softly over his broken heart. The energy of his body joining with mine was startling. It felt like a strange, low hum; a distant bass note. I had no idea how I'd managed it, but in that moment the 'hows' and 'whys' seemed very unimportant. All I really cared about was helping Jay. I don't know if it was my imagination, but I thought I felt his heart jump as my fingers connected with his chest but then he seemed to relax and surrender under my touch, and his mind finally stilled. The path of his solitary tear glistened on his cheek but no new tears came to join it. It was as though he'd entered a trance, or maybe he'd just reached that point where he had nothing left inside of him. I focussed all of my attention and wove golden threads of strength, hope and love through the tatters of his spirit, trying to mend what others had torn. I lingered at his side whispering words of comfort and support until the new day dawned and he faded into an exhausted, dreamless sleep.

# Jay

Shifting uncomfortably on the sagging couch, I cracked open a bloodshot eye and strained to see the time: 11.16am. With a groan I shoved a cushion over my head and stretched my stiff and aching limbs. It was never a good idea to pass out on this couch. The smell of stale beer and cigarettes assaulted my nose. *Christ, I need a shower.* Disjointed pieces of the crazy dream drifted into my awareness. It was a beautiful dream and now I was annoyed to be awake and realizing that it was, in fact, just a dream. I squeezed my eyes shut trying to remember everything the angelic girl had said. *Was she an angel? Well, that's a stupid fucking thought! I'm sure, if angels do exist, they have better things to do than waste time with me.*

I sighed and internally retracted my negative statement, ashamed at how quickly I could put myself down. With a deep breath I brought the vision of her to my mind. *What exactly did she say to me? I know it was really important. Damn! Why can I never remember my dreams properly?*

She had been radiant, with her long dark hair and hazel eyes that had smiles all of their own. Her face had emanated pure truth and joy. There was a wonderful glow about her, like a blazing lighthouse on a distant shore guiding you in the right direction and keeping you safe from harm.

*She'd said something about life being all about*

*learning... that's right, she said I'm a soul having a human experience...whatever that means.* It had all been so clear to me last night. Everything she said had made sense and felt like the real truth, except now I was struggling to hold onto the meaning. For the first time in a long time, I'd remembered what it was like to feel hope. I wanted to hold onto that feeling forever, to believe I could mend all my broken parts. She *must* have been an angel. She was so beautiful and loving and patient. Her compassion had touched a part of me that I had thought long lost, but it was just a dream and like all beautiful dreams, it was slipping from my grasp with each waking second.

# FIVE

## Lilly

My childhood home was nestled in the purple foothills of Clear Mountain perched on six acres of cool forest and thick grasslands. A burbling creek ran all the way from the mountain top and trickled sneakily behind the house before vanishing into the trees. On steamy summer days during the dry season, Christian and I used to make it our mission to rescue helpless tadpoles from shrinking, muddy puddles in the creek bed. With the passion and gusto of a six-year old's logic, I would persuade my parents to let us make 'frog hospital' in the backyard which consisted of countless containers filled with water to house the 'patients'. Despite their best efforts to explain to us that mother nature knew best and we shouldn't interfere with the natural balance of things, we weren't having any of it. Inevitably, weeks later, the Flights' household would be serenaded by a four-hundred-strong frog choir that kept us awake half the night.

Passing through the threshold of my family home always subtracted ten years from my age. I became aware of this bizarre phenomenon soon after moving out of home for the first time and now accepted it as normal. My mother would ask all the obligatory, motherly questions about sleep and diet while piling enough food for three people on my plate, and my father would gaze adoringly at me like I was the most precious of all jewels.

"How's your study going sweetheart?" My mother's raven hair was secured neatly at her nape and flowed over her left shoulder in a black river. Her hemp apron was spattered with colourful ingredients. She looked like a walking finger painting.

I flopped down next to her onto the faded linen sofa which had been my favourite place to nap as a child. The pattern of dainty bluebells and falling petals had lost their vibrant hue but I remembered pleading with my parents to let me sleep in the field of flowers. "This semester's workload is lighter so I've had more time to spend at healaxis," I reported. "Healer Cray is amazing. She's teaching me how to refine my energetic body scanning technique. The other day, I managed to detect a patient's condition before I entered the consultation room. So that's progress, I guess."

"That's brilliant, Lilly," my mother smiled proudly, her eyes flashing with glee. Despite her age, there was barely a line on her face. The faint creases would only appear when she laughed or smiled.

"Well done my little flower," said my father in his usual soft tone, "sounds like you're getting stronger every day."

"Speaking of keeping you strong, I'd better go check on dinner." My mother rose from the sofa, giving me a squeeze and breezed from the room.

"Hmm, it smells good. What is she cooking?"

"Who knows? She's been working on new recipes for her cooking school again. I hope you're hungry because she's made enough for eight people." We both rolled our eyes and laughed. "Come with me. I want to show you something," he winked.

I followed him down the hall and into his cramped, musty study. It wasn't that the room was small, it was the sheer volume of books shelved floor to ceiling that made you feel like you had somehow slipped into the pages of an encyclopaedia and become trapped there. Thousands of coloured spines crowded silky oak shelves, standing tall and ready like an oversized box of artists' pastels.

My stomach growled. The smells wafting from the kitchen had followed us down the hall. It reminded me of something I'd forgotten from the other night with Jay. I supposed that with everything else that had happened, it had seemed inconsequential. But was it? I could have sworn I smelt toast cooking when I was watching him make his 4am pre-hangover breakfast. I knew it wasn't possible. The energetic boundary between worlds meant that we could see and hear, but not physically touch, taste or smell. Yet I'd well and truly disproved that theory by reaching out and touching him. But the smell of toast had happened *before* I'd reached through the veil. It didn't make sense. "Dad?" I asked slowly. "When you're speaking to Souls on earth, do you ever...um, smell things, like you normally do here?"

He chuckled once and placed his hand on my shoulder. "No honey, we can only see and hear Souls. Other senses of smell and touch aren't required for us to do our part. Why do you ask?" He smiled warmly but held me with an inquiring eye.

"It's just that I really thought I smelt toast cooking when I was with a Soul."

He shifted his stance further back to take in my expression. I could see a question forming in his mind. A fleeting look of concern. Then after a moment's thought, he smiled again and changed tack. "Well, you're new at this Lilly. Because we see everything so clearly, sometimes we imagine the smells and feelings that go along with what we see. It's not as though we are there to smell and touch things. We're there to observe, listen and provide support, nothing more."

He was probably right – just my imagination. A pang of guilt and worry snaked through me. "I know, it just felt really...real..." my voice trailed off. I was remembering how it felt to press my palm to Jay's heart. It had been surreal, yet the most real thing I think I had ever felt. If

I were to tell my father what I'd done, he'd... he'd what? Site rules and regulations? Or wrap me in a vice-like hug and chalk it up to curiosity and inexperience? I couldn't guess what he'd do. The flesh and blood me, that must abide by the rules, knew I shouldn't have done it. But the Soul wants what the Soul wants. It had felt right at the time – necessary even. Had Jay been able to physically feel me? Had my fingers actually splayed over his heart? Or was I just imagining the solid warmth and that strange vibratory hum, like I had imagined the smell of cooking toast?

My dad stepped in closer to me and wound me in a tight hug. He gave the best hugs in the world. He'd had plenty of practice and not just with mum and I. My father had devoted his life to placing orphans in good homes. His unwavering compassion and gift as a Syphon meant he could relieve others of their worry or sadness through touch – a welcome skill when explaining to a four-year-old why their parents aren't ever coming back. He was also a gifted Traveller. He could teleport around the country, helping those in need and be back in time for dinner. I marvelled at the responsibility he seemed to manage with impeccable grace and mastery. I wanted to be like him, to make him proud.

He pulled back, looked into me with hazel eyes that mirrored my own and planted a kiss on my forehead. "It will get easier with time as all things do. Have patience my little flower..."

"...my petals will open in their own time," I finished the phrase he'd been reciting to me since I was a child. Even now, I still couldn't justify his faith in me. It was a plucky, joyful thing that he tossed around with ease. I could tell him anything and he would always respect my point of view and guide and help me where he could. So why did I feel as though I couldn't share the whole story and tell him about Jay?

He smiled at me warmly and ran his fingers through his sandy hair. "I know it can be challenging and confusing at first. It's one thing to learn about the struggles humans face and entirely another to witness it firsthand. But never forget Lil, your wisdom comes from the countless past lives and struggles that you've faced on Earth before ascending to Panacea. While we may not readily remember the details of those past lives, the wisdom we gained from them is embedded in our Souls." He gave me a final squeeze and let me go. "Now, where have I put it?" He turned about the room and approached a teetering stack of books erected in the corner and peered at the pile.

I had absolutely no memories from my past lives on Earth. I knew that Sky and Christian had seen glimpses of theirs in dreams or in deep meditation. Random flashes or details that gave meaning or direction for their current course. Maybe I'd never had those experiences because there wasn't anything I needed to know yet. I looked back to the corner where he was carefully disassembling the stack. "Been 'cleaning up' again?" I joked.

"Actually, yes," he asserted, "and I found this." He turned and presented me with a large volume that was bound in dark leather, so worn and thin, that the edges were crumbling. My senses prickled as I took it from his outstretched hands. It was heavy and dusty and smelled faintly of healing herbs. I carefully peeled back the cover to reveal the title inked in an elaborate hand, 'The Vibratory Scale of Ascendency'. Beneath it was the name, *Grayson Flights,* my Great-grandfather.

"Dad, this is amazing! Is this Great-grandpa's original manuscript?" I couldn't believe my eyes.

"The very one. I thought you could put it to good use," he beamed. "You know, my father told me something quite remarkable about your Great-grandfather once."

"Oh?" I said, "What was it?"

"Well, he told me that one of Grayson's Earth lives was as the great philosopher, Aristotle."

"Wow! So he was already incredibly wise thousands of years ago and just kept getting wiser with each passing life."

My dad shrugged and smirked. "I don't know about that honey. I'm sure he had his hiccups like everyone else."

Grayson Flights was a celebrated scholar in the field of multi-dimensional consciousness. His insights into other planes of existence were still referenced in today's teachings and his knowledge revered by brilliant minds. The dusty pages held a combination of scientific theory and celestially channelled insight into the many worlds and levels of consciousness that Souls pass through on their evolutionary cycle. Inside the front cover was a hand-drawn diagram depicting the twelve dimensions in an unbroken circle. I touched my finger to the yellowed page and traced the progression of life and rebirth through the many worlds; the journey that each Soul has agreed to take.

Go-lites were conscious of their life purpose and these cycles of learning. The poor humans, however, often spent multiple lifetimes just to discover this simple fact and then several more lifetimes trying to come to terms with it. I thought of Jay and the pain he'd endured. I was so grateful that I'd risen out of that chaos. I was a go-lite now. I would never have to endure suffering like that again.

# SIX

## Lilly

For the next seven days, the clear sky transformed into a swollen bruise of roiling purple. Jagged swords of lightning sliced open the bloated belly of cloud, releasing hard, flooding rains. The wild waters came rumbling down the mountainside and took control of our town. Roads were cut off and healaxis and magistrument were closed until the weather passed but thankfully, there seemed to be little damage.

At the same time, our Guardian services were in high demand from earthbound Souls. Apparently, an earthquake had destroyed half of a small country and taken thousands of lives. Many were without homes and the collective outpouring of grief was palpable. The nights were long and we had to make sure we had enough energy to help those in need, so as Sky and I were relatively housebound by the weather, we relaxed during the day, meditated often, shared reviving pots of tea and laughter, and I found the new hiding place for the chocolate cookies.

After yet another night of restless sleep, I shuffled to the kitchen in search of breakfast. The house was so still and silent, I thought Sky must still be asleep. I stared through the glass, double doors and into the back garden. The torrential rain had eased overnight and was now just a fine mist against a sheeting grey sky, silently dusting the garden in tiny frosted droplets. I pushed open the doors and met the cool damp and the smell of saturated soil. Sky emerged from behind the garden shed. Her porcelain hands were gloved in rich, red mud and she was holding a limp plant by its tangled roots.

"What's that?" I called over to her.

"It *was* your sage-heart plant," she called back. "All the rain was too much for it I guess. It's pretty much rotted at the roots."

"Oh, let me see." The once silvery grey leaves had withered and curled and the stalks were a sodden, icky brown. Sage-heart was used to promote wise judgement and good decision making. It could be made into a liquid tonic or its leaves burnt for a cleansing smoke bath. "Sage-heart usually loves the rain," I said puzzled. "Are all the others okay?" I asked, assuming she'd done the rounds.

"A bit battered, but alive. How about we go to the market and pick up a new seedling for you? Do you have plans today?"

"No, nothing planned. That would be great. Let me get some breakfast first."

"No chocolate cookies!" she shouted after me.

"*O–kay,*" I returned, laughing to myself because I'd already eaten them all. I walked back inside, still slightly sleep-hazed and puzzled about my sage-heart. I knew rosemary and basil didn't like being waterlogged, yet they had survived. The sage-heart should have thrived.

♡ ♡ ♡

By the time we reached the square the skies were clearing and the sun was peeping through windows of happy blue. People were out and about again, relieved that their confinement had come to an end. We picked our way around the muddy puddles looking for the plant stall.

"I think it's over here," Sky strained to see over a gaggle of clucking women that had milled excitedly around a stall of silver wind chimes, tinkling angelic scales.

In a wildly coloured tent, the old gypsy fortune-teller, Swahelia dozed on and off. She must have been a hundred and two and was completely blind. Her failing body was cocooned in a fantastical, technicolour shawl fringed in golden tassels that twisted in the breeze. Tendrils of aromatic smoke spiralled from a bronze burner in the corner and her collection of divining crystals sat waiting for the next customer. I had lost sight of Sky in the crowd and decided to stand here and wait for her. She couldn't have gone far.

Swahelia stirred from the velvet cushion that threatened to swallow her shrinking form and raised her stiff, knobbled fingers toward me on shaky arms. I stared at her, a little confused and wondered what she was doing. Time had carved deep rivers and valleys in her umber face. She was a permanent fixture here. She had sat so long that under her full skirt I was sure she was growing roots. Her rheumy eyes opened wide and turned to me; two still pools of milk that saw nothing and everything. A current of intuition came over her like a breath of life, uplifting her hunched posture and temporarily arresting the tremors of age. She was poised as still as stone, like a classical statue with her arms outstretched, trying to catch a falling star. After a moment, her thin, weathered lips parted and she spoke just one line to me in a time worn-voice. "Be careful, little one."

My heart skipped a beat. I acted purely on instinct and found myself walking hurriedly away, fleeing before she could say any more. Although, I didn't really know why, my body just seemed to act without my permission. I belatedly realised she had been burning sage-heart in her tent and turned the connection around in my mind. Before I'd managed to form any coherent thoughts, Sky pranced up to me bearing a little seedling and a loving smile.

"Where did you get to?" she questioned, searching my hands for additional purchases.

"I got distracted and when I turned around, you'd

disappeared."

She handed me the fragile little plant and I thanked and hugged her warmly.

"Come on," she said, "let's go put the *new baby* in the nursery."

We spent the rest of the day together doing a bit more tidying in the garden and then some well overdue study. It was incredible to see how much progress Sky had made over the last year. She was sitting quietly now, wreathed in a circle of beeswax candles, eyes closed with determined concentration. I looked up from my enormous botany reference to see the wicks flicker to life one by one. Her auric field was aglow with a whirling rainbow that illuminated the room.

"Wow," I breathed and she cracked open one eye and grinned at me. "Well, it's only taken five years to master," she laughed. "How about you? You seem to be doing really well at healaxis, which reminds me, can you take a look at my sore wrist? It's still bothering me a bit."

"What? From our handstand competition two weeks ago?"

"Yes," she admitted sheepishly. "I should know better than to challenge *you* of all people."

"I don't know what you mean," I said with feigned innocence and batted my lashes. If there was one thing I knew I was good at, it was handstands. For some reason I'd been obsessed with them as a child, always trying to beat my own record. My mother had concluded that I must want to study the world from a different perspective to most.

"Well, let's just say we don't all have your incredible awareness of every cell in our bodies," she rolled her glassy blue eyes.

"Let me see," I laughed, taking her hand and closing my left palm over her slender wrist. I took a few centering breaths and allowed my sight to permeate her skin to see the bone, sinew and tissue. I magnified the vision and was energetically drawn to some muscle fibres that lacked the vibrant appearance of surrounding areas. It was a muscle strain with some microscopic tearing - nothing serious. Now that I had the diagnosis, I set about healing the wound. I opened myself to the universal flow of healing energy and saw my body ignite with a white hot glow. I conducted it through my hands to the inflamed area and watched as the tiny muscle fibres stirred and knitted themselves back together. When the revitalized colour I was looking for returned, I was done.

"Wow Lilly, that was fast. You're getting much stronger." She twisted her wrist appreciatively. "Thanks, it feels great!"

"You're welcome," I smiled shyly.

"Hey, is that your uniter I can hear?" she pointed over my shoulder.

I dug through the bottomless pit that is my handbag and found the vibrating crystal. As I brushed my finger across its clear surface, Chris' face wavered into view.

"Christian! How are you?"

His contagious warmth lit up his face as he relayed what he'd been doing the past week. "Anyway, there's an important reason I'm calling," he said. "I wanted to ask you and Sky to the Midsummer Ball."

Marking the day that our sun would shine the longest, the Midsummer Ball celebrated and gave thanks for the life-giving powers of the sun. Without light and warmth, there can be no life.

Sky looked genuinely touched. "Oh, you're sweet and very charming, Chris, but I'm going with Gabriel."

"I'm not charming," he scoffed. "I was looking forward to going with the two smartest and most beautiful girls in Citrine. The benefit would have been all mine. Guess I'll just have to settle for one gorgeous woman instead."

"I haven't said yes yet," I shot back.

"But you will," he said and there was a protracted pause as he waited patiently for my reply. He sat perfectly still with an expectant smirk. The silence stretched out until Sky and I couldn't contain our giggles anymore.

"Okay, yes, I'll go with you!" I laughed. "Anything else?" I asked, rolling my eyes at Sky.

"That will do for now." I saw his thumb casually swipe across my view of his satisfied grin as he disconnected.

"Ugh, he just blanked me!" I said laughing at the

vacant crystal.

"So, it's a date then," said Sky. It was a statement, not a question.

My head snapped around at the mention of the word, *date*. "No, it's not a date," I said quickly and then paused to think about that.

"Are you sure?" she asked, "Because I think *Chris thinks* it's a date."

I stared at her wondering if she was right. "If he thought that he wouldn't have invited both of us," I reasoned.

"I guess not," she shrugged. "You're probably right, but I don't understand why you two aren't together. He's absolutely gorgeous and you're perfect for each other."

She surprised me with her thoughts on the subject. I didn't even know it *was* a subject so I just stood there dumbly.

"How do you feel about him, Lilly?" The laughter had left her eyes and she studied me now with careful interest. Her head tilted slowly in that catlike way while her sharp, watchful eyes read every inch of me.

I stared at her trying to form my answer. "Well, as you know we grew up together..." beyond that, I wasn't sure what to say.

"Yes, and..." she coaxed smoothly.

"And, I don't know. He's funny and smart, confident, loyal, attentive and caring..."

"Precisely," she agreed, "and you love him," she

smiled triumphantly, as though she now had the mouse pinned beneath her paw.

"Of course I *love* him but I don't have romantic feelings for him. We're friends. I don't see Christian that way," I said shaking my head. My voice had taken on a nervous tone.

Her smug smile remained and she almost purred, "Are you sure?" She left the question hanging in the air and try as I might, I was unable to remove it.

I suppose in a way I took Chris for granted. He had always been a part of my life, so I tried to imagine a world without him and failed. I only managed to prove how many pieces of my memory were tangled up in pieces of his. I didn't even really know how to measure what I felt for him because I didn't think I'd ever been in love before.

My last boyfriend, Asher had been wonderful in every way, yet it had just felt like a polite exchange instead of the bone deep connection I knew was out there. Chris had been out with some beautiful girls, on the inside and out, and there were no shortage of them lined up either – a fact he was either oblivious to or was simply ambivalent. He could have dated someone different with each new moon had he been inclined.

Now, Chris and I were both single and had effectively been joined at the hip, reminiscent of childhood days. It was like a default setting with us, encoded in our cells that we'd always be in one another's lives. Thinking about it, I supposed our interactions had been bordering on unexplored territory for a while, only it had been happening so naturally that I'd not noticed. All of a sudden I felt nervous. Maybe this *was* a date! Snapped from my reverie, I realised that Sky was no longer in the room. I marched to her bedroom door and knocked. "Sky, I need a new dress!"

♡ ♡ ♡

We circled the bolts of luxurious fabric with unrestrained delight. Floating chiffons, slinky silk, crisp satin and lace as delicate as cobwebs, all begging to be touched by admiring hands.

"Ooooh, I'll never be able to choose," I whined.

The kitsch little shop belonged to Abigail Rose, a talented local designer. "Let's decide what style of dress you'd like first, then we can discuss fabric choices," she suggested. Her smile was full of excited mischief and she had a haphazard way about her, as highly creative people often do. Her eyes were so dark they were like onyx, flashing within the frames of her rose pink glasses. Her curly hair was bunched messily on top of her head and secured with a collection of coloured pencils, while coils of it forced their way free like metal springs bouncing around her pretty face.

We followed her over to a workbench overflowing with piles of design sketches, pattern pieces, orphaned buttons and stray pins. Behind her were several dressmaking dummies wearing yards of material swept, gathered and ruched every which way, waiting to become her next triumph. She cleared a space and rummaged for her sketch pad.

"Did you have something in mind?" she asked, pushing a jangling row of bangles up her arm. She eyed me up and down and seemed to almost visibly bounce as her next dazzling creation began to burst forth in her imagination.

"Not really. I thought I'd leave it in your capable hands," I smiled.

She said nothing, twirled the pencil in her fingers a few times and set it on the page in a flurry of passionate movement. Her feverish strokes made her look like she was conducting an orchestra. She finished the sketch with a few staccato notes and sat back to admire her work and wait for the inevitable applause. The silhouette was simple and elegant; a fitted, bias-cut shift that skimmed over the breasts and hips and flowered from mid thigh into a fluted hem. The neckline was softly cowled and the shoestring straps were studded with tiny crystals.

"It's beautiful," Sky and I said in unison.

Abigail smiled, nodded and guided us back to the fabric bolts. "I have the perfect thing for this," she beamed, pulling out a roll of pale tangerine silk. She unrolled it on a broad cutting table and lifted the corners to shake out the wrinkles. It billowed up in a weightless sail, seemed to hover mid-air, then floated back down on a long, silent sigh. I was admiring the silk's matte lustre when she produced a bottle of crystals in the same pastel colour and poured a few into my palm. They sat there, winking in the light. "These will be perfect for the straps," she nodded at me assuredly and went to work with her tape measure.

After much draping, pinning, flourishing and primping, we had the beginnings of a ball gown and by far, the most gorgeous thing I had ever worn.

# SEVEN

## Lilly

The last fortnight had been hectic. There were extra lectures to make up for the magistrument's week-long closure and the influx of human Souls in need hadn't eased much since the earthquake. I had not seen Jay again… or Sky, or Chris for that matter. We had all been extremely busy and I had been looking forward to the Midsummer holiday for a much-needed rest.

Somehow in between all of this I had managed to attend dress fittings. Abigail's masterpiece was stunning. I only hoped I could do it justice at tonight's ball. I lay in bed admiring the floaty tangerine dream hanging on the back of my bedroom door.

"Lilly, are you awake?" Sky called from the hall. "Chris will be here in an hour. Do you want breakfast?"

"I'm up. I'll just eat something on the way." I stretched and forced myself to abandon the cosy nest I'd made in the covers. We were heading to the beach to pay homage to the sun and relax. Of all the things in this glorious world, the ocean was sacred to me. Although we only lived thirty minutes from the coast, I dreamt of one day living in an open, airy pole home overlooking the sea.

Sky had invited Gabriel to join us. He was an amazing person and I couldn't have asked for anyone better for my beautiful friend. She seemed to blossom when he was around and I knew that this was the beginning of something true and lasting. As for me, I had put the idea of Christian and I as a couple from my mind. After Sky had first questioned me about it and I had failed to arrive at any conclusion, I had let it go and concentrated my focus on the present. I wasn't about to worry and ponder like a human. Go-lites took things from moment to moment, always responding to what was right in front of them and not becoming emotionally caught up by dwelling on the past or wondering about the future. I didn't know how I felt right now but I trusted that when it was time for me to know, I would know!

Chris had picked up Gabriel on the way and had arrived at our place right on time. The four of us sang badly and laughed at each other as Chris steered around the winding ribbon of road that hugged the coastline. As soon as we arrived, I threw open the car door and hurtled down the sandy track leading to the sea. An early morning storm was clearing in the path of the sun. The whitewash of pale sand, the glittering green of the sea, and the intense lavender sky all competed for the eye's adoration. A hint of a rainbow ghosted behind the flight of an eagle, while dolphins frolicked on foamy crests. I dug my toes into the fine powder and flopped onto my back, arms outstretched, sifting handfuls through my fingers. It was silky soft and still cool below the surface. The others wandered up moments later and plopped down with satisfied sighs.

"Happy?" Chris winked, knowing that the beach for me was as necessary as oxygen, followed closely by chocolate, or anything containing sugar for that matter.

"Perfectly," I replied. I drank in the sound of the sea. My love of the ocean was so much more than passing admiration, it was a sustaining need. It filled me as nothing else could.

I walked to the water's edge and inhaled deeply as another perfect wave swelled to life, lifting my heart with it. Without pause in its eternal rhythm, it collapsed in a wash of foam and spray, the rush of water sliding up the sand and nipping at my feet in bursting, effervescent bubbles. I advanced hypnotically into the champagne wash and plunged in. Every muscle in my body surrendered to the feeling. I swam out behind the wave break with the taste of salt on my tongue and floated peacefully on my back, rocked on the cradle of a wave.

An hour later, I reluctantly dragged myself from the sea and sauntered back.

"Nice swim?" Chris asked. He lounged casually

with his head propped on his hand smiling quietly to himself. His long fingers were woven through his ebony hair and his smooth chest was caked with sand.

"Heavenly," I managed sleepily, flopping back onto my towel and focussing on the delicious feeling of the breeze on my wet body. "Where are Gabe and Sky?"

"They went for a stroll down the beach. I think that's them down there," he pointed at two specks in the distance. "They seem to be getting very friendly," he observed.

"Yeah, Sky is smitten," I snickered. "Did you know he's a Hand?"

"Really?" His eyebrows shot up at the mention of the rare gift of time manipulation. "What length of time can he bend?"

"Sky told me he's studying Greater Science with his major in time-space continuum. He's managed to break his own record and stop time for thirty-seven minutes within a three mile radius."

Chris whistled low and long. "That's impressive." His slate blue eyes glinted appreciatively then stilled, as an unwelcome thought struck him. "Hold on, does that mean I might have been unwittingly frozen at some point while Gabe has been practicing?"

"What do you mean?" I scrunched up my face in amusement.

"I don't know, I can't say that I'm totally comfortable with the idea." He waved an indignant hand.

"How do you know we haven't been frozen for the last half an hour and he didn't just unfreeze us again?" he said dramatically, daring me to rule out the possibility. "We should check our mouths for bugs. They could have flown in while you were frozen in laughter at my irresistible wit and charm," he grinned.

"I'm pretty sure the bugs would have been frozen too," I laughed and flicked sand at him, which he annoyingly didn't react to. "Apparently Master Clay takes him outside of the city limits to practice." I wondered what it would be like to have a gift like Gabe's, or Sky's. As an Elemental, she could exert influence over fire, water, air, earth and ether. "Gabe's gift *is* pretty impressive, but Sky is evolving so fast it makes my head spin."

Chris had caught the flat tone in my voice – because he was Chris and he always noticed when I began questioning myself. "

How so?" he asked patiently.

"Well, I saw her fill a glass with water by directing moisture from the air."

"Hmm, handy," he shrugged. "Were you thirsty at the time? Stranded in a desert, were you? Do you think she could direct all of my missing socks to return when she has a free moment? Because *that* would be genuinely useful." He wore a smug grin to drive home his point.

"Very funny. You know she can't manipulate matter, just the elements."

He jerked his chin at me. "Meanwhile, I hear *you've*

been knitting muscle tissue and bone back together."

I flushed. The truth was, I'd always felt different from my friends. I couldn't describe exactly what it was, but while they danced through their lives with grace, joy and ease, I sometimes sensed a piece missing inside me. I didn't know if I'd imagined it long ago and now accepted it as truth. I didn't know what the piece was or what it looked like, but it meant I never felt exactly whole.

Chris sifted sand through his long fingers. I cleared my throat and focussed the conversation back on Sky and Gabe. "Anyway, apart from the fact that they're both extremely gifted, I think it's a foregone conclusion: I can't imagine two people that are better suited to each other." As soon as my words were out, I realised the implication.

Chris held his open expression and my gaze, without flinching. It was like he willed himself to stay still; waiting for something that may, or may not, come.

His lack of response was not lost on me so I quickly changed the subject. "Aren't you going to have a swim?" I fumbled.

"Maybe later," he murmured. He studied me for a moment more and stood up. "Come on, let's go for a walk up to the headland," he suggested, grasping my forearm and bringing me to my feet as though I were nothing more than a wisp of cloud.

The sun was climbing steadily in the sky and warmed my cool, wet body, raising goosebumps on my skin. We walked slowly, turning over sea shells and looking at crooked lengths of driftwood, bleached white like bone. The craggy headland was home to the Record Keepers; a mountain of rock, where the histories of Panacea were captured in ancient layers of stone. Go-lites understood that minerals were magnetic in nature, meaning they held the energetic memory of all that had come to pass. The headland's Record Keepers had watched over this beach and its surrounds since our planet's creation. They had remembered and recorded it all and would share their stories with anyone inclined to listen.

We scrambled up the jagged rocks, peering into tidal pools alive with fleeting fish, anemones, and crabs with intricately patterned shells; like little miniature seas. Higher still, were hidden caves that weren't visible from below, but we knew they were there. This had been one of our greatest playgrounds as children. Even then, the sea had an undeniable claim on my heart so I had hounded my parents to bring me here often.

As we wound higher and deeper into a maze of stoney blades and spears, the breeze stuttered against the enduring obstacles, raising the temperature considerably. Sweat trickled down Christian's neck and the metallic sheen across his bare back made him sparkle like some sort of god immortalised in bronze. We moved in comfortable silence to the foot of a scramble climb below the cave's mouth, Christian striding confidently ahead, with me chasing his shimmering form.

I watched in fascination as he mentally assessed the easiest line to climb and methodically negotiated the first leg. "Watch your footing there," he pointed at a section of loose shale. It was the first time either of us had spoken for quite some time. His velvet voice hugged the rocks around him and then dropped down to me like a rope. I nodded and followed his instructions. I was breathing a little heavier as he grasped my hand and helped me up the last ledge to the cave's entrance.

The air was still and I could hear an eagle cry in the distance. Inside, there was an instant feeling of reverence. You could feel the history sleeping in the sediment, layer upon layer stretching all the way back to the beginning of time. We picked our way around the rocks on the cave floor and stopped at an unusually shaped stone in the centre. Veins of crystal cut its surface and captured the dim light pouring through the mouth of the cave. Christian took my cold, clammy hand and pressed my palm onto the boulder. "Listen," his eyes flickered excitedly and we crouched quietly as we had when we were children, heads bent together and closed our eyes.

At first, there was only blackness. Then remote, echoed voices and snippets of hazy faces flowed into my mind's eye. I relaxed into the connection and saw a much younger version of my mother lounging on the shimmering sand, her face turned skyward, lids closed to the blinding, golden light of afternoon. Her fine hair was blowing about her face and her palm was pressed to the swell of her belly. She looked radiant.

"Can you feel the enormity of her heart?" my father whispered, next to her.

"Yes," she smiled, "she is like her father; pure and strong and true."

He leant toward her and settled a devoted kiss on her lips and then her belly. My parents' faces faded in a swirl of sand, the sounds of the beach were sucked away and my sight darkened.

Through a red mist, I could hear a light, steady patter. I floated toward the sound, and there was my tiny body growing in my mother's womb. I was only about four months old; so delicate and fragile, cushioned in the peaceful warmth. I felt safety and contentment bloom around me in eternal promise. I lingered there watching my little form stretch and curl, testing its limbs. The sublime sensations of peace and wholeness were absolute. I was immersed in that glorious feeling when I was disturbed by the sensation of time rewinding, and my unborn body became smaller and smaller until I could see nothing but blackness.

Ice crept into my bones and I felt an escalating panic. Confusion overtook me as my lungs caught fire and my chest constricted with a crushing pain. I couldn't breathe. I saw arms flailing and desperate hands clawing in front of me and realised they were my arms, my hands. My body felt weak, I was trying to kick to the surface but I couldn't. It was too heavy... too far... I was drowning.

The world was growing dark and everything slowed and softened. The gripping fear ebbed away, my perspective skewed and then there was just silence and the push and pull of dim, watery shadows.

I gasped, yanking my hand from the rock and toppled backward in a violent coughing fit. Chris's warm hands were cupping my face and I could see his lips moving but my ears weren't working. I blinked, stunned and slumped weakly into the dirt. He scooted around the rock and scooped my head up into his lap, brushing the hair out of my eyes.

"What happened? What did you see?"

It took me a little while to find my voice. *What did I see? Myself drowning, that's what. It was me... but it wasn't me.* I calmed my breathing and willed my heart to slow, thinking over what I'd seen. "I was drowning," I told him. "It must have been a past life memory from Earth. It was me, but it was another version of me," I stifled another cough.

"Are you all right? How are you feeling?" He held my hand and waited, the concern clearly showing on his face.

"I'm okay. Just a little rattled," I trailed off thoughtfully. "It's kind of an odd, disjointed feeling to witness your own death."

"I know. Do you have any idea why that would have been shown to you now?"

"No, not a clue," I shrugged feebly and tried to sit

up. Chris saw me struggle and lent a guiding hand.

"It will come to you. These things always do." He wrapped an arm around me and rubbed his warm palm over the goosebumps on my shoulder. "Merciful Source, you're freezing! Even more than your usual reptilian temperature." He wrapped me in a tight hug. "Let's get you out of here and into the warm sun. Do you think you're okay to head back?" He asked helping me onto my feet.

"Wait, what did you see?" I asked him.

He grinned. "Oh, you know, just memories of us as kids. You running around naked in the creek at your parents' place, that sort of thing."

"Christian!" I swatted at him while he delighted in my embarrassment. Although he laughed and joked, I must have looked a bit green or something because he kept a watchful eye on me as we drove home for the Midsummer ceremony.

♡ ♡ ♡

All over town, ceremonial flames were lit and prayers of gratitude were sent up to the blazing sun. Our town was designed in a perfect circle. In the centre was Ophanim Dome where the Elders carried out their duties, and centuries of knowledge were preserved in vast libraries and ordered catacombs. The structure, as the name suggested, was an enormous lustrous dome, made entirely from infinity quartz. It was said that this type of crystal was not of this world and the dome had stood since the dawn of time. The earliest records indicated that it was a gift from the One Source of All so the energy of unconditional love would always be concentrated in this place to lend the Elders strength to guide us.

Hundreds had gathered at Ophanim Dome to see the spectacle that only occurred on Midsummer. The sun's rays would strike the dome's elaborate, faceted crown at just the precise angle shooting rainbow light in all directions and bathing everything in loving colour. Excited children were wide-eyed and bouncing out of their skins while their parents told the story of this magical moment. "When the rainbow light reaches out and touches you, you'll know that you are adored, treasured and loved, always and forever. You need never feel afraid of anything or ever feel alone because the rainbow light touches us and connects us all. This, a go-lite knows in their heart, never to be forgotten." I could hear my mother's voice reciting the words to me as a child. Every year families would gather to marvel at the miracle of life and love.

We found a good spot under a shady tree and wholeheartedly threw ourselves into the festivities. As the big moment finally arrived, our spirits soared on the excited squeals and awed gasps of enraptured little voices. I caught sight of a tiny girl twirling around and around in a beam of rainbow light, her arms outstretched and giddy with laughter. People ate, drank and laughed together, parents and grandparents played with their children and everyone felt the brightness of the day.

We left at around two with full stomachs and hearts. Chris and Gabriel were getting along famously and I could see a great friendship forming there. I was glad, but it also meant that there would probably be more days like this with the four of us. There would be fewer outings with just Sky and me and no one wants to be a third wheel. Chris dropped us home so we could get ready for the ball.

"We'll be back to pick you up at six," Gabe called out the car window and they both waved as they drove off.

# EIGHT

## Lilly

I slipped the whisper-soft silk over my head and it cascaded down my body, floating to the floor in delicate ripples. I felt naked. The fabric was so light it had a 'barely there' feeling. The tiny crystals at my shoulders flashed in the light as I stepped toward the mirror. I decided to leave my hair down; at least then I wouldn't feel quite so naked.

Sky's gown was sapphire blue. The colour looked divine on her, intensifying the clear blue of her eyes and giving her ivory skin a luminous glow. "They're here!" she announced excitedly, motioning me over to the circle of green glass that overlooked our front garden. Gabe had pulled up and the two boys were climbing out of his car. We giggled at the satisfying sight of them in crisp black tie. It was ridiculous, but I felt the nerves kick in and prayed I would get through the evening without embarrassing myself. With Christian looking like *that,* it would be a challenge.

The ball was being held in the city's Butterfly Gardens which sat on the outskirts of town fringed by a deep green river. We arrived just before sunset as a low, golden haze weighed in the air. Magnificent wrought iron gates fashioned in the shape of butterfly wings were spread wide in welcome. We stepped through and passed under an archway smothered with purple flowers, emerging at the other end, into a breathtaking scene that was almost another world. A pebbled mosaic path ran in a straight line, barely holding back the tide of freesia, lilacs, and lilies that swayed over its boundary.

The intoxicating perfume of so many blooms swirled around me as Chris bent his lips to my ear. "I haven't told you how exquisite you are," he whispered.

"Thank you," I said with a shy smile and took his outstretched hand. His fingers curled lazily around mine and I felt settled for the first time in days.

Velvet lawns collided with winding beds of pink roses, powder blue hydrangea, and gardenias of pure white, dashed around clusters of delicate peonies, ran into smartly sculpted hedges, and yielded at the feet of yawning trees. Floating in their branches were a hundred crystal chandeliers bursting with points of light that cast a fraudulent night sky into a still mirrored pool.

The spectacle of the guests formed a garden of its own, a vibrant display of every colour and hue. Their high laughter, the clinking of cut crystal glass and an intense beehive of conversation wavered against a climactic backdrop of the wildly setting sun. Beyond them, an extravagant, lacy rotunda comfortably received a whole orchestra. I noticed my parents taking a spin on the dance floor that had been constructed on a bare expanse of lawn in the centre of the gardens.

Christian gripped my hand a little tighter as we moved into the milling crowd. The four of us reached a table where bowls of golden punch were being served and surveyed the general splendour. The fizzy liquid bit at my tongue and was wonderfully icy. I was still feeling flushed from Christian's compliment and the beguiling smile that had accompanied it. Despite the incredibly romantic setting I still wasn't sure if this was a real date and I wasn't sure if I wanted it to be. Whatever happened, I was going to have a fantastic time tonight. How could anyone not? It was an enchanted evening straight out of a fairytale.

Chris took my hand again and led me onto the dance floor where couples were assembling for the traditional Midsummer dance. It would mark the turning of day to night, the men symbolising the sun, the women, the moon. Sky and Gabriel lined up next to us and the music began. Chris placed his broad palm at my waist and I felt the heat of it through the barely there silk, his other hand closed around mine.

The dance began in slow weaving circles, Chris leading me strongly about the floor. He held my gaze until he twirled me several times and I was passed to partner with Gabe who looked like he was on cloud nine and so did Sky. I was sure this evening would finally make a couple out of them.

The girls danced with each boy in turn and were twirled down the line until we arrived back with our original partners. I returned to Chris and he lifted me by my waist into the air and turned slowly on the spot, smiling up at me the whole time. This was the end of the dance, symbolising the moon rising into the sky.

He slowly placed me back down, the orchestra fell silent and everyone raised their glasses to the last ray of sunlight as it withdrew over the horizon. We all paused and silently sent our own words of thanks, then cheers rose into the air and the music started up again. This time, a waltz. He offered me his hand again and we glided around the floor carried by the lilting notes of violins.

"When did you become such an amazing dancer?" I asked.

"I was about to ask you the same thing."

"I suppose it's been a while since we've danced together. Remember ballroom classes when we were kids? I swear to the Source, you hated it! You were always trying to get out of going," I laughed, remembering a gangly Christian testing his charms on our teacher. Sometimes it even worked.

"If you'd been my partner I wouldn't have minded, but because I was late all the time, all the other boys would snap you up and I'd get stuck with Sophie Hallows. Do you remember her? Lovely girl, horrible dancer! I was sure she had a vendetta against my feet for some reason. I'd literally come home with bruises!"

"Ha! That's right! I'd forgotten about her."

He leaned to whisper in my ear. "Please Lilly, if we happen to see her tonight, you'll protect me, won't you?" he pleaded.

We laughed and spun in circles. He was devastatingly handsome in that suit. What was it about a man in a well-cut suit that always made you weak at the knees? We sat the next dance out to catch our breath. Sky and Gabe were still glued to each other on the dance floor, their mutual adoration plain to see. I spied my parents not far from where we were standing so we went to say hello.

"Christian," my father extended his hand.

"Jonathan, Dawn, lovely to see you both," Chris returned.

"You look beautiful honey." My mother wrapped me in a tight hug.

"Thanks, mum, so do you. Hi, dad." I gave my father a big squeeze.

Chris and dad settled into a conversation that I couldn't hear over all the chatter and my mother drew me aside.

"So…" she said conspiratorially, "that's a very handsome date you have there."

I was quite taken aback. In all these years she had never even hinted at what she was hinting at now. I wasn't sure how to respond so I gave her a reproachful smile.

"It was merely an observation," she said, her mouth turning up at the corners, "an observation that many females have made this evening, I'm sure," she raised her eyebrows and laughed at my dumbstruck look. "Goodness!" she exclaimed, "Is it such a surprise that he'd be interested in the beautiful Soul that is my daughter?" She gave me a long, studious look and placed her hands on my cheeks with a loving smile and kissed my forehead. "I love you, Lilly."

"I love you too, mum." I gave her a hug and rested my head on her shoulder. It was nice to take a breather there for a moment and I felt some tension melt from my body that I wasn't aware I'd been carrying.

"What are you two up to?" interrupted my dad as he and Chris wandered toward us.

"Our daughter is sharing some of the love in that enormous heart of hers," she said, giving me a final squeeze before we separated.

"Hi, Mr. and Mrs. Flights!" Sky came prancing up towing Gabe behind her.

"Sky! How are you darling girl and who is this lovely man?" asked my mother.

"This is Gabriel Tropane," Sky beamed.

"Nice to meet you both," said Gabe extending his hand, "and congratulations on your nomination Mr. Flights."

"Thank you, Gabriel."

After a good chat with my parents, we moved through the party catching up with friends and acquaintances alike. I became entwined in lengthy conversation with Healer Cray, she was a fascinating woman and so knowledgable. She wore earrings that looked like mini chandeliers and I couldn't decide what sparkled more; her ears or her voice? All the Council Elders were present and she introduced me to Elder Tunes, an endearing old man of eighty or so, balancing on his walking stick and having the time of his life. His face was filled with joyful crinkles as he laughed merrily at just about everything. His eyes scrunched at the corners with each burst of laughter and his whole body shook with gay abandon. I think he was the happiest person I'd ever seen.

"Elder Tunes, I'd like to introduce Lilly Flights, Jonathan's daughter, and Grayson Flights' Great-granddaughter."

His eyes were the palest of blue and glistened with unshed tears of joy and excitement.

"Hello, Elder Tunes. It's a pleasure to meet you," I smiled.

"The pleasure is all mine dear," he said graciously and kissed my hand. "Your Great-grandfather was a credit to the academic community. No!" he exclaimed, raising a crooked finger, "he was a credit to us all! What a mind! What a heart!" he hooted and burst into another fit of laughter.

"My father recently gave me Great-grandfather's

original manuscript," I told him.

"Oh, how magnificent!" he gushed. "Written in his own hand I believe, how splendid! Have you read it yet?"

"Not yet, but I intend to."

"Good, good," he nodded. "I sense there are great things on the horizon from you too, my dear," he winked. "What is the area of your special gifts?"

"I'm an Acolyte Healer," I replied.

He inclined his head and a fleeting change raced across his expression, a shadow of uncertainty, then it was gone. "Well of course you are, of course you are! I can feel your compassion. It radiates from you like sunshine. I would be very honoured if you would permit me to see the manuscript at your leisure. Perhaps you might join me for tea and put some sunshine in an old man's day?" he chuckled.

"Thank you, I'd love to," I said, "but I'm quite sure that it would be the other way around."

Waiters wafted through the crowd with silver trays of dainty morsels and a rainbow of coloured drinks. The orchestra retired for the evening and was replaced by a jazz band, a grand piano and a female vocalist who's voice dripped with honey. We danced until our feet hurt, swaying with her sultry tones.

"Are you tired?" Chris asked some time after midnight.

"A little, but I don't want to go home yet."

"How about a walk then?" he grinned.

"Sure," I nodded.

He caught two crystal champagne flutes from a passing tray and nodded in the direction of the hill behind the band. We strolled along the mosaic path that extended behind the rotunda and away from the twinkling lights. It ended at the foot of the hill with an ornately carved, circular fountain. Lights shimmered up from below the surface and in its centre sat an innocent maiden of sparkling amethyst balancing a butterfly on her finger.

"Where do the butterflies go at night?" I asked.

"I'll show you," he said pointing at a stand of trees on the hilltop.

"Okay, but I might need to get rid of these." I sat on the edge of the fountain and removed my heels.

We left the path and picked our way through overflowing beds of daisies and irises that gave way to sturdy shrubs the higher we climbed. The thick grass was cool and soft on my tired feet, so I took my time, enjoying the delicious feeling of it. We reached the tall whispering trees and snapped and crunched our way through the leaf litter to find a seat on one of their giant roots. Chris handed me my glass and I took a long sip. The music drifted up the hill in thin, honeyed notes, couples were dotted about the dance floor like glistening wet paint on an artist's palette and the chattering crowd became a mere twittering of birds.

"Are you having a good time?" he asked.

"It's like a fairytale," I breathed.

He flashed that beguiling smile again and said, "Look up."

I tipped my chin back and gasped. Hidden above in the crisp, dewy curtain of leaves were hundreds of sleeping butterflies, their delicate legs sticking to the undersides of leaves, their motionless wings at rest.

"Oh, sweet universe! I've never seen..."

"Shhh..." he said, pressing his finger to my lips. He stood and looked up into the canopy and motioned for me to stay seated. He slowly lifted his arm to a low hanging branch and one gorgeous creature with black and turquoise wings stirred and fluttered to his finger. My eyes were wide with wonder as he crouched down slowly and held her out to me. He reached for my hand and raised it carefully to his. We sat very still and after a few moments, she stepped lightly from his finger to mine. I could barely feel her dainty steps. Chris sat back smiling widely, watching my delight. She slowly stretched her wings of iridescent velvet in the bright moonlight and I wondered what she was thinking. She lingered for a few moments more and then fluttered up in a lazy spiral back to her secret resting place.

As we both lowered our faces from the path of her flight, our eyes met. He was still smiling and so was I.

"Thank you," I said simply, knowing that words couldn't convey the beauty of that moment but knowing that my face said everything I felt.

He nodded gently, placed his hand on top of mine and we sat silently for a long time beneath a canopy of sleeping butterflies and scattering stars.

# NINE

## Jay

I was so sick to death of myself, I'd decided to get professional help. Desperate times called for desperate measures. God help me if John heard about it, I'd never live it down. The appointment was tomorrow and I'd been tempted to cancel it a hundred times over. I kept telling myself that it couldn't hurt to try counselling, millions of people did it every day and the reality was, I was still struggling. The bulk of the pain was behind me and dealt with but her betrayal had crucified me. I don't know how many endless days I'd spent in shock and denial before I'd finally broken down and shattered into a million tiny shards. I had died inside. It had even hurt to breathe and I'd questioned whether I wanted to go on breathing. I didn't know that a person could feel that much pain and suffering and I didn't know that someone who was supposed to love you could inflict it. I'd learned to accept the beatings from my father. The man clearly loathed himself, so how could he be expected to show love when he was filled with so much hatred? This had been different. I had thought Jess really loved me and then I'd hated myself for being so trusting and naive. I was sure I would never survive it.

It was weeks since the beautiful angel had come into my dreams and given me hope that things could be different. I had thought of her every day since but she had not visited me again, so I was prepared to try anything to feel even a small measure of what she had made me feel. I doubted Dr. Ferguson was an angel, but he would have to do.

The freeway to the coast was packed, but I was dying for a surf to clear my head and no amount of traffic was going to stop me. We were all at a crawl, yet there were always those drivers that thought repeatedly swapping lanes would get them one car length in front and somehow reasoned this was a good thing. *Christ!* I cranked up my music and looked around at all the deadpan faces encapsulated in their air-conditioned bubbles. Maybe I really was an alien. The more I tried to figure people out, the more they confused the hell out of me. No wonder I couldn't find a girlfriend!

It had been a long time since I'd walked away from Jess and I hadn't been near another girl. Not because I didn't want to. It was because I never seemed to meet the right one. I had become very good at reading people's true intentions when I met them. The funny part was, I'd always had this uncanny ability since I was a kid, I'd just never trusted my instincts. Well, after repeated hard knocks, I was definitely listening now. John called it my 'superpower' because he preferred not to talk about airy-fairy things like intuition. Ryan, on the other hand, was a bit more on my wavelength and had a few super powers of his own.

There was no shortage of girls in the world and I was often amused that they gravitated to me. It made me sure that these women had an inbuilt radar alerting them to struggling males. They seemed to want to scoop you up and make it all better, bleeding if necessary to fix your problems. Then there were the 'good time girls' who wore heavy armour to protect themselves from anything that remotely resembled a feeling and were better 'players' than most guys I knew. I just wasn't interested in a shallow fling or people that were too frightened to open themselves up to another human being. I was looking for someone real and extraordinary, who understood there was more to life than work, money and material things. It wasn't that I passed judgement on people who wanted to live their lives that way, I just had a very different outlook compared to most. I knew there was more. It was hard sometimes because I'd see everyone around me playing this game called life, and I'd try to fit in and play along, but they were all playing by a very different set of rules to me. It made me feel lonely a lot of the time, but not lonely enough to throw away my integrity.

The long drive was worth it. There were some beautiful sets of waves coming in. I stood on the headland and eyed the swells and breaks. I'd gone to my usual beach that only the locals knew about. There were some other guys working the break further down and apart from a couple of dogs wrestling with a stick and their owner, I had the whole place to myself.

The sand scrunched under my bare feet. I breathed in the familiar, salty air and squatted just back from the water's edge to wax my board. I loved the freedom I always felt entering the ocean. It was like stepping into a new world somehow and it only asked that you surrender to it. As I paddled out, the waves rose in crystalline arcs and curled in on themselves in a glittering display of diamond light. The water was the perfect temperature as I sat on my board and waited for the next set. I caught a beautiful wave and was lifted and hurled forward at tremendous speed. I dropped into the barrel. The water curled around me in a tunnel of glittering silver and blue. *God I loved surfing!* The sound of churning water and wind, the perfection of being there just as the wave forms and riding it to its end, delighting in the thrill of a moment that always ends too soon. I paddled back out and waited. Salty droplets fell from my hair like stray diamonds.

I started thinking about my appointment again and what I was going to say and wondering if there was anything that anyone could really do to help. Then

I thought of the angel. She'd know how to help. She seemed to have all the answers. I'd read some stuff online about people conversing with guardian angels. It wasn't that I didn't believe it was true, I just didn't know if it was something that the average person could do. Did you have to be religious or special in some way? I didn't know. I smirked into the sun while I toyed with the idea of trying to contact her. It felt kind of stupid to try, but the worst thing that could happen would be feeling like an idiot if it didn't work. So, I took a chance and decided to ask her the question. It was a long shot, I knew, but stranger things happen every day. Don't they? I started explaining my situation out loud, addressing my problem to the briny wind.

"It's taken a long time to put myself back together. I'm mostly whole again, but some of those pieces were obliterated into dust," my voice caught, remembering the intensity of that pain. "I don't know, maybe I'll always have holes now," I sighed. "I mean, how do you ever completely heal from something that... devastating? Is that even possible? I don't know if those lost pieces of myself can ever be replaced, no matter how hard I try. Maybe I'll always be a little bit... flawed."

I closed my eyes, thinking it might help, and waited and listened for a reply. I conjured the vivid memory of her in my head, imagined her slender body, the dark, flowing hair and huge shining eyes, until there she was, painted on the dark screen behind my eyelids.

I could see her drifting nearer, illuminating my darkest places. I drew her image even closer to me so it appeared that we were face to face, only inches apart. "Oh my God, you're so beautiful," I breathed.  Her serene, angelic face froze and so did she. She looked like she was in shock. *Did I say something wrong?* I wondered, hoping she wouldn't disappear.

"Can you... see me?" she asked softly.

"Um, yes," I replied feeling extremely stupid because I'd just realised that I was sitting in the middle of the ocean, on a surfboard, with my eyes closed, talking to my imaginary angel!

"You called for me... and you can see me?" she said with exaggerated slowness. "This shouldn't be happening," she whispered breathlessly, almost to herself and then there was a slight shake of her head. Her eyes grew even wider with surprise.

"What do you mean?" I asked her, puzzled. "It's my daydream. I'm talking to you because I *want* to talk to you," I started laughing, thrilled that I had such a brilliant imagination. She cocked her head to one side.

"Is that what you think this is? A daydream?" Her question was delivered in measured tones.

"Yes," I replied, but some uncertainty had crept into my conviction.

"I assure you I'm not a figment of your imagination, Jay. I'm here to help because you asked. Help is always given to those who ask," she looked at me expectantly.

My mind started asking questions. If this was a daydream I don't think this is how I would imagine it playing out. Her beautiful eyes didn't waver from me for a second. My heart had begun beating faster as I entertained the unlikely possibility that she was real. So... why couldn't I bring myself to open my eyes? Curiosity... blind faith... desperation... complete insanity? But I had to. If this was some supernatural encounter and I had achieved the unlikely feat of summoning an angel rather than imagining one, I had to test the theory. I forced my eyes open and blinked into the sunlight. Bobbing on my board I looked all around and dunked my head under the water for good measure. *Yep, definitely awake and fully conscious.* I took a deep breath and very slowly closed my eyes again. "Holy shit!"

A glorious smile lit up her face, and seemingly, the rest of the world too, and then there was that feeling again; an indescribable, expanding joy. It was palpable, instantaneous and unarguably real because I felt it in every cell of my body as an incredible lightness, filling me to bursting point. If I were capable of magically conjuring this feeling, I wouldn't be seeing a counsellor tomorrow, that's for sure! No, it was all her. This must mean she was real. *Holy crap!* I could feel the ecstatic, dopey smile spreading on my face as I asked the million dollar question. "Are you an angel?"

She laughed in high melodic notes. "No," she shook her head, "I used to be human and now I help humans in need."

"So... you're a spirit?" I guessed.

"No, I'm very much alive," she smiled.

"So...where are you exactly and how can I see you if you're not in my imagination?" My head was whirling, trying to figure out a plausible explanation.

"I don't know how you can see me. This is an... unusual situation." She paused, seeming a little perplexed herself, then recovered. "Jay, you asked me if you would always be flawed and my answer is, that's entirely up to you. Is there a reason you *think* you should be flawed?"

She was clearly changing the subject but I tried to calm myself and answer her question. She gazed at me intently, as though every single word I said was precious.

"I don't think I *should* be flawed, I just don't see how I can avoid it. The damage has been done and I've repaired as much as I can. I think maybe this is as good as I'm going to get but I'm hoping, that by some miracle, I'm wrong. I'd be happy to be wrong."

"If you're happy to be wrong, then you'd best start being happy," she laughed.

I pursed my lips and thought about that for a second. "Are you saying that I don't have to be flawed?"

"I'm saying you should do what makes you happy. You can sit in the ruins of your past or you can rebuild in the present moment. Those are your choices."

I examined the so-called choices and determined that there wasn't a choice at all. "I don't really have an option, do I?" I frowned.

"You'd be surprised how many choose the ruins," she said shrugging her shoulders. "What will you do now?"

Her question stumped me a bit. "Aren't you supposed to tell me?" I asked uncertainly.

She smiled and shook her head. "It's not my place to tell you what to do, Jay. Besides, you don't need me to; you've always been perfectly capable of deciding what's best for you." Her expression was filled with compassion and certainty. "You just need to trust yourself a little more and act on it."

I wasn't entirely convinced. "What makes you think that?"

"I don't think... I know. I see who you truly are beneath all the pain and self-doubt, I see a beautiful, shining Soul who is only limited by prisons he builds for himself. Knock down the prisons, Jay. Start building bridges."

Her sincerity was so infectious that I immediately believed she was right. She made me feel like I could conquer Mount Everest, as though it was obvious to her that I would. No, it was even more than that; to her, I was already triumphantly standing on the summit. I felt a soaring sense of freedom mixed with relief and excitement. My body tingled with it. I didn't want her to leave... ever! I tried to think of something else to say. "You know my name but I don't know yours," I said.

She paused, deliberating whether to answer or not. "It's Lilly," she said finally.

"Lilly, I don't know who you are or where you came from but you've given me hope when nothing else has. I don't know how to thank you," I said shaking my head. "Just being here with you makes me feel like I can do anything. You *must be* an angel and right now I'm hoping that you're a guardian angel and I'm praying that you're mine... no-one else's... just mine."

Her eyes never left me as I said what I felt and they showed me the unfettered love and devotion within her; the love she shared so freely. "You needn't thank me, Jay. I was once where you are. I understand how you feel, but I also see things as they really are and I promise you will be fine." She placed two fingers to her lips and blew me a kiss, my heart faltered and she was gone.

# TEN

## Lilly

My heartbeat was so loud it woke me. I rolled onto my back, stretched my sleepy limbs and collapsed into satisfied giggles. *That was amazing.* I didn't have a clue how he'd seen me, but I felt as though I'd been of more help that way. He had really understood. I had seen the promise of change in his eyes and felt his spirit lighten. Maybe now he could finally let go of his past and move forward into the beautiful life I was certain he'd have. I was so excited for him! Had I blown him a kiss? Oh, well, I'd meant it. It was moments like these that made Soul Guardianship so rewarding. We were ever hopeful that Souls would choose the path of light instead of shadow, but it was always their choice. There was no right or wrong way, of course, they all had to make changes in their own time and I had learnt that change on Earth was slow; often painfully slow. Not for us watching, but for those who needlessly dragged out their suffering, usually by trying to pretend that it wasn't there.

When I'd looked into Jay's heart, I'd seen the constriction loosening and the walls around it begin to crumble. He would learn to trust again and I hoped I would be the one to guide him through it. *I'm praying that you're mine,'* he had said. His words had stirred something inside me that I couldn't name, and I had, again, felt that strange sense of familiarity. I didn't bother explaining to him that isn't how it usually works because this clearly was an unusual situation. He had called *me,* had asked specifically for *me,* which meant he had seen me before. It must have been the last time we had contact when I had reached out to him and placed my hand on his heart. I remembered feeling as though he were looking right at me, but I had dismissed it. The thought sent a little wave of shock, panic and excitement through me.

*So what now?* I checked my conduct and was satisfied I'd not broken any rules apart from the obvious fact that I'd touched a human. There wasn't anything in the rules specifically saying that I shouldn't, but I knew I'd overstepped my duty and now he could see me. It seemed too much of a leap to just call it a coincidence. Besides, there were no coincidences. The urge to comfort him had been so strong and it had felt like the right thing to do. I couldn't explain it. It just had. Well, I didn't have any control over the fact that he could see me now and I decided that this was the way it was supposed to be. The

Soul wants what the Soul wants. I resolved to go with the flow, accept the way things were and maintain faith that anything that happened from here on in was for Jay's highest good. What else could I do? And who was I to question the will of the Universe?

Soul Guardians were not usually assigned specific Souls to care for. We gravitated toward Souls that resonated with our past human experience and they naturally drew us to them, energetically sensing which of us would serve them best. I thought of my past life vision at the Record Keepers. Had I known something of Jay's pain in that life? Were we brought together because somewhere deep in my subconscious I knew how he felt?

Jay had been tested since birth, struggling through the pains of an abusive childhood, only to continue the pattern in his adult years by enduring a partner who lied and cheated and made him feel that he was never good enough, no matter what he did. My job was to help him see that he could choose to remain a victim and blame others for his unhappiness, or he could start discovering and believing how wonderful he was. Once he did that, beauty would naturally flow into his life. Whether or not he could find the strength to do it in this lifetime was another matter, and entirely his choice. There would be no shame or failure if he couldn't. Human life was hard. There were many lessons to be learnt, which was why Souls kept reincarnating back to Earth until they understood them all.

Jay's dazzling smile and warm, open face were clear in my mind. There was a childlike innocence about him that many adult Souls had misplaced and forgotten, or had purposefully put away in favour of 'sensible' and 'serious' pursuits. He led a simple life, with simple things. He was uninterested in material possessions beyond basic comfort. He preferred the company of a night sky or a tranquil rock pool to wearying crowds. I had seen him revelling in the unpredictable power of the ocean waves, delighting in the sublime beauty of mother nature; a gift that was on offer for all to enjoy, but received by so few. His innocence would be his greatest strength and saving grace.

When I got out of bed, Sky was napping in the garden. She was curled up like a cat on a mountain of soft pillows in the warm sun. We had both needed a nap after last night's festivities. It had been after 4am when Chris dropped me home and Sky had breezed in mid-morning, having spent the night at Gabe's. I had not spoken to her yet, but judging from her cheshire smile, it seemed that things went well. I brewed two mugs of croyberry tea and made my way outdoors, settling on a cushion of my own. She yawned and smiled even wider.

"Here," I said, handing her the steaming amber infusion.

She reached for it gratefully. "Mmm, thank you. So, how was your night?"

"Oh, no. You first," I laughed. "That smile demands

an explanation!"

Her cheeks flushed rosebud pink. "Oh Lilly, he's just gorgeous," she gushed. "I had the best time! I didn't think it was possible to be any more blessed in life and then I met Gabe. He's so… so…"

"Gorgeous?" I offered.

"Yes!" she laughed and squealed all at the same time. "When I saw him in that suit I thought I'd die, with his luscious nutmeg locks and soft brown eyes!"

"He's not hard to look at," I agreed. "So, is it official? Can we start calling him your boyfriend now?" I asked hopefully.

"Yes, I think you can," she squeaked, glowing with excitement. "And how was your night?"

I had to pause and think back. My conversation with Jay made last night seem distant. "It was lovely." A butterfly caught my eye across the garden. I smiled and turned back to Sky lounging on her pillow pile. "Christian made me feel like a princess. We had a great time together like we always do." We really had. He was doting and attentive and distractingly handsome.

"He couldn't tear his eyes away from you all night," she twittered.

I could feel the heat rising to my cheeks. He'd been the perfect gentleman and it had been comfortable and effortless as we'd slipped into our easy banter, laughing and spinning in dizzying circles on the dance floor. The only evident awkwardness was when the lines of friendship became blurred in his arms. My body buzzed with remembrance.

I could feel Sky studying the emotions passing on my face and turned to look at her. "Are you seeing something I'm not?" I asked.

"Maybe," she said gently and diverted her inquisitive gaze toward some low hanging branches, laden with fuchsia blooms.

I stared into my croyberry tea and tried to change the subject. "Are you doing anything for the rest of the day? I thought we could head up to the crystal pools and relax."

"Ooooh, perfect," she grinned delightedly.

♡ ♡ ♡

We laughed and joked as we skipped our way through the still forest, our voices bouncing off the rough trunks only to be swallowed again by dense green. We walked to the water's edge, teetering over the smooth, warm river stones and climbed higher along the creek's twisting path until we reached a wide, deep pool with a plunging waterfall. The crystal clear water rained down in sheets making a gorgeous shushing sound and pierced the pool's still surface. A cloud of fine mist sprayed up from the impact and captured the light in occasional rainbows. The pool was perfectly round and so deep that it resembled a green glass pot brimming with ink. The edges encircled with clear, pale green, descended to black in the centre.

We plunged in, squealing from the shock of the cold water and swam over to the cascading falls. Giggling, we each found a stone to perch on and let the water pound down over our backs in a liquid massage. I closed my eyes, the noise of the falls blocked all other sound and the steady pummelling sedated me. Eventually, I slid from my perch and drifted lazily from one end of the pool to the other, stopping to watch a water spider skating on the surface or catch the glint of a dragonfly's wings. Sated, I glided to the shallows and dreamily rose from the water. I lay my towel on a bed of hot stone and stretched out face down, listening to my heart beating against the rock. The sunlight on my skin was magic as I drifted in and out of a blissful afternoon nap.

My eyes fluttered open when I heard footsteps quite close by. Sky was dozing next to me. I looked behind us and saw a boy picking his way over the loose river stones. He seemed to be in a hurry. It was the lanky teenager from the healaxis. "Garrick, hi!" I waved. His head jerked in my direction and he stopped abruptly. He was all of sixteen, with rust coloured hair and a spattering of freckles over his nose and cheeks. He eyed me with suspicion, I supposed, trying to place my face. "It's Lilly Flights," I smiled and paused for his response. "I examined you at the healaxis." I tried for a reassuring tone. My explanation seemed to have the opposite effect I was looking for because he now looked alarmed. "So, how are you feeling?" I continued, trying to put him at ease.

"Oh, hi. I'm fine, thank you," he mumbled, but looked very far from it as he shifted restlessly from foot to foot.

"That's good to hear," I smiled. "Have you been for a swim yet? It's a beautiful day for it."

He seemed to be at a loss for words and his eyes were darting in every direction to avoid contact with mine. Sky was awake now and sitting up, stretching with a satisfied yawn.

"Oh, Garrick, this is my friend, Sky," I gestured.

"Hi Garrick, nice to meet you," she chirped characteristically. "What do you have in the basket?"

I'd not noticed that he was clinging tightly to a cane basket that he'd swung behind his back. It was covered over with a tea towel and whatever was in there, was moving.

He was fidgeting uncomfortably as he addressed his response to the rocks beneath his feet. "It's an owl I found injured, that's all, but I've been caring for him and he's better now. I came here to release him."

"Oh, let me see," I said walking over to him. He almost leapt back as I closed the short distance between us. He was acting like a scared animal himself.

"You know, I have another friend Chris who's a Translator. He loves animals like you. Are you sure the owl is completely well? Chris could ask him if you like before you release him."

"Yes, no, I mean, yes I'm sure he's well and no,

I don't need any help," he said nervously. "Thank you anyway. I have to go now. Bye Acolyte Flights. Bye Sky."

He scurried away into the trees clutching his basket and was swallowed by dense green within seconds.

"Bye," I called after him, doubting he heard me. "That was odd," I said turning back to Sky.

"He's either very nervous about something or very shy," she offered.

"I don't know. I've only met him once at healaxis. Healer Cray asked me to examine him for a second opinion but I don't know if she's arrived at a diagnosis yet."

I stared through the trees in the direction that Garrick had fled. I saw nothing but a dark tangle of twisting branches competing for the light.

# ELEVEN

## Jay

The traffic was typically horrendous as I drove through the city. A bleak, obscuring haze clung to the skyline, sent up by the drone of stationary cars below. Faceless suits carved weary paths in the pavement with all the purpose of a mechanical army. Blank masks marching to perform empty tasks from office cubicles like battery hens.

I dropped my hands from the wheel and waited for the lane to move. I remembered a day long ago when I thought I'd never find my way back to myself; when I was still consumed with understanding why Jess had cheated on me. I'd been sitting in traffic, just like this, and I was so tired at that point in my life that I'd given up on energetically cursing the world in favour of greeting each day with exhausted indifference. A beaten up old van had passed me, travelling in the other direction. Reggae music had spilled from the open windows and in the passenger seat sat a caramel skinned woman with the plump, dark shape of an islander with crimped hair and dazzling white teeth. Her head had tilted out the open window, unabashedly basking in the glorious feeling of sun and wind on her smiling face. Her joyous eyes had found me as she'd sailed by and she had gifted me with the most beautiful and brilliant smile. I'd never seen a smile like that. I'd felt cracks forming in the wall I'd built around myself. I had felt more of a connection with that stranger than I had with anyone else in years. She had been there and gone in an instant. A moment in time that we'd both shared. And it had struck me then: how could she be in the same time and place as me, feeling true joy, while I battled apathy punctuated with despair?

It was years ago, but I still remembered it as the moment I had decided that every second of this life was precious because that lady had shown me that every second holds the potential for real joy. We spend a lifetime striving to find joy when the truth is, it can be found in seconds. It was one of those cathartic moments that we stumble upon from time to time. Or more accurately, the moment stumbles into you, just when you need it the most. And here it was again, reminding me of a feeling I'd forgotten. Maybe happiness was that simple. Maybe all I had to do was choose it.

I looked at my watch thankful that I'd allowed plenty of time. I queued with impatient drivers at the entrance of the underground car park and waited for my ticket. The slow crawl down the ramp was like descending into hell; the temperature raising by ten degrees and the air so thick with petrol fumes it was almost unbreathable. I half expected the devil himself to be manning the ticket booth. It took me another ten minutes of driving in circles around the concrete dungeon to find a vacant space.

♡ ♡ ♡

After a short wait in the leafy reception area, Dr. Ferguson came out to greet me. He was younger than I had pictured; around forty or so with a kind, tired face and the beginnings of a receding hairline. He seemed to almost sigh with relief when he saw me. I was still walking on air from my angel encounter and assumed he was unaccustomed to smiling patients in his line of work. He led the way down a bland hall where the carpet was worn and flattened like a runway and opened a chipped wooden door.

His office was simply furnished and homely which immediately put me at ease. I noticed a Buddhist statue on his overflowing bookshelf and caught a few titles like, 'The Power of Now' and 'You Can Heal Your Life' on well-worn spines. He invited me to sit in an overstuffed armchair with gigantic, puffy cushions after shaking my hand.

"So, Jay, what brings you to see me?" he smiled congenially.

I relayed the story of my broken heart, how I'd

always remained faithful to Jessica and how idiotic I felt for being so gullible and trusting, how I no longer felt anger or resentment toward her but was still angry for putting myself in that situation and allowing it to go on for so long. On a subconscious level I had known there was something very wrong. I'd even questioned her about it on several occasions, but she had always denied it so convincingly which left me riddled with self-doubt and with the feeling that I was losing my mind. I had allowed myself to believe her lies because the alternative was just too horrific to accept.

Dr. Ferguson asked only a few questions as I went through it all. He scratched occasional notes on his pad and when I was done, he sat back and took in my expression. "You look relieved," he said and poured me a glass of water from a plastic pitcher with orange slices printed on the side.

"I suppose I am," I agreed. "I've never said all of that out loud to anyone before."

"Not even your friends?" he queried as perplexed creases appeared on his forehead.

I shook my head.

"Jay, what's the most important thing in this world for you?"

Straight out of the gate, that was a pretty huge question. This guy didn't mess around. I didn't know what answer he was looking for, but I knew instantly what the answer was for me. It was something I'd often thought about. "Love. There can't be a world if there's no love."

His expression remained smooth, giving no hint of whether he agreed or disagreed. "Do you understand the difference between love and unconditional love?" he asked.

"Unconditional love? Like the love a parent has for a child?" I wondered out loud.

"That's traditionally the example that's used but a parent's love isn't always unconditional."

He watched me, I think, expecting me to argue or protest. When I merely looked puzzled, he continued. "A parent will often show love to a child when he or she is well behaved, yet they might get annoyed, yell, or threaten a child when they are judged to be misbehaving – in other words, in those moments, they are withholding love from the child because the child isn't doing what the parents want." He paused again, gauging my reaction and waiting for his words to sink in. "Unconditional love doesn't switch on when another person is doing what we want them to do and switch off when they're not," he explained. "I'm not saying a parent shouldn't teach their child right from wrong, I'm saying there are loving ways to do so.

"The same goes for how we treat ourselves. We might say that we love ourselves, yet we get angry and punish ourselves when we do something we're not proud of, we find faults with how we look, act and behave and sometimes, we even hate ourselves. If we truly loved ourselves we wouldn't abandon and turn on ourselves so quickly. We would adopt loving ways to nurture ourselves and allow ourselves to make mistakes and grow. It's like being the ideal loving parent and the child at the same time. Do you see?"

I sat there stunned as his words sank into my brain. This guy was like Buddha in a bad suit! "That actually makes perfect sense," I said after a long silence. "I've noticed how quickly I put myself down sometimes and I've been pulling myself up on it lately."

"Good. You can't fix a bad habit if you don't know it's there, so well done," he smiled faintly at me as though he was very tired, but it was sincere just the same. "Jay, you said earlier that you're still angry at yourself for being gullible and trusting in your last relationship."

"Yeah," I rubbed my hand over the stubble on my jaw, "I suppose I still feel like an idiot for believing her lies."

The worn out springs of his puffy armchair squeaked as he leaned toward me and nodded his head. "It's very hard when someone we love turns out to be someone different, but you've learnt something from it, haven't you? What do you think you'll do differently next time?"

"Next time I'll listen to my gut. I'll trust myself and how I feel instead of allowing another person's words to distract me from my instincts and emotionally manipulate me."

He grinned and kept nodding. "So you learnt quite a bit from that relationship and one of the things you learnt was to set healthy boundaries for yourself and not allow destructive or disrespectful behaviour in your life. Again, well done," he smiled reassuringly.

"Yeah, I suppose I did learn something," I shrugged."

That's what life's all about Jay, learning," he smiled.

"So why do I still feel like I'm just going through the motions in life? I don't ever really feel happy. I just want to feel good again and I don't know how to do that."

Dr. Ferguson leaned back in his chair and put aside his scratchy notes. "You let Jessica go because her behaviour was unhealthy for you – destructive and disrespectful. I would like you to examine your behaviour toward yourself for a moment. Do you always trust and respect yourself Jay? Do you treat yourself well or is the way you treat yourself sometimes destructive too?"

I thought carefully before I answered. "I know I can be very hard on myself. I have high expectations and standards and am always trying to do better," I answered honestly, "but I know I fall short of the mark a lot of the time."

"And when you fall short of the mark, how does that make you feel?"

I thought about that for a moment. "Angry and like I'm not good enough."

Dr. Ferguson looked at me squarely. "So, you become like the parent that withdraws their love when the child isn't behaving the way they would like."

"Ah…." He was right.

♡ ♡ ♡

*Wow! That went well.* I drove home feeling very glad that I hadn't cancelled the appointment. I began to realise that my unhappiness had less and less to do with Jess and more to do with how I felt about and treated myself. In a very brutal way, the whole fiasco with Jess cheating had just illustrated that I didn't feel good enough about myself as a person or a partner. If I didn't feel good enough about me, how was she supposed to, or anyone else for that matter?

The memories of what she did still hurt, but I was starting to see it from a different angle. Dr. Ferguson had said life was all about learning and Lilly had said something about soul contracts and learning too. It seemed like a cruel way to learn, but what if that whole crazy situation happened so I could finally see that even though I'm not a frightened little boy anymore, suffering at the hands of an abusive drunk, I've never really found my self worth? Jessica hadn't given up on me, I had done that to myself, long before I even met her!

Life was suddenly looking like a whole new ball game where I had the ball, not other people. Now I just had to learn how to run with it. When I got home I checked my messages. There was a text from Ryan wishing me luck for my appointment. I'd sworn him to secrecy so John wouldn't give me any crap. *Went great. Thanks, man. Fill u in later,* I typed and pressed send.

Tomorrow I was starting work on the landscaping for a community permaculture garden one suburb over. It was the biggest job I'd ever landed. I would be heading a team of six guys and I was keen to get started on it. I picked up my sketch pad and the final plans to look them over. I hadn't had any work for the last two weeks which was probably why I'd been feeling a bit flat as well. I couldn't wait to get out there and get my hands dirty. Working in the earth and with plants was amazing.

I loved being outdoors with the sun on my back and the satisfaction of creating something beautiful; places where people could enjoy and appreciate nature. Yep, I was a greenie and proud of it! I was really happy with the sustainable design. It would be an oasis in the middle of suburbia with fruit trees, beds of vegetables and herbs that would be tended and cared for by the community for the reward of fresh produce. What could be better?

I sat back, with my sketch pad still in my hand and noticed I was smiling. I was feeling good, freer somehow. Today was a very good day. I decided to celebrate with a beer. That first cold swig was always the best. I grabbed my sketch pad and my beer and went to lie in the hammock in the back yard. The early spring air was still a bit chilly in the mornings but it had warmed up to be a perfect day.

The grass was coming back to life after a frosty winter, new shoots were appearing on the trees and birds were busily tending their nests.

I threw myself into the hammock and rocked away while I listened to the buzz of insects and the warbling magpies. It felt so good to be relaxed and happy... content. I was on a roll now. I almost couldn't wait for my appointment with Dr. Ferguson next week. I just wanted to plough in and get all this sorted, I wanted to move on and live my life.

I flipped through the pages of my sketch pad to a fresh, white sheet and let my hand roam. I'd always loved drawing and painting, but it had been quite a few years since I'd picked up a brush. Any drawing I did these days was mainly work related. I preferred pencil and paper to a computer design program, it was just more real that way.

As the graphite tip wandered freely over the page, my thoughts strayed to Lilly. Staring at the shifting clouds, I wondered for the millionth time where she was and what she was doing. My pencil began forming the slim curve of her cheek, the arch of her brow, the alert shape of her eye, the huge shining circle of her iris, a thicket of long, black lashes. I drew the line of her nose and her heart shaped lips, my hand gliding over the cartridge with familiar ease. I stroked my finger over the silvery lines, smudging and softening the half face that stared back at me. I added her glossy hair in long fluid strokes; silky strands dancing on the wind.

I closed my eyes to envision her and compare my likeness. I conjured every bright thing that beat within her and burned without, an intense light that kept me awake at night and dulled my days. I'd pictured her so often I knew her by heart, and then, without warning, she was right there. "Lilly?"

She drifted close enough to touch and her face lit up. My sketch was a poor imitation. The life and love she exuded was magnetic.

"Hello Jay," she smiled sweetly.

"You're here!"

"Yes."

There was a long pause. I didn't know what to say. Had I done this? Had I brought her here just by thinking about her? "How are you?" I asked, lacking something more interesting to say.

She looked slightly confused and then broke into a laugh that burst from her lips like a song. The joy that radiated from her was infectious and I found myself laughing back.

"What?" I asked her, confused.

"Sorry. It's just that I've never had a human ask how *I am* before, but I'm wonderful thank you and how are you?"

"I'm great," I shrugged, shaking my head in amazement and awe.

"Really?" she said, her eyes warm and wide, inviting me to tell her more.

"I went to see a counsellor this morning," I said. "It was pretty amazing."

She remained silent, so I continued. "We spoke about unconditional love and how I haven't treated myself very well." I lowered my eyelids like shutters of regret.

When she didn't respond for a while, I looked up to see if she was still there. She remained placidly focussed, carefully watching me.

"I admitted to him that I've never really felt good enough," my words were exhaled in a stumbling rush and I looked at her for any sign of a reaction. She was perfectly still, her expression had not changed and I breathed a sigh of relief. I suppose I had been expecting her to recoil in horror or even worse, pity me. "So, you'll be happy to know that I'm starting to see how those flaws aren't from Jess, they're from me, which means I can mend them."

She broke into that incredible smile and just nodded slowly. "So, I'm building bridges...no more sitting in ruins," I added. She just kept nodding and smiling and her eyes glistened with emotion. "Why won't you say something?" I finally asked.

"Because I don't need to. I already told you you're amazing, and you are. Look at what you've done in 24 hours."

It was such a strange feeling to have someone speak about me that way. "I still have a long way to go, though," I shrugged while trying to accept her compliment.

"Not as far as you think. Your whole perspective

has shifted and you no longer see yourself as a victim. You're taking responsibility for your life and your happiness. I'm overwhelmed with joy for you, Jay!"

I just sat there grinning and shaking my head, blown away by the way she made me feel. I felt so light and happy I thought I'd burst like a lost balloon that dared climb too close to the sun. "Now you're the second person in the world I've ever said that to out loud. Except, you're not really in my world are you?" I decided to just come out and ask her directly. "Lilly, what are you and where are you? How is any of this possible?"

"Honestly Jay, I have no idea. This isn't usually how things work."

"So it's never happened to you before? People can't normally see you, I mean?"

"Not that I know of," she shook her head.

"Lilly, are you my guardian angel?"

"I'm not an angel, but I am a guardian, a Soul Guardian. We guide and help Souls who need us."

"Okay, so have I just become one of those people who can see ghosts and spirit guides and things like that?" I laughed with an equal measure of mocking and nervousness.

"That's a bit different. They're all a little less... um... solid than us."

I thought about that for a second. "Hang on, so, you're flesh and blood? Is that what you meant when you said you're very much alive?" I gaped.

"Yes," she replied matter-of-factly.

I let out a nervous huff. "Hang on, let me get this straight. You're not an angel, you're a soul guardian. You're not a spirit, you're alive and you used to be human and now you're... um... what are you?" I searched her face as though I might find the answer etched there.

"I'm a go-lite. We're the same as humans except for the functioning of our hearts and minds. We see life from a... higher perspective, the beauty of every moment, and it's our job to help Souls on Earth see that and join us here."

I found myself nodding at her in slow motion, trying to take in this surreal information. "So, what do you mean by *join you?* Like, reincarnate there?"

"Yes," she grinned.

"And where is *there* exactly?" I could feel my face scrunching up in anxiousness and disbelief.

"Panacea. A planet in a different dimension to Earth."

I took in a deep breath trying to accept what I was hearing. It didn't work. "Right... okay... I think I need another beer. Actually no, make that a scotch," I scrubbed my hands over my face, trying to make sense of what she was telling me. I felt as though someone had taken to the contents of my skull with an egg whisk.

"Well, you asked!" she laughed. Then she paused and a look of concern crept onto her face. "I'm sorry. This is a shock for you, maybe I shouldn't have said anything, but I do have a *terrible* habit of telling the truth. Kind of comes with the territory," she beamed at me again, this time with a certain amount of cheekiness.

I found myself laughing along with her. Her laugh sounded like crystal glasses clinking, while mine came out of my constricted throat with unfortunate, hysterical strain. I quickly closed my mouth and cleared my throat. "It's okay, I'll be fine in a minute," I said, not believing myself for a second, "and duly noted about the truth telling. Thanks."

There was something in her smile that quivered at the edges of a long forgotten memory. It was a momentary spark of recognition and then it was gone.

"But seriously, are you all right?" she asked.

I shook my head a little to clear it. "Actually, yeah. Perfect," I smiled. "I've always believed in reincarnation I just never expected to end up living in another dimension of existence one day." I heard myself say the words that at once seemed utterly absurd and comfortably true; as though a voice very deep inside of me said, *but you already knew that, didn't you? Remember?*

Her expression smoothed and she gazed at me as though I were a sheet of cellophane, her eyes wide and piercing. "You remember, don't you?" she asked softly.

There was a long pause as the reality of it settled into my awareness. Lilly just waited patiently for me to catch up. "It's hard to explain, but I think I do," I said slowly. "What you're saying sounds crazy, but it's as though I've always known that's the truth, it's just been buried so deep, I didn't know it was there."

"The Soul remembers everything, Jay. It's a person's mind that gets in the way and prevents them from remembering. So whenever you feel that glimmer of recognition, that deep inner knowing that you can't explain, trust it. That way you'll always find the truth."

# TWELVE

## Lilly

I let him digest that for a while and watched as the lights switched on. I could see it as energetic pulses of colour and light that flickered and surged through his whole body, reconnecting his Soul memory to his physical form. It didn't matter how many times I had witnessed this it still left me spellbound. To think, that I was once exactly where he was now, after so many difficult human lives, to finally start remembering the truth of who you are; an inherently loving and limitless being. He had opened his eyes and it was as though he was seeing the world for the first time.

"Lilly, will you stay with me a while?"

"Of course," I answered.

He smiled contentedly, stretched his smooth, brown arms and relaxed even further into the hammock. It swayed him gently in the breeze as he watched wisps of cloud feathering across the sky. The two green worlds in his perfect face were tranquil and reflective, the pain and empty longing replaced by peace. It touched me so deeply to see him this way. I watched the sunlight dance on those tawny streaks in his hair and my eyes wandered to the sketchpad resting on his chest. There I saw the soft, delicate lines that formed a half-drawn face. I looked closer and was surprised to see it was my face. In place of the other half, he had written one word – eternity. My heart became louder and I had that feeling of being caught in a riptide again, just like the first time I'd seen him.

There was a pattern emerging here that I didn't understand and I couldn't ignore. I felt a very strong connection to Jay and it clearly wasn't one-sided. He was able to draw me to him at will, with an intensity I'd not experienced from any other Soul and I had to admit that I liked it. I wanted to be near to him. I knew these were not the feelings of a Soul Guardian carrying out a selfless service but sometimes when he looked at me I felt as though I would melt. I didn't know if this strength of feeling came from past Soul memories of being human or if it was something more. Why had he written the word eternity? A warm feeling flooded my chest then his dreamy voice interrupted my thoughts.

"Are you still there?" he asked, gently closing his eyes again. A gorgeous smile lit up his face as he saw me still hovering in his mind's eye.

"Mmm-hmm, still here," I murmured, suddenly

feeling just as relaxed and happy. Then without any warning at all, the happiness died on his face.

"Every time you leave I never know if I'll see you again. What if this time when you disappear, it's forever?" His expression became stricken in an instant as though pain and anguish had swooped, seized, and carried him off with sharp talons.

My own feelings performed a backflip as a roller coaster dipped and looped through my insides. I could feel my eyes filling with torment and suddenly, my mouth opened. "Would you be sorry if it was?" I was staring at him desperately waiting for his answer. *What did I just say? Where did that come from?* I had not consciously formed the words, they had materialised on my tongue and tumbled from my mouth without my consent. It sounded as though I was listening to myself from a distance, like an echo returning to me across an impassable gorge.

His eyes became trembling arrows locking on their target. "I'd be more sorry than I could ever tell you," he whispered. "It would take me a lifetime to make you understand how much I wished you would stay."

His sorrow and regret found their mark, piercing my heart with a sickening pain. Jay's expression was wretched, contorted with the hurt that arrested him. Neither of us could speak and the dizzy silence stretched out between us until I felt like two hands were crushing around my heart, squeezing the life from me and I couldn't make it stop. I could feel his grief and wanted nothing more than to erase it. *What was happening? Oh, merciful Source! I can't breathe. Why can't I breathe?* My chest constricted tighter and my lungs were burning. I couldn't see Jay anymore. I wanted to call out to him but I had no air, no voice, no fight left. Everything dimmed and wavered and slowed and melted into a quiet, still softness. I love you, I thought and everything faded to black.

♡ ♡ ♡

"Lilly! Lilly! What the hell? Lilly are you all right? Please, say something?"

Jay was almost screaming at me. I saw his face come back into focus, frantic with fear. "I'm okay," I managed to choke out. My throat felt raw.

"What the hell just happened? I felt... and then you... oh God! I thought you were... dead." He said the last word in a haunted whisper, eyes glistening with tears, and fell into stunned silence.

Wordless emotions passed between us. I couldn't think straight and I couldn't bare to see that agony in his eyes. I had to make it stop. Without thinking, I reached out to him with both hands. It wasn't a desire, it was a consuming need. I had to close the distance that separated us. I had to get to him, now! My heart began to race. The air quivered as I gave a desperate push forward. There was no resistance this time, only a loud crack and flashes of blue lightning surrounded my body as I surged forth on an invisible wave. White and blue sparks erupted around me and electrified my arms as I reached for him. I felt momentarily airborne and then my feet hit something solid - grassy lawn.

I slowly opened my eyes and saw Jay sitting bolt upright and motionless in the swinging hammock with his eyes about to pop out of his head, mouth hanging open and deathly pale.

"Holy shit!" he breathed.

I looked down and saw my bare feet planted a metre away from where he sat. *Oh!* I could feel the heat of the sun on my skin, hear the calls of birds above. I looked down at my hands, my arms, my whole body, I was actually here. *Oh, sweet Universe!*

Jay slowly stood and blinked at me. He took a small step closer and reached out a trembling hand toward me, I could see his anticipation battling the fear that I was a hallucination. I didn't hesitate, I moved forward and wrapped both my hands around his. My fingers reached his skin and I felt like my whole body was heaved up onto the crest of a wave. I was weightless. It was incredible. My whole body vibrated with that low hum.

"Oh my God! I can feel you touching me!" he gasped in awed relief. He looked like someone had just saved his life, his face filling with a sweet sadness. He cupped his other hand around mine and touched our hands to his bowed forehead. "I can't believe you're here," his eyes were closed and he shook his head slightly. I wanted to scream with happiness and cry all at the same time. I felt a surging sense of completion. I felt whole, I think it was the first time I ever had. Was Jay my missing piece? He inhaled deeply and raised his head to look at me. I don't know how long we just stared at each other.

"Lilly, I could easily spend the rest of my life looking at your beautiful smiling face, but I wish you would please say something," he gently shook our still clasped hands, prompting a response.

I knew I was supposed to say something but I was fixated on the glorious swell of energy that flowed between us in dizzying waves. "Here, sit down," he said, releasing my hands. I floated down onto the warm grass and he settled opposite me.

## Jay

There was a heavenly creature gracing my lawn wearing a thin singlet and lacy boxer shorts. She was absolutely stunning and unnervingly silent. What on earth was happening? She had delicately arranged herself with her slender legs crossed at the ankles and knees hugged up to her chest. Her eyes were wide and glistening and her hair blew softly around her shoulders on the playful breeze.

"Is this the official Soul Guardian uniform?" I asked, grinning and pointing to her clothes. She started as though waking from a dream and a crimson blush rose to her cheeks.

"Oh! No, I was asleep," she blustered.

"Shame," I said cheekily, "I like it. Well at least we know you can still speak."

She was smiling but I could see how embarrassed she was. "Wait there," I said, "I'll be right back. Please don't go anywhere." I got up and bolted inside, rummaging through my drawers and returned with my favourite blue tee shirt which she took gratefully and pulled over her head. It was huge on her tiny frame and came down to mid thigh. "Better?" I asked.

"Yes, thank you," she nodded shyly.

"So, you were asleep? Does that mean you visit me in your sleep?"

"That's right, like in a dream except I usually wake up in my bed," she said, looking all around the back yard now.

"Did I do this?" I asked her.

She looked back to me. "I think it was both of us, but I don't really know. I just know I felt how much pain you were in and…" her voice caught a little "…I just had to come to you. I couldn't bear to see you that… torn."

Her openness and honesty were astounding. She inspired more trust with a single sentence than anyone else could hope to build in a lifetime. In that moment, I could feel the warmth of her truth melting the last of the icy walls I had created to protect myself. I felt safe with her; safe enough to be completely open in return. "Lilly, I know it's strange, I've only spoken to you three times, but there's something so familiar about you. Do you know what I mean?" I asked softly, almost not wanting to hear her answer in case she said no.

"I do," she nodded.

Before she had materialised here, the thought of never seeing her again had overwhelmed and broken me in two. I couldn't explain it, I thought about her all the time and had been secretly dreaming she'd fall to earth. It was just a silly dream, but now, she had. If this meant I was insane, I would gladly live out my days in blissful derangement. Having her right here with me was mind-blowing. I felt like a plant that had been starved of sunlight, now basking in her life-giving warmth.

"Jay, are you okay?" I nodded while wondering if I was going cross-eyed through brain strain.

"Are you?"

"I think we're both in shock," she said shakily.

"Probably. What are you supposed to do for people in shock again?"

"Usually warmth, rest, and fluids." It rattled off her tongue like a mantra.

"Huh? Are you a doctor as well now?" I laughed.

"Sort of, I'm a healer. Well, I'm in training anyway."

Okay, so now I'm sitting on my lawn with an angelic, half naked doctor! Christ!

"What?" she laughed at my stunned expression.

"Um, I was just wondering how you find the time

for two jobs?" I recovered quickly.

"Being a Soul Guardian isn't a job, it's something we do to be of service to other Souls. We do it in our sleep. It isn't a burden and it doesn't prevent us from having normal lives. Well, not usually anyway," she smiled.

"Hmm, would you like to come inside? I can get you a drink of water and a comfortable chair," I suggested hopefully.

"Water sounds good. Thanks." I offered my hand to help her up. As our skin made contact another wave of warmth flooded through my body. I felt light headed and had to concentrate on walking in a straight line as I led her inside. I showed her into the lounge room and watched as she turned in circles taking everything in.

"Do you live here alone?"

"Yeah, I prefer it that way. I like to have my own space. Have a seat, I'll get you that drink." I sped to the kitchen and hurriedly filled two glasses. "How about you?" I called to the other room, "Do you live alone?"

"I have a roommate. Her name's Sky."

I came back and found her sitting with her legs curled up on my shabby sofa in the spot where I usually sat. The sight of her there was so surreal I couldn't help but grin at her like an idiot.

"Um, Jay, can I have my water?" she smiled.

"Oh sorry, here," I handed her the glass and sat at the other end.

"You like music," she said eyeing the shelf

overflowing with CDs.

"I think music is my second love, after plants. Do you like music?"

"Love it! I think it's my second love after the sea."

"Should I put something on?"

"Sure, I'd love to hear what you listen to."

I went over to my collection and tried to choose. *Hmm, what was appropriate for entertaining stunningly beautiful soul guardians from another dimension?* I grabbed a Benjamin Francis Leftwich album and pressed play. When I turned back around she was looking at my acoustic in the corner covered in dust.

"You play?" she asked.

"Used to, not so much anymore."

"Why not?"

"Well, I was never that great," I laughed, "I just used to enjoy messing around with it."

"What changed?" She had seen my avoidance tactics and was intrigued.

"It was something Jess and I did together," I answered truthfully.

She nodded and let it drop. "I like whoever this is we're listening to."

I handed her the CD cover. "Yeah, he's great. Is this a lot different to your music on Panacea?"

"No, not really. As I said, we're really only different in how our minds work and how we look after each other and our world."

"So completely alien then," I laughed. "Tell me about where you live. What's it like there?"

She described a world that was so much like my own but unspoilt and peaceful. It was the world that so many of us dreamed that earth could be again. She told me about her parents and the house she lived in with Sky, how she spent her days and what she liked to do. She spoke with so much passion and vivid detail that I immersed myself in every word she said, captivated by her high, melodic laugh and animated eyes. She told me about her favourite beach spot and how she'd been going there since she was a child. Her city sounded incredible, with plenty of green space and organic farming. There were no such things as banks because their economy was largely barter and trade, or prisons because crime was non-existent! To me, it sounded like heaven. She wanted to know all about my work and we had a lengthy discussion about plants once I learned that she was skilled in herbal medicine. We talked for hours, happily lazing together on the couch like long lost friends. I was so caught up in the moment, marvelling at just being there with her, that neither of us had noticed the day dwindling away outside.

"Jay, I think it's time I got back now."

I nodded and sighed, unable to hide my disappointment.

"It was lovely spending time with you and I'm so glad you're doing better. I had a really nice time."

"Me too. Lilly, I know you have to go, but will

you come back soon?"

She paused for a moment, thinking. "I'll try," she smiled wanly.

The fear of never seeing her again began to seep back into my body. I reached over and grasped her hand. "Promise?"

There was another pause as she looked into my eyes, weighing her decision and I caught some of the raw emotion I'd seen earlier. She nodded. "I promise."

She flashed that mesmerising smile, closed her eyes and took in a few slow, deep breaths. Her body wavered in and out of focus for a moment, slowly shimmering like a desert mirage, then she simply evaporated leaving an empty space and a terrible stillness. I sat in the silence of a desolate room, surrounded by lifeless objects. Everything seemed dull for want of her light and the elation I had felt a minute ago abruptly turned into longing as I sat staring at my very empty hand.

# THIRTEEN

## Lilly

I hadn't given a moment's thought to whether or not I *could* get back home. I'd been too preoccupied with the way Jay had looked at me. Now that I was sitting on my bed, still wearing his tee shirt and feeling ecstasy and bewilderment in equal measure, I wasn't entirely thrilled that I'd managed to make it back. I felt dizzy. I stared at the hand he had held seconds ago and involuntarily hugged the soft blue cotton of his shirt to my chest. *I had been on Earth! With Jay!* It smelt like him – sandalwood, salt and rain clouds.

Every time he had touched me, it was hard to speak. The connection between us was undeniable and I needed to find out what that connection was. It appeared we both had a part to play and mine was no longer restricted to just being his Soul Guardian. I was personally involved somehow. I was still trying to process it all but

I knew that all things happen for a reason. We had been set on this course by fate and I needed to see that we both arrived safely at wherever we were destined to be.

It was possible that I had known Jay before this life, that we had shared other lives together on Earth. It would certainly explain why we both felt that sense of familiarity and how comfortable we were together. The part that bothered me was the overwhelming emotion that had spontaneously seized us both; a raw pain and desperation that consumed. We hadn't discussed it. I wasn't sure he was fully aware of the voices that had taken us over.

Hurt of that magnitude reeked of unfinished business in another life and I was uncomfortable with the idea that it may involve me. If that was the case and there were things that needed to be dealt with, I would accept it and work through it, but I was aware that it might be a bumpy ride. When I worked out what was happening between us, I would tell him, but I had seen no point in adding yet another shock to his already eventful day.

Suddenly I felt incredibly tired and climbed under my covers. I closed my eyes and saw the word *eternity* drifting behind my eyelids. Then I remembered thinking, *I love you* before I had blacked out. It was easy to see how I could have in another life. We were like two sides of the same coin. I was exhausted but I was too excited to sleep. I tossed and turned for ages until I remembered my father had provided me with the perfect tool; Great-grandpa Grayson's manuscript, proving further that there are no coincidences in life. He had found that manuscript at the precise time I needed it. If answers were to be found anywhere, they would be in those pages.

I had placed the heavy book in a box under my bed for safe keeping. I grovelled around and found it tucked up against the wall. I'd not opened it since the day dad had given it to me. It wasn't exactly light reading and I'd been so busy lately. I dragged the box out into the light stirring a small hurricane of dust in its wake. Removing it carefully from its cradle, I sat cross-legged in the middle of my bed and smoothed my hand over the dilapidated leather binding, leaving a chalky film of dust on my fingers. I opened the cover and admired my Great-grandfather's distinguished hand, 'The Vibratory Scale of Ascendency.'

I leafed through the brittle pages, scanning them for information that might help, reading random paragraphs and trying to make sense of intricate diagrams. After much reading and no answers, it became apparent that I would have to start at the beginning and work my way through. It was an extremely complex subject and my Great-grandfather was a very thorough man. I only managed to read about twenty pages before it was time to get ready for my shift at the healaxis.

♡ ♡ ♡

The traffic was banked up down Agate Street and now I

was late. I couldn't see what the hold up was but the main street into the city had been turned into a car park for the last twenty minutes. Citrine's market district stretched before me with emporiums of cerulean, golden wheat and the soft pink of seashells rising up on either side of the cobbled street. Filigree etched display windows had heavy drapes drawn closed or sat in silent dimness. All the candles had been snuffed in the window of Wax'n'Wicks, even though it was not yet noon. A bright red 'closed' sign swung from a brass nail on the door. As I scanned the street, the tailor, lapidary, art gallery and perfumers, all had signs pressed on their windows. The street had fallen under a heavy hush. People were weaving their way around stationary cars, some looking blank, others fretful. They seemed to drift aimlessly like dandelions floating on the wind. *What was going on?*

I reached for my uniter and sent a message to Healer Cray saying I was on my way. It hummed back immediately with a reply: *Healer Cray is extremely busy in casualty after the attack. How far away are you? We need your help.*

I projected a reply: *What do you mean? What attack?*

It hummed back: *The city centre was overrun an hour ago by an enormous swarm of bees. We have dozens of critically injured.*

I was two blocks from the centre so I pulled my car up onto the footpath, grabbed my bag and ran up the street. *Bees? How bizarre!*

At healaxis it was mayhem. Pinched faces and stung bodies were haphazardly sprawled over the waiting room, crowding the hallway and spilling down the front stairs. From the moment I pushed my way to the front desk, the nurse whisked me away and ushered me into a treatment room where I remained soothing swollen, angry, red stings for the next five hours.

As my last patient was treated and sent home, I breathed a sigh of relief and wandered to the tea room for a well-deserved break. I pushed open the door to see Healer Cray sitting with her hands wound tightly around a mug, staring blankly at the wall. "Healer Cray, are you all right?"

She blinked, came back to herself and looked up at me, flashing her trademark smile. "Lilly, I'm fine. A little tired. I hear you were kept very busy too."

"Yes," I breathed. "I'm so glad I replenished the poultice stores the other day but I think we've used them all again! So what happened exactly? I haven't even had time to hear the full story."

"A giant swarm of bees swept through the town centre early this morning and attacked hundreds of people on their way to work. No one knows where they came from or why they were so aggressive. What I do know is one woman in intensive care will be lucky to survive the day." Her lips thinned into a grim line. "She was stung a hundred times, perhaps, it's hard to tell when one giant welt connects with the next. She's so red and swollen she's in toxic shock. We're doing all we can, but I just don't know," she said smoothing the frazzled wisps that had escaped from her usually neat bun.

I had nothing to offer but a supportive smile and, "She's in very good hands."

Healer Cray smiled, a little sunshine breaking through the gloom.

"So what do you need me to do now?" I asked, then realised I would have to go and make more, "poultice," we both said at once and burst into exhausted laughter.

♡ ♡ ♡

The hot water pelted down in a steady stream. My tired, sore body luxuriated in it. I stood there, gratefully, for a long time with my eyes closed and my face pressed to the smooth stone wall. The exhaustion of the day swirled down the plughole as I reluctantly shut off the tap and reached for my towel. There was a knocking sound coming from somewhere. I cracked open the bathroom door and listened. Someone was at the front door. Sky wasn't home so I dashed to my room, wrapped my still dripping body in a silk robe and ran for the door. "Coming!" I shouted. "Who is it?"

"The man of your dreams."

*Christian.*

When I opened the door his steely grey eyes raked me from the puddles at my feet to the top of my dripping head. I involuntarily tugged at the neckline of my robe to ensure it wasn't gaping.

He grinned and raised his eyebrows, saying nothing.

"What?" I rolled my eyes. "People *do* shower you know. Perhaps if you'd called ahead."

"*Per-haps,*" he annunciated, "if you didn't answer the door like *that.*" His eyes flickered pointedly down at my chest and then back to my face and he was biting his bottom lip while trying to stifle a smile.

I looked down in confusion to find that my silk robe was somewhat see-through when wet. I fought the urge to scream and ran back down the hall to my bedroom, leaving Chris in hysterics at the front door.

"So can I come in then?" he shouted after me.

I was mortified. This was a far cry from being two and splashing nude in the creek together. I could hear him tramping down the hall anyway. I was so embarrassed.

*Don't be ridiculous, Lilly.*

*You're both adults and a body is just a body.*

*You're an Acolyte Healer for the Source's sake!*

"Feel free to come on out when you're not the colour of a big angry bee sting!" he called from the lounge room.

I slipped on my favourite jeans and an extra loose tee-shirt, forced my fumbling fingers to wind my wet hair into a messy knot and marched into the lounge room before I lost my nerve.

Chris' tall frame was seated in the single armchair with his hands over his eyes. "Is it safe to look yet? Are you sure you're decent this time?"

"Yes," I huffed, grateful he was making light of it.

"Are you absolutely positive," he stressed, "because I don't know how much..."

"Christian!" I scolded, wishing he would drop it and forget it had ever happened. I lunged at him to yank his hands from his eyes but tripped on one of his long legs. He tried to catch me mid-stumble and somehow I ended up sprawled across his lap with my arm around his neck. Our faces were only inches apart.

The wicked grin faded from his lips and his eyes became still and wide. They were like storm clouds just before it rains. He seemed to search my face and hesitate for a moment, then confessed in low, velvet tones, "As I was saying, you *have* to be decent because I don't know how much more I can take."

My breath hitched at his confession and then he bowed his head so his cheek rested against mine. His skin was cool on my flushed face and his breath warm. The slightest shadow of charcoal stubble grazed along my jaw and before I knew what was happening, his lips touched mine with a soft, thoughtful sweetness.

He lingered there, lips barely parting, and it felt as though a cocoon was being woven around us. Its silken threads encircled us both in a soft, glowing sheath that kept out the rest of the world and cradled us at its centre.

In this moment, there was nothing but us, we were the entire world. I melted into him, into the simplicity of it, and kissed him back. His palm smoothed a molten line across my shoulder blade. His lips were deep velvet like his voice, meeting mine with a sighing breath and all the laughter and secrets we'd ever shared.

His kiss was golden… precious… pure.

It asked nothing of me.

It just was.

"Hey, just me! Wow, what a crazy… day…" Sky stopped short, her voice trailing off into stunned silence. Startled, I had jumped to my feet and stood staring into her wide eyes. I could feel the rising heat of embarrassment scorching my cheeks.

"Christian, Lilly," she grinned. "So how is your day going?" She stood with her hands on her fine hips smiling smugly.

Both of them were looking at me as I stood there. I was aware that my mouth was gaping open.

"Lilly was just telling me how red a bee sting can get." Chris arched a perfect brow as his lips twitched up into a smirk. His body was perfectly relaxed as he stretched his toned arms and clasped his hands behind his head, reclining in the tapestry armchair with absolute ease. The storm clouds had been chased from his eyes and they were now the misty blue of a mountain range just before dawn. The smooth lines of his golden torso were showing through his elegantly pressed white shirt. A golden slice of his chest peeped through his open collar and although he looked completely peaceful, I could see his pulse working rapidly in his throat.

Sky couldn't stifle her laughter any longer and my hands flew to my inflamed cheeks. "Oh, be quiet, both of you," I squirmed, lowering my gaze to the floor.

"Well, I hear you were the hero of the day," Sky turned to Chris, changing the subject and graciously taking the attention away from me.

I looked up then, wondering what she meant. Chris shrugged. "The Council called me in to try and work out what was going on."

"And," she pressed.

"And, I tried to find out where the swarm had come from and it was really strange because they didn't seem to know. They had lost their hive and were completely disoriented and very agitated. I ended up directing them out of the city towards Laurone Forest. There are plenty of wildflowers there. I hope they'll settle into their new home."

"There are a few people in critical condition with multiple stings," I said. "The whole thing is just so odd."

"There's been a lot of 'odd' lately," Sky reflected. "Flooding rains, marauding bees, what next?"

Christian's uniter hummed interrupting our reverie. "You had to ask?" he said raising his eyebrows at Sky. He drew the clear, tabular crystal from his pocket and peered at its shimmering, flat surface. "It's the Council." He got up and strolled into the kitchen to take the call.

Sky stood, hands on hips, wearing a wide grin. "Sorry I interrupted you two," she purred.

"You didn't. I mean… I don't know what I mean," I shook my head, exasperated.

"Oh for love of the One Source, Lilly! You're like a school girl with a crush and no idea what to do when the boy actually likes you back."

"Yeah, something like that," I replied, not wanting to tell her the real reason for my uncertainty. It was Jay. As crazy and unrealistic as the situation was, I felt a commitment to him. Was that even the right word? Or was it closer to devotion that I felt? But it was impossible! We were from two different worlds. Besides, I had a job to do and I would see it through. That was the most important thing.

"Well, it seems I'm needed at a farm out by your parent's place Lilly," Chris breezed back in waving his uniter. "A horse has appeared out of thin air and no one knows who owns it or where it came from."

"And the weirdness continues…" Sky smiled.

"You wanna come for a drive Lil? I have to head out there now." His mountain blue eyes looked hopeful and I found myself agreeing, unable to say no.

# FOURTEEN

## Lilly

Chris put on some music and hummed most of the way out to Clear Mountain. He didn't seem to notice my comparative silence, or if he did, he was being very patient because we had yet to discuss the kiss. Which was a very good thing because I had no idea what to say to him. *Christian, you are the perfect dream guy and I do love you but I also have an undeniable connection with a human that I need to figure out and I'm very confused.* Obviously, I couldn't say that. I think I was in shock. It would be untrue to say I'd never imagined what it would be like to kiss Christian. When you've been friends with a guy your whole life, it's bound to cross your mind at some point. I had never imagined it would be like *that!* That soft, gauzy glow I'd felt came flooding back to me.

I snuck a sideways glance at him; at the face I knew as well as my own. We'd known each other for so long that every expression was as clear as the written word. He was smiling now, drinking in the scenery, content. Christian was a flame that burned quietly, yet everyone felt his heat and saw his light. I loved him, I always had. I just wasn't sure what form that love took. Maybe I owed it to the both of us to at least find out. After all, I had no idea of what this strange connection to Jay meant. Was I really prepared to compromise my sanity and future happiness on the off-chance that an impossible relationship might bloom between Jay and I? How could it? He was on Earth, and I was here. It wasn't reasonable to put my life on hold for feelings that I wasn't even sure were my own. What if the connection I felt to him was purely residual emotions from a past life: emotions waiting to be cleared so we could both move on? When here, sitting beside me, was my best friend. My constant, steady flame.

We turned onto a dirt driveway with rolling paddocks on either side. The sound of music was replaced by the crackle of tyres on loose stones and we left clouds of dust in our wake as we weaved around the potholes, gutters and divots in the compacted dirt road. The setting sun ignited the distant hills to gold and the scudding orange clouds jutted in relief of a pink sky. As we reached the farmhouse, a beautiful black mare trotted over to the car. She bowed her head through the window to nuzzle at Chris' shoulder.

"Hey there," he chuckled and stroked her coarse forelock. He reached out to her in peace and friendship.

He was in his element. Every touch, every breath, each subtle movement, a secret language passing between them.

The farmer was already approaching us with a lantern in his hand. He moved with swift efficiency for an elderly man with a limp.

"Mr. Summers, I'm Chris Palladen. The council sent me about the stallion."

"Thanks for coming on such short notice Chris," he extended his hand in welcome.

"And this is Lilly Flights," Chris said as I rounded the car to join them.

"Lilly, nice to meet you. Well, he's this way if you'd like to follow me."

The mare trailed behind us as farmer Summers showed us to the stables and I could tell that Chris was half listening to what the farmer had to say and half listening to the mare. Inside, the stable was dim in the afternoon's failing light and farmer Summers raised his lantern so we could see what looked to be an ordinary, run-of-the-mill horse standing in the corner of a stall, munching contentedly on some oats.

"I've asked everyone around and nobody has claimed him. He's not wild either, completely tame. A little too tame if you ask me. He seems kinda hollow or sad, but the strangest part is, he keeps walking on his hind quarters. Never seen anything like it. It's like he's been trained to do it! Who would train a horse to walk on two legs when they walk perfectly fine on four?" The farmer scratched his head looking genuinely puzzled.

We both watched in silence as Chris slowly approached the stallion. The broken looking creature warily stopped munching and wedged himself further against the stall. Chris extended his broad hand in greeting and I wondered at the silent conversation that passed between them. Farmer Summers and I watched as Christian worked his magic. A beautiful feeling of serenity settled over the stable as Chris worked hard to calm the frightened animal. By the end of it, he was patting the stallions cheek reassuringly. When he finally rejoined us, leaving the stallion to his oats, he looked tired.

"Any luck?" the farmer asked.

"Not really," Chris told us. "I seem to have more questions than when I started. What I can say, though, is the stallion is not from around here and doesn't seem to have any memory of how he got here. The last thing he remembers is feeling the crack of a whip which cut his rump and being left to nurse his wounds. He said it's as though he appeared here by magic soon after. Mr. Summers, can you look after him while I consult further with the Council?"

"Sure can. I've already tended to that wound. We'll look after him, won't we Molly?" The farmer smiled patting the mare at his side.

Chris paused, listening to the mare. "The name her mother gave her is Jana," Chris smiled at the farmer, "but she likes Molly just fine. The poor old stallion doesn't know his name, so I gave him one. Houdini."

"Houdini? Well, that's an interesting name," said the farmer, once again scratching his head.

"I'll be in touch when I know more. Maybe tomorrow?"

"All right, thanks again and drive safe."

Once we were in the car I turned to Chris."Houdini?" I laughed.

"Well, I heard it straight from the horse's mouth. He did say he just appeared here by magic. I thought the name was appropriate."

"Naming him after a famous magician from Earth is appropriate?" I asked puzzled.

Chris manoeuvred carefully down the dark, rocky drive. "There's something very strange going on here Lilly. If I didn't know better, I'd say that Houdini was a circus animal from Earth. His spirit is all but broken and his hind legs and rump are covered in scars."

"Oh, the poor thing," I cringed, "but who would do that to him?"

"Exactly. No one in all of Panacea would treat their brother so cruelly. He is not from our world and I'm starting to think those angry bees weren't either." His voice was low and filled with warning.

A strange feeling washed through my solar plexus. "Hang on, what are you saying? You think these animals are from Earth?" I stared at him incredulously.

"That's impossible."

"I know it's impossible but what other explanation is there?" he looked at me waiting to hear an alternative, the muscle ticking in his jaw.

"I don't know. None of this makes any sense," I said. We both searched for a plausible explanation and found none. "If animals could magically materialise here from Earth, then why hasn't it ever happened before?" I argued.

"How do you know it hasn't?" he countered, raising his perfect brows.

"Well, obviously I don't know for sure."

"If anyone does know, it will be the Council. I need to notify them right away of my suspicions. I'll drop you home first."

Christian's face was placid but I could see the cogs turning in his mind. There was little conversation for the remainder of the drive. What conversation we might have had about our kiss this afternoon had been replaced by more pressing matters. We were both absorbed in our own thoughts as we wound around the hills. I stared out the open window and watched as they turned from pink to violet, to black as though a blanket of dark velvet had been thrown over the world. Saffron windows were illuminating one by one to sparsely dot the hillsides while the hazy glow of our headlights cut a crooked path through the fuzzy landscape.

Pulling into my driveway, the little house sat in

darkness. Sky must have gone to Gabe's.

"I should probably get going," Chris smiled and leaned across to kiss me on the cheek. It was easy, natural and sent a giddy rush through my insides.

"Yes, you should," I stammered.

"I'll talk to you soon, though," he said reassuringly.

I waved him off and negotiated the stepping stones to my peacock blue front door. The key slid comfortably into the brass lock and released it with a satisfying click. *Home.* The tension drained from my shoulders as I stepped over the threshold and closed the door behind me. *What a day!* I was glad of the reprieve and some time to think. I went to get changed out of my jeans and made myself a comforting cup of tea. I was suddenly feeling very tired.

Recent events had turned my peaceful little world upside down; not in a bad way as such, there was just a lot to digest. In the last twenty-four hours, I had witnessed marauding bees and a prancing pony and what if Chris was right? What if these animals were from Earth? How did they get here? My head was spinning with questions. On top of that, I had kissed my best friend which I couldn't even think about right now, and I'd somehow found myself on Jay's sofa in my pyjamas experiencing a barrage of emotions that I couldn't even be sure were my own. I felt tired in my bones, yet as I padded to my bedroom with the intention of lying down for a while, I stopped short at the doorway.

There was a strange feeling in the air. An intent

presence that felt other-worldly. I flicked on the light and scanned the room. The water sprites carved into my teak bedhead were all accounted for. I grinned. My patchwork quilt remained tangled at the foot of my bed where I'd left it. The hand-painted pots and jars crowding my baby pink dressing table were still in a neat row. I cast my eyes to the lapis blue feature wall with a diamond window punched in its centre. It was closed. There was nothing here, but the air was suspended in stillness, a stillness so powerful it seemed time had stopped altogether.

I tentatively crossed the threshold and opened myself to feel where it was coming from. As I stood with my palms outstretched and my eyes closed, the energy intensified. It hummed through my veins like silver chords, turning the branching map of my nerves into musical strings. I took a tentative step forward… and then another and the sound permeated every cell of my body. The music was coming from within and without.

Notes clear and bright were plucked inside and resonated to my core, drawing me further forward until my legs bumped into my bed's wooden frame. "Ouch!" The music cut off abruptly and I opened my eyes. My Great-grandfather's manuscript! I was sure the music had come from there. I stooped under the bed where it was resting in its dusty nest. As my fingertips contacted the worn leather, I had expected the music to swell back to life, but nothing happened.

The yellowed parchment smelt of age and

something slightly medicinal – lavendulum and briarweed? My fingers tingled whenever I turned a page and I felt as though Grandad was there with me in some way, guiding me on. The pages had called to me, I was sure of it, as though they wanted to be read. I carried it out into the living room and nestled into the huge tapestry armchair. As my eyes trailled line after line, the lavish script on the page became more like music; the words forming a melody in my mind and my own thoughts creating the harmony. I turned the page.

'*Karma can be simply explained with one word: healing. Yet this small word encompasses so much.*'

My eyes danced across page after page while my Great-grandfather spoke of karma as an opportunity to make better choices in the present to heal wounds of the past.

'*The purpose of reincarnation is to heal ourselves and others.*'

I woke slumped in the armchair with a kink in my neck. Groaning, I forced my legs to carry me off to bed and remembered nothing until I sat up with a start in what seemed only moments later.

# FIFTEEN

## Jay

"Hey man, I don't want any trouble. Just take the money."
I had stopped at an ATM to get cash out on my way to the
pub. The streets were empty marking that time of night
that was too late for families to be out and about and too
early for the party-goers. In any case, my last minute stop
meant that I was late. The guys would be waiting for me
and by the look of the three menacing figures surrounding
me, they might be waiting a while.

My eyes were instinctively drawn the biggest
guy, lurching behind the others. I sized him up as the 'all
brawn, no brains' type and cast my eyes left at his weaselly
friend. He was dwarfed by the lurcher and was missing
a front tooth. A detail made apparent by his slack jaw
and stupid grin. But the one that worried me most stood
poised before me. He was lean and catlike and calculated
every small movement. I could see him devouring every

detail through unblinking eyes. I held out the brand new notes with as steady a hand as I could manage. "Here, just take it."

"How 'bout I fuck you up first and then take your money?" he sneered. "Sounds like a lot more fun to me. I just got this brand new, shiny knife and I wanna try it out. My boys here think I won't do it. I plan on proving 'em wrong." He shifted his weight ever so slightly toward me. He was like a panther ready to pounce.

"Look, I have no reason to fight you. It's senseless. Just take the money and go." I had tried to make my voice cool and even. It just seemed to antagonize him further.

"Who the fuck do you think you are? Yoda?" he screeched with incredulous bitterness. "I've got the fuckin' knife, Yoda! The only way you're gettin' past us is to take a swing, so do it!" He spat the words like a volley of razorblades, the force of them raising prickles down my spine.

I willed myself to take a deliberate pause and tried to control my panic. "I'm not going to fight you," I shook my head. "I just want to go. Please just take the money and let me go." My heart was slamming out of my chest and sweat was beginning to trickle down my temples. Each weighted second seemed to crash by in my mind as I stood like a man with his neck in a noose. He took two stealthy steps toward me and craned his sinewy neck forward. Cords of rage strained beneath his muddy skin as he advanced with another catlike step and almost whispered,

"I'll say when you can go."

The bravado was eerily absent from his voice now. Instead, the delivery was cold, measured and menacing. All taunting had left his face as he loomed defiantly over me with an expression like cold steel, his eyes, the only things still animated, blazed with a mad and sinister flicker. My feet were cemented to the pavement and my muscles were rigid and poised to fight for my life. *Christ, maybe this guy really was more interested in beating me to a pulp, or worse, than he was in taking my money.* There were three of them and one of me. I knew I didn't stand a chance in hell so my only option was to run.

Instinct took over and my whole body caught fire as adrenalin shot through me like lava erupting in my veins. Within a split second I took off towards my car, the fire fuelling my body to push harder and faster with each stride. I couldn't feel my feet pounding the pavement or the wind on my face. All sense of sound was gone too, so I heard nothing as multiple hands clawed and ripped at the back of my shirt and yanked me backwards, hauling me off my feet and wrestling me into a chokehold.

The heels of my boots dragged across the ground as the first fist connected with my cheek, spinning my head sideways, followed by an iron blow to my ribcage. The pressure around my throat was gone and for a moment I was thrust forward, free and gasping. All I could hear was my own heart pounding in my ears. They had surrounded me, jeering and snarling and goading. I steadied myself and bent my knees so I could drive my elbow backwards into the stomach of the lurcher behind me. I caught him off guard and he dropped in a heap with a surprised grunt. I lunged forward at the ringleader landing an uppercut that rattled his jaw and sent him sprawling. The weasel swung his right arm around my throat trying to get me in a headlock but I was already mid-swing with a left punch to his stomach. The air whooshed from his lungs and I followed through with a right hook that sent him floating to the ground like a slashed sail.

Then it hit me with a jolt – like the angry fire of a giant scorpion sting plunging into my side and dispatching vicious venom. A poisonous heat seared through my ribcage and made my vision dim for a moment. Confused, I forced myself to turn slightly and saw the ringleader with his arm outstretched toward me, frozen in his strike pose, flaunting a mocking, satisfied grin. I stared uncomprehendingly for a second at his deranged expression, burning with a wild, impersonal hatred that can't help but destroy whatever is in its path. His eyes were maniacal and his snarling teeth were red and gleaming with blood. Then I looked down to see his filthy fist closed around an object buried deep in my side. I sucked in a breath and stared obliviously, waiting for my mind to catch up to what my eyes were seeing. There was no pain now, just shocked numbness and a sense of detachment born of disbelief. I could just see a curved sheen of dull silver encased with insubstantial looking red plastic – the handle of a pocket knife.

"Now, you can go," he sneered, and grabbing my shoulder, casually shoved me off his blade as though he was flicking at a dead mosquito. The slick metal sliding from my flesh was the strangest sensation, like my flesh willingly parted to expel the violent intruder. There was a wet, sucking sound as I slid smoothly from the blade's tip and I felt like a puppet whose strings had been cut and now there was nothing to hold me up.

I reeled and swayed until my knees buckled and the grey pavement rose up to meet my face with a sickening crack. Straining through heavy lids, my dizzy, sideways vision transformed the solid pavement into a wavering ocean and I could see my car bobbing on the distant, blurry horizon. It was so far away. A seeping warmth pooled beneath me but I began to feel very cold and wondered if I *was* perhaps lost at sea, drifting in icy waters, waiting to be rescued, while the slow, creeping numbness gradually overtook and blotted out the world until eventually, there was nothing... nothing at all.

## Lilly

I woke up with a scream, clutching at a vicious pain in my side. I wildly threw back the covers and yanked up my shirt, frantically checking my torso for the source. There was nothing. I gulped in some ragged breaths and smoothed my palm down the unbroken skin, wincing as the sensation dulled to an ache. I checked and rechecked;

twisting my body, pressing my fingers to my flesh. I was baffled. There was nothing wrong with me.

I had forgotten to draw the shades and pointed spears of light were shooting through my bedroom window and stabbing into the wooden floor. My sleep-filled eyes smarted into the brightness and for a split second, I thought I saw a limp figure, face down on my floor beneath the sharp rays. *Jay?* I gasped and blinked into the blinding light but it had vanished. "Jay?" I said again, this time out loud. I paused, not knowing what I expected to hear.

The world outside was still, apart from the melodic twittering of birds. The calm was splintered by a sharp noise at my window and I started in alarm, jerking my head up, not knowing what I expected to find. It was a sapient bird, clutching the windowsill and pecking urgently at the glass. The dark beads of its eyes fixed on me as its needle-like beak struck at the glass, again and again with insistent jabs. It looked like the bird I had seen on Jay's windowsill. I could feel the blood drain from my face. It was a sign. "Jay? Jay!" I could feel the panic rising up into my throat. Something was wrong, very wrong. "Jay, can you hear me?" *What was I doing? Oh merciful Source, I feel sick.* "Please answer me." The excruciating seconds wound down and toiled into minutes as I sat blinking into nothingness and waiting for a reply that never came.

*What should I do? I don't know what to do.* I got up, splashed some water on my face and examined my reflection in the bathroom mirror. "Get a grip Lilly!" My fingers drummed on the vanity while my mind searched for a solution. This went on for a while until I finally realised what I was doing. I was thinking like a human! *Oh, for the love of the Infinite, what is happening? All right, focus, centre, breathe! You can't be of any use this way.*

I went back to my room and seated myself comfortably in the centre of my bed. The beautiful bird was still on my windowsill, watching me, so I focussed on every colourful feather in his fine plumage and breathed calmly and evenly until I felt myself again. Then, I knew what to do. If Jay could summon me at will, perhaps it could work both ways. Maybe I could lift the veil and find him through sheer will, like he had found me. I had to know if he was okay. I had to try because we shared a connection and I cared for him and I couldn't ignore the signs.

I inhaled deeply and evenly, focusing my intent, feeling the Source of life enter my body in a surge of euphoric warmth and light. I held the image of Jay's face in my mind, tracing the features I knew so well and willing him to be near to me. Then, they began to gather; the broken voices and fragmented people wavering in and out of focus as I searched each one for his unmistakable smile and sea-green eyes.

It was so faint at first that I could barely make it out, but a sense of connection made me pause and gravitate toward the ghostly image. As I drew closer, the scene looked just like the flash I'd seen on my bedroom floor; a figure lying face down and motionless. My heart stuttered as I peered closer trying to see. The scene refused to come into focus. It was like looking at a smudged watercolour painting.

Without wasting another second I reached out and pushed forward. The air around me became electric, crackling and sparking as I held Jay's image in my heart. My arms still outstretched, became entwined with what looked like vines of blue and white lightning. It felt like hot static striking my skin followed by thousands of tiny shocks prickling my body. It wasn't painful, but it wasn't pleasant either. I pressed on, waiting for the wave-like feeling I had experienced before to scoop me up and hurtle me through the veil. It never came. Instead, I found myself trudging forward, my entire body now cocooned with the electrical vines which were starting to burn. White and blue sparks flew as I gritted my teeth and threw my weight forward, never letting my vision of Jay go. With a thunderous crack the veil finally separated and my feet hit solid ground.

It was night. I was standing in a dim, deserted street in a pool of blood. A dog yelped and howled under a heavy moon, pasted in a starless night. The streetlight made Jay's form blend with his elongated shadow, making a ghost of him. I had landed in the sticky, scarlet river that seeped from his limp body.

I almost passed out.

He was sprawled face down on the cracked concrete, his head twisted to the side like a broken doll. His cheek was split, bleeding and swollen. In the lamplight, he looked preternatural; drained of his golden olive colour to an unearthly shade, his jaw slack and eyes unseeing. His shirt was torn at the back and soaked with blood at the front. *I'm too late. He's dead.* "Jay! Jay!"

Through blinding tears I dropped to my knees and raked the matted hair from his eyes. My whole body was shaking with terror. I fumbled to find a pulse and sent a silent prayer to the heavens. *Oh, thank The Source!* It was very weak but it was there and he was breathing. I had to roll him over and stop the bleeding. "Jay, I'm here. I'm going to do everything I can. Just hold on. You need to hold on," I pleaded.

God, he was so heavy as I struggled to roll him onto his back. His shirt was soaked through with blood and caked with dirt from the sidewalk, and there, in the middle of the muddy, red mess, was a small, neat slice in the fabric. *Oh no...*

My head swam in a vertiginous stupor.

I lifted his shirt.

There was a puncture wound in his right side, winking like a slitted eye crying blood.

I ordered myself to stay calm. It was possible that it might have missed his organs but I didn't know how deep the wound was or how much blood he had lost. He wasn't dead yet but there was blood everywhere. I placed both hands on the wound to stem the flow. They trembled with panic. I knew that I shouldn't interfere, that I was supposed to remain an impartial observer of human events. But did that mean I should sit here and watch Jay die? It was absurd! The rules were completely useless in this situation. I was no longer just an observer. I was here and I was involved.

I engaged my inner sight and delved into the puncture wound to see how deep it went. It looked as though it had been a single stab entering between his ribs and angling upwards. The flesh was sliced neatly which meant faster healing, but I was getting ahead of myself. I looked deeper to see that his liver was punctured and checked the hepatic portal vein. It was unharmed and his surrounding organs were also intact. *Okay, I just need to stop the bleeding and he needs a transfusion.* I knew that without it, he would die. He was already so cold.

I had been kneeling up over him until the weight of my body became too heavy to bear. I swayed as dizziness closed my eyes and buckled my knees. I almost toppled onto Jay but managed to correct and fell backward instead, landing roughly on the heels of my hands. I breathed deeply, trying not to pass out. *Hurry Lilly! Jay needs you.* I didn't know whether I wanted to throw up, or pass out, or both, but I had to save him. I forced myself back up and mustered all the strength I could and funnelled it into his wound.

The universal flow of healing energy ignited my

body with a white hot glow. My hands vibrated with it as I hovered them just above the entry point and magnified my sight to see his damaged cells flooding with healing light. It was beautiful. The cells looked like star nebulae as they pulsed and flowered into wholeness. My vision blurred and the starlight streamed across my view in long silver beams and shooting tails. I fell back again, my body hollow and wanting nothing more than to sleep. I impatiently rubbed at my eyes and pushed myself back up again.

The bleeding had stopped but he still needed to get to a hospital for a blood transfusion. I checked his breathing and circulation again and fished around in his pockets for a uniter... a phone, as they called them. I fumbled around with it, stabbing my shaking fingers at the screen. Thank the Source I'd witnessed enough humans making emergency calls to know what to do. I called an ambulance, giving them the name of the shopping centre over the road and the street name on the nearest sign. I had done everything I was able to do to save him. Now I would have to wait.

I slumped beside him, exhaustion making me nauseous. It would have alarmed me if I hadn't been so overwhelmed and desperate to save Jay. I gathered his cold hand into mine and stroked his bruised knuckles. He had been in a fight and whoever had done this to him had just left him here to die. I ran my hand lightly over his clammy forehead and touched my fingertips to his cheek. "I'm so sorry this happened to you," I whispered. "Help is coming. You have to fight a little bit longer, Jay. Please fight… for me." I lowered my face to his and placed a single kiss on his forehead.

# SIXTEEN

## Christian

I paced the crystal hall, waiting for the Council to discuss the evidence at hand. I had addressed them the night before, endured a fitful night of sleep, and returned early this morning to find the chamber door still closed while the symposium continued. Had they been in there all night?

Lil was probably curled up peacefully in bed. The thought relaxed the creases in my forehead and brought a smile to my lips. I would go see her when I was done here. Yesterday, we had kissed. Neither of us had planned it, although I'd been thinking about kissing her for a while. If we hadn't been friends our whole lives, it would be simple. I would have acted on my feelings at the Midsummer Ball and kissed her under a canopy of sleeping butterflies. I would have told her I love her as more than a friend and waited for her answer. Instead, our first kiss, that I think took both of us by surprise, had been cut comically short. Now, all I wanted to do was take her out somewhere and do things properly. I wanted to talk to her, laugh with her, watch the light play in those wide eyes that were sometimes blue and sometimes green. I had only recently admitted to myself how deeply I felt about her. Now that I knew, I wanted to shout it from the mountaintops, but I couldn't until I found out if she felt the same.

It was nearly quarter past eight. I'd been waiting for over an hour. *What could be taking them so long?* I decided to step outside, give Lilly a call and see if she was free tonight. My footfalls were a dull ring against the solid crystal floor as I made my way towards the entrance. The grand hall of Ophanim Dome ran in a perfect circle around the structure's perimeter. The floors, the walls, the entire building, was solid infinity quartz crystal. The high, curving walls, at least a foot thick, were semi-opaque and drank in the sunlight, trapping it and amplifying it in a translucent white glow. It almost had the appearance of an ice cave. I walked to the main entrance where a high, ornate archway with imposing pillars on either side were heavily etched with sacred geometric shapes. It opened onto an expansive cascade of scalloped stairs that were polished to a dazzling sheen.

Outside, oasis' of green swallowed some of the reflected glare and offered welcome shade. I crunched my way along the gravel paths that wound through the gardens. Sweat was already beading on my neck and back, soaking into my linen shirt. I sought refuge on a low stone bench hidden in a damp, dewy pocket of trees, the cool moisture not yet burnt up by the heat of the day.

I focussed on the crystal screen of my uniter, thought of Lilly and waited. It hummed in my hand as it amplified my thought and sent it out to her. No answer. Maybe she was still asleep. I left a message instead and hoped that she'd cleansed her uniter for once. There were only so many messages that a crystal could record and if it was full, it wouldn't record mine.

"Oh, hey Lil. I'm still at the Dome waiting for the Council and I guess you're curled up sleeping… I'm jealous. If you feel like delivering a fat, fluffy pillow to break my fall when I inevitably slip into a comatose state through sheer boredom, I won't object. Anyway, no decision from them yet, so I'll try you again when I hear something and I was wondering if you're free tonight? I thought we could go to dinner? Okay, talk soon." I swiped my thumb across the crystal and looked at my watch again.

The gardens were deserted and quiet apart from the occasional rustle of a lizard through the fallen leaves or the birds singing overhead. I stretched out my legs and leaned back onto a conveniently positioned tree trunk behind me. The bark was cool on my heated shoulder blades. My thoughts wandered to where I should take Lilly tonight. Gabe had told me about a new restaurant that had opened up across town and it sounded perfect for a romantic date. Each dish was so lovingly prepared that eating it produced a natural high and sated patrons apparently floated out of there with full bellies and hearts.

Lilly had a sweet tooth and the deserts sounded sublime. I was sure the whipped chocolate mousse with toffee spun rose petals would make her weak at the knees, as all things chocolate did. I chuckled at the childlike delight I had witnessed so many times when she was about to bite into something delicious. Her hazel eyes would grow wide and sparkling and her whole face would light up like she was about to explode. I shook my head, still smiling. I should probably make a reservation.

I reached for my uniter on the bench next to me. As I went to pick it up, a small flash of colour brushed my knuckles and fell limply on the hard stone bench. It was a butterfly. Its delicate wings were deep magenta with soft swirls of black and violet and they had ceased to beat. I carefully stroked its beautiful wing with my finger. It was dead. I picked up the flimsy body that weighed no more than a cobweb and held it in the palm of my hand. A flash of turquoise whispered past my shoulder as another lifeless body joined the first, and then there was another... and another, until they fell like coloured rain.

I looked up and gasped. Confusion flowed through me like a cold river. The air was moving in a whirling rainbow. Hundreds of butterflies of every colour were dropping from the sky as life simply abandoned their fragile bodies. They were in motion one moment and still the next, falling to a silent death; their weightless frames tossed on the breeze like dried out autumn leaves. It broke my heart. They rained down all around me, falling in my lap, in my hair and burying the grass in a kaleidoscopic graveyard.

I tried to connect with the thoughts of those that were still airborne and alive, but there were too many speaking all at once. The confused pleas of small voices blurred to an incoherent hum and all meaning flitted from my grasp. As the final few dropped to the ground, I stood bewildered in a mass of lifeless colour. It was over. I knew that whatever had caused them to die wasn't natural. I had to tell the Council. They needed to see this.

I went to take a step and realised that I couldn't move without standing on and crushing their dainty bodies. I closed my eyes and shuddered at the thought. But what could I do? I was surrounded. I swallowed down the sick feeling rising from the pit of my stomach and fixed my eyes above ground level in the distance. I took a shuddering breath and walked forward.

# SEVENTEEN

## Jay

"...Fifteen are confirmed dead including the gunman who took his own life, refusing to surrender to police. Another eight were injured in the massacre. In other news now, protesters have gathered in their hundreds to allay the slaughter of dolphins in Taiji, Japan. Each year the seas run red as thousands of dolphins are herded and killed..."

"Christ, that's disgusting. Turn it off." Ryan's voice penetrated the fog of my unconsciousness and I clutched it like a lifeline in a sea of morbid words and nightmares. I tried to say his name but my own voice wouldn't work. I tried to swallow only to find something lodged in my throat. Panic rose. I couldn't breathe. My eyes refused to open and my arms wouldn't be moved. I couldn't lift my hands to remove whatever was choking me. I was going to suffocate. I was going to die.

I must have managed a strangled whimper because

a nurse was called and there was a rough scraping up my throat and the choking sensation left me. Then there was pain. Sharp and bruised and raw, all tangled up together. My body still wouldn't work but I was fully conscious now. I made my next inhalation shallow. It hurt less.

"Jay? Are you with us?" The nurse's voice was at my left ear. "I've just removed the airway. You were having some trouble breathing earlier but you're okay now. Just rest. Doctor will check on you later." I heard the clatter of a trolley wheeling away powered by her brisk, efficient steps.

"Jay?" Ryan's voice came close to my ear.

I was glad. I think my mouth managed the beginning of a smile but ran out of the energy to complete the gesture.

"Hey, you're okay. You're in the hospital. John and I are both here." A reassuring hand pressed into my shoulder and I was finally able to peel back my eyelids. Ryan was stationed next to my bed, perched on the edge of a chair and John was standing rigidly at the foot. Their serious expressions were fixed on me, their postures vigilantly poised like soldiers on watch.

As I found my voice, it was hoarse and rasped up my throat like sandpaper. "Have you been watching me sleep? 'Cause that's kinda creepy."

They both started laughing and Ryan smiled gratefully at me with exhausted relief. "You gave us a decent scare, dude. How are you feeling?"

"Like shit." It was as much as I could manage and pretty well summed it up. "Well shit head, you've been dubbed 'miracle boy' around here. A real celebrity," John teased.

"What John means is that you had lost an awful amount of blood and it was touch and go there for a while. The weird thing is that your wound wasn't that bad. Anyway, you're lucky to be alive my friend. What the hell happened to you?" Ryan asked.

"I stopped to get some cash out and three guys mugged me. I tried to just give them the money but the psycho ringleader was more interested in trying to kill me." I felt sick as his twisted face sprang into my mind. I had never been on the receiving end of such vicious, indiscriminate hatred. You see it on the news but never think it will happen to you. If I'd had the strength, I would have been livid that some asshole had tried to murder me for sport. As it was though, all I felt was the fear that accompanied the horrible memory. Human beings seemed to be oblivious of their power. All too often they used it to cause harm.

"Are you okay Jay?" Ryan asked. "We don't have to talk about this now if you're not up to it."

"No, I'm all right," I sighed. "There's not much more to tell. I tried to run, they caught me, I got some good punches in, but psycho had a knife. You know the rest by the sound of it."

"God, you're a lucky son-of-a-bitch," John shook

his head smiling.

I shot him a hard glare. I was stunned and incensed at John's lack of empathy. "I hardly think someone trying to kill me qualifies as lucky," I spat at him.

"You will," he said raising his eyebrows at me with smug amusement.

I looked to Ryan for a translation to see his face had taken on the same amused look. I was tired and my head ached. "What?" I asked exhaustedly.

"You haven't asked how you got here yet. To the hospital, I mean," Ryan began.

"Okay then, how did I get here?" *Did I really have to play this irritating game?*

"On the wings of a freakin' angel, that's how," John sniggered excitedly.

I snapped my head around to look at John. "What did you say?" I waited in alarmed confusion. He just continued to grin his idiotic grin. "What is he talking about?" I looked back to Ryan.

"He's talking about the woman that found you dying in the street and called the ambulance," he smiled.

"A woman? Huh, well I guess I owe her my life. I'd be dead if it weren't for her so that does make me a lucky son-of-a-bitch, doesn't it?"

"She also came in the ambulance with you to the hospital," continued Ryan.

"Wow, that was nice of her. So there are still good people in the world after all." It was a minor consolation prize after a near death experience. The good deed of one did not atone for the horrific actions of the other.

"Oh it gets better," laughed John. He was almost beside himself now like a kid on Christmas morning that's about to open their biggest gift.

Before I had time to ask what John was on about Ryan interjected. "She came by earlier to check on you but you were still unconscious."

"Well, did someone get her number? I'd like to thank her for what she did," I looked impatiently from one to the other.

John lazily raised his arms in a yawning stretch and still had that annoying, smug grin on his face. "Oh, I don't think you'll be needing her number," he laughed and jerked his chin in the direction of the door. "Hi Lilly. Come on in."

*Lilly?* Stunned, I turned toward the door and there she was. Her slender frame was planted confidently on the threshold. The white-blue glow of the fluorescents played strangely about her form, encasing her in a subtle luminous halo that randomly threw small arcs of light into the air. The lights buzzed and flickered as she came into the room but the boys didn't seem to notice. They were transfixed by her every move.

"Hi," she smiled at them both and turned to me. "How is the patient?"

There was a long pause while I scrambled about in my mind trying to find some words... any words would do. I came up blank.

"He's still concussed," said John helpfully. "Jay, this is Lilly, your saviour. Lilly-Jay."

"Ah, hi," I said lamely, sticking out my hand. *This was surreal! My friends could see her? What had she said to them while I was unconscious?*

She gave my hand a gentle squeeze to indicate that she was really here. "Good to see you awake, Jay," she said in a measured tone. "It looks like you'll be fine."

"Thanks to you," I sighed, putting the pieces together in my mind. It must have been worse than I'd been led to believe if she had come here to help me. I probably really would be dead if it weren't for her. What had really happened? Silence stretched out in the room creating an awkward emptiness while the questions in my mind filled it up again. She turned her attention to Ryan and asked how my surgery went. Their voices were like background noise jumbled with the ambient sounds of the hospital; the faint beeping of monitors, hurried footsteps in the hall, the mechanical drone of telephones buzzing and hushed conversation from the nurses' station.

"So, how are you feeling?" she asked eventually.

"Okay, I think. All things considered," my voice sounded flat and automated. I was probably in shock... again.

Ryan came to my aid then. "He's only just come to Lilly. He's still a bit overwhelmed I think."

She nodded. "You need some rest, Jay. I just

wanted to stop by and make sure you were all right and now that I've seen that you are..."

"No, don't go," I blurted.

Still at the foot of the bed, John scoffed quietly. "Real smooth man."

"*You* can go," I shot back at him.

"I think it's time we both went," said Ryan easily. "I know I could definitely use some sleep. It was a pleasure to see you again, Lilly. Come on, John, let's go. We'll be back tomorrow, Jay. Get some rest and call if you need anything."

"Thanks, guys."

Ryan pushed John from the room before he could protest, and they were gone.

Again there was silence as her eyes raked me with careful concern, seeing more than ordinary human eyes ever could. "Are you really okay?" she asked me again.

"I'm sure you're much better equipped to answer that question than I am," I chuckled.

She didn't return my laughter. Instead, she looked at the bandaged wound on my side and held out her hands. "May I?" she asked.

I wasn't entirely sure what she wanted to do but I nodded my assent knowing I could trust her implicitly. She took in some slow breaths and closed her eyes, hovering her hands just above my body. I watched in silent fascination as her already angelic face smoothed into an even deeper serenity and then something in her seemed to lift and unfurl like the petals of a flower. I could feel a comforting warmth on my skin at first. Then it seeped deeper and spread slowly throughout my body like someone lighting lamps in every room of a dark house. I involuntarily closed my eyes and relaxed against the pillow. It felt phenomenal. If I could have painted it, it would have looked like a shimmering gold mist, winding in ribbons and tendrils to reach into every part of me, filling me up until I was overflowing with…what was it? There was a phrase I'd heard or read somewhere – 'an unbearable lightness of being.'

It built in dizzying waves and lifted me in rapture until I didn't think I could take any more. Being in the presence of so much beauty was more than I could bear. My neglected heart faltered and constricted, shying away from the foreign feeling. I don't know why but it moved me to tears. I rocketed from euphoria to heartbreak in seconds and after pushing back my tears, I realised that the feeling my heart couldn't accept, the thing that Lilly was giving me, was unconditional love. I knew that I should be grateful for this indescribable feeling that I had only ever glimpsed in the blaze of a sunset or in the wonder that you feel watching a lightning storm, but it was so beautiful, it hurt.

My eyes were still closed as I felt her smooth fingers close around my hand. She said nothing, so I kept them closed until I felt like my emotions were under control. When I opened them, she was gazing out of the one window in the room. Her eyes lingered there a while and when she turned back to me she wore a small, serious smile. I felt like jelly now and words seemed redundant. She looked down thoughtfully at our clasped hands and smoothed her thumb across my knuckles, just once. It sent a warm thrill up my arm and roused a meek smile. "I think you're just fine," she reassured me. "You have a little more healing to do but there's no permanent damage."

"Is that what you were doing?" I asked her. "Can you see what's going on in there."

"Yes," she replied softly, "and I may have helped the healing process along a little too."

"You're incredible. Thank you so much. I suspect I don't know the half of what you've done for me. How did you find me? I would be dead if it weren't for you, wouldn't I?" My last question unsettled her. Not in the way that modest people can't accept praise, it was something else.

"Neither of us can know what would have happened under different circumstances. I can only tell you what *did* happen... if you want to hear it."

"I do."

"Okay, well, when I found you, you were unconscious and had lost a lot of blood. You were still breathing and I could see that your liver had been damaged as well, but the main danger was the blood loss. I knew the bleeding needed to be stopped and if you didn't get a blood transfusion, you would die. I used your phone to call an ambulance and came with you to the hospital," she shrugged as though it were nothing at all.

"So, you stopped the bleeding didn't you?"

"Yes," her answer was direct but there was a struggle behind her eyes.

"How?"

"I healed the worst of your wound to buy you some time," her eyes skittered towards the floor when she said it.

"Now I know why they're calling me 'miracle boy' around here. Lilly, I owe you my life!"

She raised her face back to me slowly. "You owe me nothing Jay," her eyes had an assiduous glint; proving that she meant it.

"Well, obviously I'm going to be eternally grateful. I'm alive because of you."

Instead of responding she moved to examine my swollen face. Her careful fingers skimmed skilfully along my jawline and to my surprise, there wasn't a trace of pain or tenderness there.

"Wow! What did you do? Is the swelling gone?" I gasped.

That brilliant smile lit up her face. It was the first time I'd seen it the whole time she'd been here. A sort of relief flooded through me like I'd been starved of the joy it gave. She gently held my chin and turned my head left and right. Once satisfied, her fingers lingered momentarily as our eyes met. Her skin was flawless and had the radiant flush of pink rosebuds. The full arches of her bee-stung lips were stained as dark as wine. I think I froze, not wanting the moment to end, as though staying very still could somehow stop time. It didn't though and all too soon she dropped her hand and sat in the chair beside the bed.

"Lilly, how did you find me?" I whispered.

She deliberated for a few seconds before answering. "I thought about you. I held an image of you in my mind. I took a chance that it might work the same way for me as it does for you."

"You wanted to see me?" I grinned.

She ignored my blatant fishing and kept her expression smooth. "I could sense you were in trouble and you needed me," she shrugged, "and before you ask me *how* I sensed it or anything else, I think you should sleep now. You need to rest."

She was right on both counts. I did have quite a few questions and I was utterly exhausted. I sighed in compliance and relaxed completely into the crackly, plastic-covered hospital pillow. There was just one thing I really wanted to know before I drifted back into unconsciousness. "Lilly, are you going to come back?"

She smiled sweetly at me then. "If you need me, Jay, I'll come, and I'll keep coming until you don't need me anymore," she reached out and placed her hand on top of mine. "Right now though, I'd better go before I'm missed. It's morning at home. You, rest." She wavered out of focus and was gone.

I knew she had meant it as a comfort but her words sent a pang of anxiety through me. I had that feeling of wanting to stop time again, or rewind it so she had never said, *'until you don't need me anymore.'* What did that mean? Was that the only reason she was here – because I had needed her? So, was she just looking to the end; to the time when her duty was fulfilled?

I, like an idiot, had been absorbed in what I saw as a beautiful beginning, while still trying to wrap my head around how any of this was even possible. A beginning to what I did not know. All I knew was that I was completely infatuated with her. My run-of-the-mill life had been knocked sideways and I'd been shown a different view of reality, one that I did not want to lose. I kept thinking, *why me?* Of all the people on this planet, why had this glorious creature gravitated to me? Surely there were people that needed her more, yet she kept coming back. Each time she did, I became more and more swept up in the perfection that was her. I couldn't imagine *not* needing her. As I tried, it felt as though something essential was being torn away from me. Never seeing her again would be like erasing the sun.

# EIGHTEEN

## Lilly

"Where have you been?" Chris sounded hectic and a little breathless.

"Sorry Chris. I just listened to your messages and was about to call you back, but you beat me to it."

I hadn't spent that long at the hospital with Jay yet the clock on my dresser said ten minutes to twelve. *That couldn't be right, could it?*

"...they were everywhere," Chris was saying. "Hundreds of dead butterflies, for no reason that I could see. They just died and fell from the sky."

"What? Dead butterflies?" I had missed the beginning of his story and his words floated together in my mind like an audible jigsaw puzzle. "That's really sad and... strange. You've told the Elders?"

"Yes, I went inside, interrupted their meeting and took them to the gardens and showed them."

*Ah, so this happened at Ophanim Dome.* "What did they say?"

"They asked me if I'd managed to gather any explanation from the poor things before they died and I told them I wasn't able to. After that, they went back inside, closed the doors and resumed their meeting," he sighed.

"And you're still waiting to hear something?"

"Yes. We'll just have to wait and see," he sounded tired. The usually rich tones of his voice sounded thin and tinny to my ears, like a cello string that had been wound too tight.

"You sound exhausted, Chris. Are you okay?"

A smile twitched on his lips as he spoke. "All the better for hearing your voice. How about you? I don't suppose you have anything quite so eventful to report?"

*If only you knew.* "I'm fine and no, there haven't been any flying monkeys or juggling mice around here," I laughed shakily.

"Good to hear," he chuckled. "Lil, do you mind if we postpone dinner? I *am* pretty tired and I wouldn't want to fall asleep in my desert plate."

"That's fine." I hoped I hadn't answered too quickly. I was exhausted as well. "Let's sort out a day later okay? Go get some sleep."

"All right... 'night."

"Well, technically it's almost afternoon. Sleep well."

He chuckled as he swiped his thumb over his uniter and I collapsed back onto my bed, landing in a pile of embroidered cushions. My hands were shaking. What had I done? I had saved Jay's life and I had broken the first rule of the Guardians' Code - *a Guardian's role is to offer support, strength, and encouragement in times of struggle and to remain a compassionate and impartial observer.* I had definitely done more than observe. He would have been dead otherwise. *No, I don't know that for sure.* Just as I had told Jay, we couldn't know what would have happened. He may have lived anyway. I desperately wanted to tell Chris everything but I had the feeling that I was in too deep now to confess what I'd done to anyone.

Regardless, it was done now and if I had to do it over, I would make the same choices. There was no way I could justify standing by and watching Jay die because of a rule book. It was ridiculous to even contemplate. Anyone with a heart could not have done it, I told myself, but that wasn't true. I had witnessed humans die; plenty of them – in plane crashes or having heart attacks or drifting peacefully away as their frail bodies wore out. Not once had I intervened or lifted a hand to save a life. Rather, I had whispered words of comfort and peace and listened to final confessions. *And why is that Lilly? Why do you remain an impartial observer and never intervene?* I knew the answer to my own question - because we cannot *save* another from their destiny. Every Soul has agreed to experience certain things before they take a body and are born into a life. It's a contract that they make with themselves so they can experience certain lessons in order to grow. For a go-lite to interfere with a Soul's destiny is to interfere with the lessons that they went to Earth to learn.

Even still, how could I have stood there and watched the life drain away from him? I had felt the bite of the blade in my side, I had seen a vision of Jay in my room... and that bird, with its incessant pecking! Was I supposed to ignore all those things? Stay away and not get involved? The entire situation was impossible... literally. This was an impossible scenario that the Guardians' Code did not cover and therefore, the rules could not be applied. Besides, I had felt from the outset that the connection between Jay and I was important and was happening for a reason. Just because something like this had never happened before didn't make it wrong. I had already decided that whatever happened was the will of the Universe and I would go with the flow. I just hadn't anticipated the water being quite so turbulent and deep. So, I would stick to my plan and keep looking in Great-grandpa's book for anything that may help explain why Jay and I had been thrown together, why he could see me and what this undeniable connection was.

Then it occurred to me that in the last week or so, I hadn't been drawn to any other Souls in need. So much had been going on that it was a belated and confounding realisation. I put it down to the amount of energy I was expending on Jay. I had already been feeling really tired lately, then when I'd intervened to save him, I'd been exhausted. I'd almost blacked out. I waved it off in my mind and decided things would go back to normal when he didn't need me anymore. *When he didn't need me anymore.* The thought sent a pang of longing to my heart. It felt like a strangled beat followed by a heaving mournful note from a violin.

I rolled onto my side and hugged the pillow tightly to my chest as though I could wring some solace out of it. This is how it had felt when I'd seen him lying motionless and discarded on that deserted street; when I had thought he was dead. All I could think, as the life force drained away from him, is that this wasn't how it was supposed to be. Every cell in my body had revolted against it as though I were suddenly qualified to judge how another person's life path should unfold! My mind had screamed, *'No, please let him live!'* and yet, I knew perfectly well that I had no right to ask it. However painful death and loss are for the ones left behind, it's an inseparable part of life. Whatever lives, must die. They are two sides of the same coin. If people lived forever, they would never appreciate the gift of the present moment. It is easy to believe that life is a gift, but the truly wise know that death makes it so.

My refusal to accept that Jay might die had been so deeply emotional that I was convinced now, more than ever, that we had shared a past life together. What

I couldn't figure out was how much of what I was feeling belonged to me and how much of it was energetic and karmic remnants of that past life. The lines of distinction were becoming blurred and I was starting to have problems differentiating. I kept seeing the soft graphite sketch that Jay had drawn of me with the word *eternity* next to it. It had been coming into my mind like an unexpected and persistent knock on a door. Groaning, I got to my feet and retrieved my Great-grandfather's book, turning to the page where I'd left off. I had work to do.

"Lilly? Are you in there?" My eyes flew open as Sky waltzed into my room, waking me abruptly. "Sweet Universe, you must have been sleeping like the dead! I've been knocking for an age." She stood with her hands on her svelte hips and an air of maternal concern about her.

"I'm fine," I said, trying to wake myself up by shaking my head, which happened to directly contradict what I was saying.

"Uh-huh." Her eyes roamed over my dishevelled state, which seemed to be happening a lot lately, and then took in the open volume on the empty side of my bed. "What's that?" she pointed.

"It's my Great-grandad's manuscript. I'm trying to wade my way through it."

"Is that why you're looking so tired and why you've forgotten about our outing today?" She was dressed in a light voile sundress the colour of ripe watermelon with cheery mint pinstripes that wrapped around her diagonally.

"What time is it?" I lurched onto unsteady feet.

"It's past two in the afternoon." She folded her arms and waited.

I was tempted to ask what day it was. Everything was becoming a warped blur between Earth and here. "Sorry I overslept. I can be ready in thirty minutes. Just let me have a shower to wake up properly."

"It's perfectly fine. It's not like I'm in a hurry. I just wasn't sure if you were even home, that's all." She paused and examined a buffed fingernail. "I didn't mean to burst in and wake you. I guess curiosity just got the better of me," she smiled impudently.

"Where else would I be?" I asked, not grasping her inference.

"With Chris of course," she purred and widened her eyes.

"Oh, um, no... I'm not."

"All right, get dressed then. We'll talk about it on the way." She spun from the room like a ballerina pirouetting in a bubble and swiftly closed the door behind her.

♡ ♡ ♡

I nestled into the headrest as Sky drove us west out of town. The multi-coloured clusters of city cottages thinned out and were replaced by grander homes with rambling gardens until finally, we were gliding through the clean expanse of untouched landscape. We had left the gentle lull of emerald hills and valleys behind us and were following a straight, flat line of road that pierced the sunburnt horizon. The Whispering Plains stretched distantly before us in an undulating expanse of tall golden grasses. The unobstructed wind was stirring their heights and bending them in hypnotic and ever-changing patterns, like the sweeping movements of a waltz.

Despite her curiosity, Sky had not raised the subject of Chris again. Perhaps she was waiting for me to speak first. As I had no idea of what to say, I remained silent. The warm wind on my face felt glorious and smelt like toasted wheat, dry earth and dust. I caught back the loose strands of hair that were whipping around my face and secured them more tightly into my ponytail. It felt like we were flying. There wasn't a single cloud in the sky and it was a hazy pale blue as though someone had pulled a plug, draining away most of its colour.

"What about here?" Sky asked pointing out the window.

"Looks perfect," I said. "Pull over."

"All right, Flights, this is round two. You won the handstand challenge but I think you're outmatched today. Do you want to hide first or shall I?"

Sense and seek, a children's game, was the purpose of our trip. Every year, Sky and I came to the Whispering Plains to play. Our 'Summer Games' was a fun challenge we'd come up with when she'd first moved here. It began with the handstand challenge (which I had won), then sense and seek, followed by the ultimate brownie bake off. The best out of three won the games. For sense and seek you were on the clock. You had exactly five minutes to hide and the other person had ten minutes to find you using their intuition to guide them. The dense, head high grass with its constant whispering movement meant you couldn't rely on your eyes or your ears to find the other person, you had to sense where they were and walk in that direction. Victory went to the player with the quickest seeking time.

"I'll hide first," I laughed. "Did you bring the timers?"

"Of course," she grinned, handing me a small five-minute sandglass hanging on a ribbon. We both looped one around our necks.

"Are you ready?" I nodded and she closed her eyes. "Okay, go!"

I took off toward the pale, straw-coloured wall of grass and plunged through. Arms outstretched in front of me, I waded through the head-high growth, parting it like a golden curtain. I walked in a diagonal line from where I began and after a few minutes of walking turned sharp right. I kept going in a straight line until the sand had drained through the glass and my time was up. I stopped walking and flipped it over. Now, I would wait.

The grass swayed in rhythmic waves like the surface of an ocean and broke all around me in a series of whispers and sighs. I tipped my chin to the sky, the tall blades whipping across my view and wondered if this is what it felt like to be a bug - lost in a sea of moving giants. It was nice to be lost. I closed my eyes and listened to the rise and fall of the wind - *sssshhhh...*

Soft prickles rose on the nape of my neck and my hands began to tingle. The breeze caressed my face like the whisper of a soft kiss. I could sense someone not far from me and opened my eyes. Warmth rose in my chest and my heart became louder, pushing my breath to match its pace. I turned a circle on the spot, scanning every direction. I couldn't see anything, I could feel it though and it didn't feel like Sky. It felt like... Jay.

The heat in my chest escalated, it pulsed fervently with a mind of its own. I fought back the ludicrous notion that I was having a heart attack and looked into my own heart. Blood slooshed through the chambers of smooth muscle, the tissue fit and vibrant. Of course nothing was wrong with my...

Something caught my eye and I peered closer. It began with a white spark that glowed in the centre of my heart, igniting it from within. It illuminated like a pulsing ruby, shining brighter with every beat. Then a needle of pure white light ruptured through the wall and snaked into a coiling thread of blinding brilliance. It beamed, circling out from itself as I gaped in shock and blinked against the glare. *What in the name of the One Source was happening to me?*

An urgent feeling outside of myself dragged at my attention. I prised open my eyes and peered toward a mirage-like vision quivering just a metre away. The tall, blurred figure had broad shoulders and an easy, casual posture. I could make out the hue of faded denim on long legs and a tousle of tawny hair, then a familiar smell - sandalwood, salt and rainclouds. "Jay," I stated incredulously. His voice came back in fragments like someone was fiddling with a radio dial. "Jay I can't hear you. Can you hear me?" I took a step closer and the hazy vision seemed to tug toward me as though magnetically drawn and I could see him clearly for a second. He seemed electrified, surrounded by blue and white sparks. He had an enormous grin on his face! "Jay, what on earth are you doing?" All I caught was, *don't think I'm on earth* before he wavered like a reflection on water and dissipated into the pale, brittle stalks, vanishing from sight.

Was Jay almost standing here... in Citrine... on *Panacea*? I felt faint. How had he managed that? What did he think he was doing? My breath came in shallow, rapid puffs and my stomach made a woozy loop. If I hadn't known any better, I would say I was displaying all the signs of a classic human panic attack. I bent over with my head towards my knees and took deep breaths as I had seen some humans do. It didn't seem to do anything except send blood rushing to my head and make me nauseous. After a few pointless moments I abandoned the idea. I sat on the ground, placed my palms in the warm soil and made myself meditate.

Sky found me a short time later and thankfully, I had managed to almost pull myself together. It was no surprise that she ended up as the clear winner of the day. My mind was numb with what had just happened, I still felt weak and I kept worrying that Jay was going to materialize again at any given moment. And what in heaven was that blinding light in my heart? I kept checking to see if it was still there but there was no sign of it. My heart looked perfectly ordinary now.

The feeling of Jay seemed to linger and it touched me in fleeting wisps that brushed my arm, or smoothed through my tangled hair, but that I could never quite hold onto. I *wanted* to hold onto those feelings, to make them sit still between my cupped hands so I could turn them over and examine them closely. I wanted to measure their weight, feel their purpose. I couldn't tell if it was residual energy from his appearance or more an internal pull that conjured images of his soft green eyes and olive skin. The feeling of him was irrevocably familiar. It had found me, *he* had found me. How had he appeared on Panacea? Was there nothing that could hold this feeling back?

# NINETEEN

## Jay

"Does it still hurt miracle boy?" John's colossal frame was hunched over me and his face was pinched with serious scrutiny as he poked at my bandaged ribs.

"No, not right now it doesn't, but I don't know, maybe if you keep poking me some more! Cut it out!" I wailed, swatting at his hand.

"Sorry, It's just really freaky how quickly you've healed," he flopped onto the couch next to me and its tired springs protested under his weight.

I had been released from the hospital yesterday and the boys, as promised, had swung by to check on me. Lilly had been right. There was no permanent damage. I was looking down the barrel of four weeks off work, *'at least,'* the doctor had said. Bah! What did doctors know? I had an angel on my shoulder. My liver would heal itself completely and apart from feeling a bit bruised, I was fine.

No, I was more than fine. I was on some kind of high. I had seen movies where people had near death experiences and suddenly saw the world with new eyes and a new appreciation for the gift that life was. I was sure there was a good dose of that contributing to my mood but I had done something incredible.

I had lain in the stark hospital room and had tried to accept that Lilly's presence in my life was temporary; an impossible gift that couldn't last. She was not of my world and was just doing her duty, I had told myself. I had recited the words over and over but they reached my ears with an echo that was hollow. Every fibre of my being told me it was a lie. There was something special between us and I knew she felt it too. She had said that ours was a unique situation. Humans weren't supposed to be able to see go-lites and they certainly shouldn't have them landing in their back yard and visiting them in the hospital and meeting their friends! The whole thing was crazy and mind blowing and she was the most amazing thing that had ever happened to me. I had rationalised that if everything that had already happened was possible, then nothing was *impossible*. So, I had decided to pay her a visit. It had almost worked too.

"You're in good spirits," Ryan came in from the kitchen balancing three mugs of hot coffee on a warped metal tray.

"You would be too if you'd been rescued by a goddess," beamed John and raised his thick eyebrows at me, waiting for a response.

I gratefully took a mug from Ryan and drank in a hot gulp. They were both staring at me now like I was a science experiment. Ryan sank casually into the threadbare armchair. His expensive clothes could not have looked more out of place against it, like a king had just sat down to dine in a slum.

"Oh Christ, say something, it's killing me," whined John. "What did you think of her?"

All I could do was sigh. "There aren't words," I shook my head and I couldn't help the dazed smile that said too much and gave me away.

"She seems like a great girl," nodded Ryan.

"Dude...she's hot!" John almost moaned, accentuating the last word.

"Yes, that too," Ryan agreed wholeheartedly.

We were all nodding now like those bobbing toys that stick on car dashboards. It seemed I had my friends' stamps of approval.

"So, are there plans to see each other again?" Ryan asked.

"We talked about it, yes."

"You lucky bastard! The sooner the better. Girls like that don't stay single long. I'm amazed she *is* single. Go get her man," John punched me affectionately in the shoulder, smiling broadly.

"I intend to," I winked.

I just had to perfect my technique when I tried

again. I had mustered everything I felt for her and drawn her image in my mind and focussed all my concentration on reaching out to her. Instead of pulling her into me as I'd done before, it was more a feeling of sending what I felt out to her instead. My mind was made up. I didn't care that we were in two different worlds. I couldn't ignore how I felt and I wasn't going to let the best thing that had ever happened to me slip away without at least seeing where these feelings might take us. If I did, I'd regret it forever.

The conversation shifted then to the purchase of Boy and Bear concert tickets next month, who would fill in for me at touch football next week, and then they started quizzing me about my hospital bills and the fact that I was off work and not earning money right now. After the guys left, I found an envelope on the kitchen table with $800 in it. On the back of the envelope John had drawn a huge love heart with his name inside it and what I think were supposed to be lovebirds flying around it. They looked more like mutant rats with wings. Ryan had written, *We don't want to discuss it and we don't expect it back. We're just glad you're still with us, R.*

I got a bit emotional and pressed the envelope back onto the scratched surface of the table. I just stared at it, shaking my head. I had always fended for myself after leaving home at a young age to escape the abuse. I never borrowed money and I'd always managed to survive within my means. Independence was my middle name and I was proud of the fact. What rattled me now was that the boys had recognised that I needed help and had selflessly and freely given it. I was overwhelmed with gratitude and touched so deeply that my heart constricted and tears pricked my eyes. It was too much. I didn't know how to accept such a huge gesture. Nobody had ever offered to put their hand in their pocket for me before and it hadn't occurred to me that anyone ever would. My independence meant that I didn't have any expectations of support or kindness from anyone really.

I stared in shock at the envelope full of money and in that moment, the independence I had claimed as an admirable trait, became a lie. The truth was, my independence wasn't something I had worked hard for and earned. It had been thrust upon me through necessity and lack of choice. It was a sort of forced independence that came from never having anybody around to help me when I was struggling. Opening that envelope was like opening a boarded up window. Through it I could finally see and feel all the love and kindness that I had been missing in the world. I just hadn't known it until now.

Then there was Lilly. She had saved me and had done so much more than heal my broken body. She had restored my faith in myself and showed me how to heal my broken heart. People show love in different ways and it isn't always how you would have pictured it. I had three people in my life that loved me enough to do all of that. It made me think that I must be deserving of it or they wouldn't bother. I wondered if I could ever love myself that much. From now on, I was going to try.

"Jay?" Her voice was a gentle whisper behind my left shoulder. I jerked awake from my thoughts and turned. She was standing barefoot on the pine floorboards wearing a pale cream dress that floated above her knees and hugged her hips. A feminine frill wound around her breasts and there were no straps, leaving her sylphlike shoulders bare. Afternoon light was pouring through the window behind her and it ignited her skin like she was dusted in gold. She was so stunning, I sighed, out loud.

"Are you all right?" A look of concern deepened the well in her eyes. "I could feel that you were sad. What's upsetting you?"

"I'm not sad really. I'm just thinking."

She didn't say anything and I knew it was an invitation to explain if I wanted to.

"I was thinking about the amazing things that people do for me, like John and Ryan and… you, and how they're all different ways of showing love. It made me a bit emotional, that's all."

She nodded thoughtfully. "I think when you're used to being alone in the world and someone finally shows they care, the relief can be overwhelming. It's as though you've been in the process of drowning for years and one day, someone finally hears you shouting and throws you a lifeline."

I smiled, instantly relieved that she understood.

Her dark hair swirled around her shoulders as though the faint breeze through the window breathed life into it and her whole body glowed, wreathed in a halo of light. "Anyway, I was in a fantastic mood before I started thinking about all of that, and now I can get back to it," I resolved.

She looked at me quizzically.

"I'm just really glad to see you," I laughed. "Ouch!" The full expansion of my ribcage tugged at my wound sending a shock of pain through my side.

She was instantly in front of me, her smooth, delicate hand resting over the bandages. "You should be resting still. Does it hurt much?" she lifted her gaze and watched me through the shade of her long lashes.

"Not much," I told her, "thanks to you." She was so close I could have circled my arms around her and breathed in more of the dizzying vitality she exuded, but I didn't. Her angelic features were schooled into a look of careful consideration and something else. Uncertainty? "How are you?" I asked her.

She took a few steps back from me and paused before she spoke. "Honestly Jay, I'm a little concerned. Your 'visit' took me by surprise," she began. Something I had not seen before welled up in her then, like a shadow that stole some of her light. "What were you doing? You almost materialised on Panacea. I need to know how you did it."

"I just wanted to see you," I breathed. "Did I do

something wrong? Lilly, are you mad at me?"

"No... no, Jay, I'm not mad," she bowed her head and shook it back and forth, "I'm just trying to make sense of this. You... me... all of it."

She actually sounded tired. It was the first time I had ever seen her look anything but vibrant and bursting with life. I felt terrible. Had I done this to her? Made her feel this way? "Here, come and sit down. Let's talk about it," I held out my hand to her and she hesitated for a moment then wound her fingers around mine. That impossible sense of euphoria shot through me as our hands joined. I led her to the lounge room, as if I was floating instead of walking, and sat her beside me on the couch. She kept hold of my hand while her eyes stared straight ahead and it was a long time before she spoke again.

Twisting her body to face me she looked imploringly into my eyes. "I'm not mad at you," she repeated, "I'm... *confused.*" She seemed to struggle with the word, as though it were new to her and she wasn't sure if she was using it in the right context.

"Why are you confused?" I couldn't guess what someone as brilliant and wise as Lilly could be confused about. My disbelief must have been clear in my puzzled look.

"Jay, I came here to see that you were all right and I also need to know how you managed to appear to me." The steadiness had returned to her voice now.

The excitement I had felt at my *almost* successful

materialisation was leaking away like air escaping from a punctured balloon. The concern on her face was filling me with the uneasy feeling that I had done something incredibly stupid instead of fantastically clever. "Lilly, I'm sorry. I just wanted to see you. So I thought of you and instead of wanting you to come to me, I willed myself to go to you. I didn't think I was doing anything wrong." It came out in a slightly desperate tumble.

"That's just it," she said pointedly, "I don't *know* if we're doing anything wrong."

"We? What do you mean? I thought this was about me?"

I could see something strange and unsettling stirring in her again. "It is, but it's about me as well because I don't know why you can see me. I don't understand how I can be here with you and I don't know why I..."

She bit back what she was going to say but I could see it written all over her face. I felt it radiating from her; the feelings that mirrored my own. It was a need. Want or desire were flimsy sentiments by comparison. This feeling was urgent, demanding, and refused to be played down or pushed aside. There was no denying it. You could no sooner stop ocean waves from breaking.

This was not how I'd pictured telling her how I felt, but the moment had come. "I know," I said quietly, "I've known it from the first time I heard your voice." Her spine straightened as though she were being pulled by invisible strings and her hazel eyes grew wide. "Every time you're near me I come alive as though without you, an essential part of myself has been missing. I feel connected to you somehow. I don't know how else to explain it. I only know I feel it, in here," I raised our joined hands to my heart and paused, searching her face for her reaction. Her rosebud cheeks were flushed to scarlet and wild sparks danced in her eyes like stars shooting across the surface of a mirrored pond. Her neutral, carefree demeanor had fled her.

"Jay, I don't know what to say." Her voice had become breathless and edged with something raw. She visibly struggled with it like she was trying to extract sound from an instrument she'd never learnt to play.

As I tried to put my finger on what was different about her now, it dawned on me. She was vulnerable. Radiant, angelic Lilly who was always at peace, always so sure, looked like she was standing on a crumbling cliff asking me to catch her.

"I feel connected to you too Jay... like I knew you before I ever met you. The first time you drifted into my dreams my heart stopped. There was something in your eyes that drew me in and held me, and now," she sighed, "I don't want you to let me go."

That was all I needed to hear. I reached for her, slid my hand around her neck and moved closer so that our faces were only inches apart. Her flawless skin felt like silk under my fingertips and her scent was an intoxicating swirl of a flower I couldn't name blooming in summer heat. It felt like I had waited an eternity to touch her this way. I smoothed my fingers through the dark waterfall of her hair, sweeping it back from her delicate shoulder and placed a gentle kiss there. Her breath came hot on my cheek and I lifted my head to find her lips. I had dreamt about it often but all of my thrilling imaginings paled and disintegrated as her lips met mine. Kissing her was like nothing I'd ever known. Her mouth was soft and all consuming as we melted into one another. Stars exploded behind my eyes and just when I thought it couldn't get any better, she laced her fingers through my hair and drew me in deeper.

My heart had already galloped out of my chest and was circling the moon. I ran my hands down her back and pulled her closer to me. I was lost in the bliss that poured out of her and didn't care if I never found my way back. Something seemed to ignite in my chest. Something that had lay dormant for a very long time, a pure, golden fire that burned hotter and brighter, the deeper we kissed. She reeled back from me and broke away gasping.

We stared at each other in a stunned daze. Her wet lips glistened like crushed cherries and she blinked slowly, her long lashes dipping like feathered fans. She extended a slight hand and slowly pressed her fingertips to my chest, gazing thoughtfully at where she touched my heart.

"Now I know how you managed to appear to me yesterday," she lifted her eyes to mine. "It came from here.

You projected what you feel for me."

"Mm-hmm," I nodded and raised her hand to brush my lips over her fingertips. "When you told me you'd stay with me until I didn't need you anymore, I panicked. The thought of never seeing you again just felt... wrong. I had to know if you'd really meant that or if you were feeling the same way I am. That's why I wanted to see you. I had to know, I had to try. I know we're not supposed to be able to see and touch each other and we're from two different worlds, but it's *because* all of this is so impossible that I believe it's right. I believe we were meant to find each other, Lilly. Why else would all this be happening?"

# TWENTY

## Lilly

There wasn't a flicker of doubt as he expressed the things I'd been wrestling with so feebly. The assured strength that shone out of him was dazzling and infectious. I smiled at him and the blazing enthusiasm in his eyes softened to reveal their deep, green depths.

"I believe that too Jay, but I have to explain why it's not as straightforward for me."

His lovely face was searching my every expression and the muscle in his jaw jumped. I gathered both his hands into mine. He needed to know exactly what the situation was.

"I'm a Soul Guardian and there are rules to be followed." He sat attentively while I recited the Guardians' Code for him and made the necessary explanations when he asked. "Following the Code ensures we do not overstep our boundaries and the free will of all Souls is preserved,"

I explained.

"So that's why you're confused," he affirmed. "Because what has happened between us doesn't fit in with the rules?" The soft, thin cotton of his t-shirt hugged his chest and shoulders showing the curves of his well-muscled body. He was reflexively clenching and unclenching his right hand - a nervous gesture that accentuated his broad forearm.

"Yes, I've been trying to do what's in your best interest and give you what you need but it's been... challenging without clear guidelines of what to do in this situation. And to complicate matters more, it's been hard to not be influenced by my feelings for you. When I found you dying, I intervened because I couldn't stand the thought of losing you." *Not when I had just found you,* a small voice echoed in the back of my mind.

"Well, obviously I'm glad you did. Look, Lilly, I know you have a job to do and you're an amazing Soul Guardian. You've helped me in more ways than I can ever tell you." He leant over and kissed my cheek and an excited shiver rippled through my body. "I want to ask you though, how did you know I was hurt? Did I call for you then?" he asked.

I thought back to the blinding pain that woke me that morning. "I could feel your pain," I said simply. "It was like that knife went through *me...* and then I saw a vision of you dying on my bedroom floor, and then there was a bird..."

"A bird?" his eyes scrunched up in puzzled amusement. "Like a live bird?"

"Yes, a bird," I nodded.

He was grinning at me now like I might be just a little bit crazy.

"It doesn't matter," I waved away his curiosity in frustration. "Anyway, I knew I had to get to you. I knew you needed me so I just willed myself to be near you."

"But I didn't call for you?" he asked again, confirming his point.

"No, I suppose you didn't."

"Don't the rules say that a Guardian can only assist souls who request assistance?"

"Yes. So are you saying that I broke that rule because I went to find you even though you didn't ask for me?"

"No, Lilly. You're being too literal," he said with a sympathetic smile. "The rule means that a Soul Guardian can only find someone to help *if* they call out for help. Otherwise, how would you know who needs help and who doesn't? So that's how the whole thing works, right? A Soul Guardian answers a suffering soul's call? The thing is, I didn't call out for anyone, so maybe you weren't there as a Soul Guardian. Maybe you just felt that someone you care about was hurt and needed you," he paused while I digested what he was saying. "Do you usually feel physical pain from other souls when they need a Soul Guardian? Do visions of them appear in your room?"

"No, never like that when I'm awake," I concluded. "Only when I'm sleeping."

The seriousness left his face and the corners of his mouth began to twitch up. "Do you usually see *birds* when other souls need your help?" He was teasing me now. "Fluffy bunnies? Aardvarks? Sloths?"

"No," I laughed, realising that what he'd said made sense.

"I don't know why you're laughing. Sloths are very cool animals," he said with mock indignation. "I don't suppose you've ever seen the movie 'Ice Age'?"

I had no idea what he was talking about but a wave of relief washed over me, releasing the tension of the past weeks. We both laughed and he gathered me into his arms, cradling me against his chest. It felt just as I had imagined it would - warm and solid. "When did you get to be so smart?" I teased.

"I had a good teacher," he grinned and lifted my chin to kiss me again.

♡ ♡ ♡

I hadn't wanted to leave him but I could no longer ignore the study I had to do for my exam the following day. Sky had made me a draught for concentration which I'm not sure she got entirely right. The steaming liquid was a bitter-looking brown instead of the rich amber it should have been and bits of dried herbs were clinging to the insides of the mug as though they sought rescue from a particularly horrid death. It wasn't her forte but it was the thought that counted. I had pushed the cup aside to make way for my reference books which were strewn across the kitchen table with all the organisation of rubble in a construction site.

I had been neglecting my studies because my world had been turned upside down by a gorgeous, green-eyed boy. It was difficult to remember what the healing properties of silver spice were when you had been kissed like that just hours before! Now, I felt like I was soaring. After talking to Jay, I realised that he had not asked for my help as a Soul Guardian since the day he was sitting on his surfboard wondering if he was permanently flawed. Then the next time I had seen him, the day I landed in his back yard, he'd been nothing but happy after his session with Dr. Ferguson and hadn't needed my help at all.

It was all starting to make sense. Jay and I were not being pulled to each other because he still needed my help. It was because of how strongly we felt about each other. I was certain that nothing that felt so wonderfully and completely right could ever be wrong. I was free of my duty and my obligations to him as a Soul Guardian. I was free to be myself. Just Lilly, a girl that wanted to fall in love. I hadn't forgotten our past life connection, but maybe it wasn't as important as I'd first thought. Today we had just been ourselves, Jay and Lilly. There hadn't been any voices haunting us from the past.

I gazed dreamily out into the back garden.

The rooftops of neighbouring houses, all looked silver beneath the lowering disc of the sun. A weathervane capped with an ornate crescent moon was eclipsing it, and from the neighbouring rooftops, a whale was suspended mid breach and a flock of geese frozen in flight. A gentle breeze curled through the open glass doors, picking up the sheer curtains and lifting the scattered papers on the table. The sheet in front of me was blank apart from the doodles I had made in the margin. *Oh for the love of the Infinite, I have to concentrate.* I grabbed at the textbook entitled 'The Encyclopaedic History of Herbal Remedies' and leafed to the page on silver spice.

*Silver spice, botanical name Silvertonium Cassis, is an evergreen tree originating in southern Avalon and is widely cultivated there and in surrounding countries (Vivantine, Septaria, Danbrite and Covella). It is one of several species of Silvertonium that are used primarily for their aromatic bark which is commonly harvested, dried and ground for healing and culinary purposes. Less commonly, the oil is extracted for use in perfumery and as a food essence. The later is not useful in the healing arts as the integrity of the plant's properties are compromised during processing...*

I became aware that my head was sinking closer to the words as the type became larger and my eyelids were feeling impossibly heavy. I laid my head down onto the page and closed my eyes. *I'll just rest for a minute,* I thought and drifted into a deep sleep.

In my dream, she walked cutting a path of silence through the cicadas' shrill ring. The narrow scrubby track that led to the beach wound through a maze of half naked trees with silvery paper bark. The damp earth beneath her bare feet was replaced by sand as she walked up the rise to where the ocean stretched out before her. Silver green grasses swayed peacefully in the dunes, yielding to the will of the sea breeze. The sunlight flared and dimmed between the fast moving clouds, their bruised underbellies hanging heavily from their fresh, white tops. Uniform dimples were left in the sand from the fall of recent rain. The superficial shell it formed crunched and collapsed under her feet as she walked toward the water, shedding her clothes as she went. The beach was entirely deserted and she paused at the water's edge to drink in the solitary peace. Her body was relaxed and she looked content as though she were... home; in that place of comfort and happiness that can only be found within yourself. I knew the feeling well.

There was joy on her face as she stepped out into the waves and dove through the giant walls of water. They exploded as they crashed toward the shore in showers of salt and foam. Further and further she swam, diving through the fast moving water trying to get out the back, behind the breaks. There was a heavy undertow that she'd not anticipated and I saw the tension rising within her. It pulled her out further like a weightless piece of driftwood and I felt her fear as the freak wave loomed up out of nowhere. It built, towering over her; a dark, solid mass, and crashed down on her body with shattering force.

It drove her down into the ocean's depths, her limp limbs tangling as it threw her upside down and tumbled her over and over. The air was gone from her lungs and she opened her eyes searching for the surface as the water continued to roll and toss her fragile form. Panic set in as her lungs constricted painfully and she kicked out in the direction of the sun. She reached desperately for the light that was guiding her to the surface and burst up out of the water. Before she could take a breath, another wave pushed her back down and she was lost and direction-less again. She tried to kick but her body was too weak. The fear ebbed away. Peace had returned to her and she almost looked happy as her heart beat its final beat.

I jerked my head up off the table and took in a sharp gasp of air followed by a spasm of coughing. Sky was sitting opposite me. "Are you okay? Were you having a dream?" She handed me a glass of water.

It was the last thing I wanted and pushed it away, shuddering. "Remember how I had that vision of a past life when Chris and I went to the Record Keepers?"

"Yes," she nodded, "you thought you might have drowned in your past life."

"Yes, well I just had a very vivid dream about it."

She sat up alertly, like a deer startled from its' grazing. "What did you see?"

I relayed it to her in as much detail as I could.

"So why do you think this is coming up for you now?" she asked.

I deliberated for a moment and decided there was no harm in telling her part of the story. "How much time do you have because it's a long story?"

"Wait," she commanded, throwing up her hand, "I think this requires tea."

I watched her select two porcelain teacups from our collection that we reserved for proper tea parties. They were all hand painted in dainty florals and planted proudly on the highest shelf like a miniature flower bed. "Which tea would you like?" she asked, whisking the baby blue kettle to sit over the flame and turned back to me.

"Vanilla please."

"Good choice. I think I'll have that too. Okay, you can start now," she urged, waving an excited arm in my direction.

"Thanks," I laughed at her. "I think it has to do with a human Soul I was called to help."

"Oh?" was all she said.

"When I first saw him there was an instant feeling of connection. It really took me by surprise because there was a strong emotional pull. I recognised something in his face and his eyes, he was so familiar to me Sky."

"That's... unusual," she said slowly. I could hear the cogs ticking over in her head. "And you think this connection was because you knew each other in a past life?"

"I'm sure of it. That's the second time I've seen that girl drowning. Once at the Record Keepers with Chris and just now in my dream."

"Okay, back up. When did you get called to help him?"

I paused, shooting her a sheepish look. "Around a month ago," I said slowly.

She frowned. "So what stopped you from telling me until now? Have you told Chris?"

"No!" It came out more forcefully than I'd intended. Maybe telling her had been a mistake. She was looking right through me, trying to understand. "Look, I'm telling you *now* because I'm ready to talk about it *now*. It's been confusing for me and I just needed to work through it on my own. I'm fine. I promise. But there are parts of this story that are going to be hard for you to understand. I just need you to listen with your heart, but it must stay between us for now. Please, Sky."

I went and turned off the kettle just as it began to whistle and filled the teapot. Sky was silent, waiting for me to continue. I sat down and placed my hand on top of hers. "He can see me Sky."

Her hand twitched beneath mine and then she froze in place. "What?"

"He can see me, he can draw me to him at will and we have conversations."

"How? That can't happen, can it?" Her dry lips hung open as she tried to accept what I was telling her.

"Well, it has happened. I was just as shocked as you are. It's not as though I asked for it, it just happened. All I know is that the first time I saw his eyes I felt as though I was drowning and now I'm having past life visions of drowning. There's a connection there that gets stronger each time I see him…"

Her body stiffened and she threw up a halting hand. "Do you mean you're still in contact with him?" she asked incredulously.

"Yes," I told her, "his name is Jay." There it was. I had told her the truth, or at least the beginning of it. She slumped into the wicker cane chair. Her face was blank and her eyes were still and glazed like two polished gemstones. Was it the light reflecting off the cheery lemon walls or did Sky look a little ill? "That's a lot to take in," she whispered.

"I know. I've spent all this time questioning it and wondering if I'm doing the right thing, but I'm certain now that I am. I haven't broken any rules because he doesn't need my help as a Guardian, at least, not anymore." It came out in a rush. I wanted to put my friend at ease and show her that there was no need for concern. I also wanted to tell her the rest but could see that it would have to wait until another time. She was still digesting the truths I had just shared.

She sipped absently at her tea and began to come back to herself. "Lilly, this is unbelievable. Maybe you were someone he loved and lost in that past life. Do you think that could be it?"

"The girl did look quite young in my vision. Maybe they never got to have the life together that they'd wanted because she died."

"What are you going to do?" Sky asked blinking.

"I don't really know. I've been looking through my Great-grandfather's manuscript for clues or answers but I think I need help."

"You're going to ask your father?" her eyebrows rose into high arches.

"No, I'm going to take the manuscript to Elder Tunes. I promised him I would and now seems like a good time. Surely with all of his knowledge, he'll have some answers for me."

"So you're going to tell him about Jay?" Her eyebrows were now climbing past her hairline.

"Not exactly... I don't really know. I'll just play it by ear I guess."

There was a long silence as we both stared into our teacups, contemplating the words that had passed between us. I saw Sky shaking her head in astonishment. "Wow! What are the chances of you re-meeting a Soulmate when they're in another dimension?"

Our eyes locked as we searched each other for an explanation.

"I think we both know the answer to that," I said finally. "It wasn't chance, it was destined, which is why it can't be wrong."

# TWENTY-ONE

## Christian

The enormous double doors to the Council chambers creaked open like a slow yawn. Inside, the circular oak table that dominated the room was surrounded by Council Elders and the three Grand Masters. The room was eerily quiet, yet as I entered, I could feel the power of their collective energies as a 'vibrating hum' all around me. The lustrous domed ceiling above was a crystal mandala of pattern and light that filled the chamber with an ardent glow.

"Translator Palladen, thank you for your patience." The commanding voice resonated off the sparkling crystal and seemed to dance around me in enchanted notes, raising goosebumps on my skin. The woman who spoke was Grand Master Trill. A plush, purple, velvet hood framed her angelic face and a pair of smouldering amber eyes leapt out from beneath its shadow. The title of Elder was at odds with her youthful beauty. A pale, ivory hand floated from beneath her robe and motioned for me to sit.

"I am at your service as always, Grand Master," I nodded and took an empty seat, folding my hands upon the polished grain of the tabletop.

The hooded faces on all sides were silent and serene. Even in this time of uncertainty, peaceful smiles were fixed on their lips like steady anchors; a testament of faith that all things are as they should be. It calmed me.

"We have examined the evidence brought to us from various sources and concur with your assessment, Translator. We can only conclude that these animals have originated from Earth and are somehow breaching the veil between worlds." Grand Master Trill paused thoughtfully and steepled her pale fingers. "What we need from you is to find out how they are doing it and why. There is nothing in our histories to indicate that this has happened before, so we are in uncharted territory. We have connected with other Councils around the globe and it seems the incidents are curiously confined to Citrine. So, Translator Palladen, it is all up to you." She cocked her head to take in my bewildered expression and her amber eyes sparkled with what almost looked like amusement. Her smile was infectious and after a few moments under her intense gaze, I felt the weight of responsibility lifting away like I was taking off a very heavy overcoat.

"How would you like me to proceed?" I asked with renewed confidence.

Her head tipped almost imperceptibly into an approving nod. "There is a new case that has been brought to our attention in the last hour. Apparently, a dozen or so koala bears have appeared in the back yard of a Mr. Broadwood. Are you familiar with koala bears, Translator?"

"Yes, Grand Master. They are native to a country on Earth called Australia and do not live anywhere else on that world or any other world."

"Indeed," she nodded. "This, I think, is the most irrefutable evidence of all. We would like you to go and talk to them as soon as you can please, Translator."

"I'll go straight away," I smiled.

"Please report back when you are finished, regardless of the hour. Thank you for your service, Translator Palladen. That will be all."

♡ ♡ ♡

Mr. Broadwood's property was a wild tangle of scrub and overgrowth, most of it too dense to be accessible. So it seemed odd to me that the group of koalas were openly lazing on the fringes when they could have been safely concealed in the deep, thick growth. I had wandered from tree to tree for quite some time before one of them finally stirred from sleeping. My neck ached from looking up into the branches, so after asking permission, I decided to climb up and become an honorary bear for the afternoon. It hadn't taken long after that for the others to wake up and join us. There we sat; me on the lowest branch and sixteen yawning, but curious koalas all around me.

Each time I asked a question, a different bear would answer. The telepathic voice in my head would sound different but I never knew who the answer was coming from. It didn't matter though. They were all linked and spoke for each other.

"Can you tell me how you came to be in this place?" I asked.

*The tall one with so much pain in his heart.*

It was a strange answer. "Tall one? Do you mean like me, a person?"

They all nodded sluggishly but didn't let it interrupt their munching on leaves or gratuitous scratching.

"Who is he?" I pressed.

*He understands and he sees what the tall ones do. He's trying to help.*

"How did he get you here?"

*We don't know how he has brought us to this place of safety. We only know we're very grateful, otherwise we would have been killed. The tall ones came with their machines to knock down our home.*

"I'm sorry." The thought of it stung my eyes. "No-one will harm you here. You have my word. Do you have everything you need?"

A collective 'yes' came back to me in staggered intervals. I still needed to know who had brought them here. "The one that rescued you, is he from your world or another?"

*We don't understand. What is a world?*

You are from a world called Earth. You have been brought to a world called Panacea. They are two different places."

*We don't know. He has two arms and two legs and looks like you.*

It was obvious they didn't understand the concept of different planets. To them, this peaceful stand of trees *was* their entire world. I decided to try a different approach. "Do you know his name?" I asked.

*No, we don't.*

"What does he look like then?"

There was a lot of yawning and belly scratching before an answer returned. *He looks as you do except not quite so large and his fur is a lighter colour.*

"Fur?" That made me laugh. "Do you mean here?" I said, touching my hair and grinning widely.

*Yes, his fur.* The answer was given to me slowly as though I were a little dense, which made me laugh even more.

"I'm sorry," I gasped after I had recovered myself, "it's just that we call this hair."

A collective *'aah'* rose up around me and they all went back to stretching and yawning, and some wandered off and continued to nap.

It was clear I had gathered as much information as I was going to. As I made my way slowly back down to the ground, one little fellow was kind enough to give me some climbing pointers, even if they were redundant in the absence of a koala bear's body and claws.

# TWENTY-TWO

## Lilly

The words on the exam paper were a meaningless collection of lines and shapes. I was exhausted, distracted and under-prepared. I tapped my pencil impatiently on the desk and watched the thin hand of the wall clock beat out its seconds until it became a smooth, hypnotic blur. The room was heavy with concentration. An almost stifling sensation that made my jaw clench and my chest feel tight. There were only five minutes to go and some of the questions on the stark white exam paper before me would have to remain unanswered. It was something I had never done before. I was an honours student. I did not leave questions blank, but in this case, I didn't have a choice. I simply did not know the answers. Again; a foreign feeling to me.

How could I have been so careless and irresponsible? I had been too wrapped up in everything that was happening with Jay and had pushed my own life to the side. Now I was seeing the consequences. The sigh that escaped my lips was amplified in the oppressively silent room. A mousey girl sitting next to me fidgeted and shot me a concerned look. My disappointment must have been written all over my face. She smiled a meek, compassionate little smile and went back to frantically scratching out her answers. I however, sagged into my seat and waited for the end.

My mind sifted and twisted through the events of the last few weeks and tried to justify how I hadn't had a choice. *Jay needed you, it told me. If it weren't for you, he'd be dead. You needed to be there for him.* That part was true. But I had also spent a huge amount of time reading my Great-grandfather's manuscript and dreaming about Jay in general. Time I should have spent studying and paying attention to my own life. Jay's glorious face was clear in my mind. His image triggered the memory of his arms around me and his lips on mine. A giddy heat rose to my cheeks in an instant. I watched my own reactions and how swept up I was in the very thought of him. The feeling was incredibly strong and it unnerved me to think that my balance could be so easily tipped and my control so easily shaken.

"Time is up. Please place your pencils down and pass your exam papers to the front."

The voice struck me like a hammer and I snapped out of my thoughts and back to the room. Strained silence was replaced by the rustling of papers, the urgent scraping of chairs against the polished floor and the usual post-exam chatter where everyone compared and debated their answers. I watched their carefree smiles, the gentle encouragement and support they shared with each other, the ease with which they accepted that they had done their best. Then I felt my own expression. I was not smiling and I was not at ease. I was *disappointed* in myself. I had witnessed it enough times in humans to know what it was. The realisation frightened me. I sat there staring numbly and tried to identify where these feelings were coming from. All I could feel was a sense of separation from everyone else. *What was happening to me? This wasn't normal!*

I dragged myself to my feet and shuffled through the chattering crowd as volleys of pent up nerves and wild relief were released all around me. The bag on my shoulder felt like it carried the world. The noise in the room suddenly felt thick and hot. A clammy sheen clung to my skin and I found myself moving with more urgency now. The distance between the door and I seemed to increase with each unsteady step, as though an invisible hand had reached down and stretched it like a rubber band. I felt sick. I had to get out. The door to my freedom resembled a narrow crack leading out of a stifling underground cave. I burst through and into the corridor like an animal freed from confinement. I gulped in the decongested air with my hands braced against my knees. They felt about as stable as melting butter.

# Jay

I had promised Lilly I wouldn't try to 'visit' her on Panacea again. At least not until she had done some digging and found out if it was safe for me. Admittedly, I hadn't stopped to think about the possible dangers of attempting to materialise in another dimension. It wasn't exactly something you usually needed to consider in life. I didn't look or feel any different, except of course for the uncontrollable grin that was making my face and jaw ache and the ecstasy that ran through me like an electric charge.

I put my sketchpad down and took another sip of coffee. "Ugh!" It was cold. I spat it unceremoniously back into the mug and peeled myself off the couch to fetch a glass of water. I was to start back at work in two weeks and I'd been trying to finalise the design for the community garden. Two hours of staring at the page had resulted in a few scribbled notes with multiple question marks attached. My mind swam with thoughts of her in spite of my best effort to remain focussed.

I opened the cupboard door looking for a glass and was met with an empty shelf and one lonely spider cowering in the back corner. I turned toward the kitchen sink. It was piled with every piece of cutlery and crockery I owned. I groaned and fished through the greasy mess looking for a glass. In the end, I resigned myself to cleaning up the mess that had been mounting up. At least it was some small achievement to show for my day.

It was hard to go back to the sketchpad. The day outside was golden sunshine and brilliant blue and the walls of my house were acting as a prison, separating me from the freedom of bobbing peacefully on my surfboard. But I'd promised myself that today was the day to get this finished. My eyes trained studiously on the sketch as I examined the placement of the raised beds, the flow of the walking paths, the irrigation system. I blinked at the precise black lines against the smooth, white paper, until blinking lost that snappy quality and my eyes refused to open at all. Slumping into the couch cushions, I descended into the blank, black space of sleep.

In my dream, there was a broken face. Tears and sweat made rivers of the tortured creases around his eyes and fell unchallenged down sagging cheeks. His heavy mouth was shut with lips like immovable boulders. All the things he wished he had said to her were trapped inside forever: the apologies for all the suffering he had caused; the unguarded outpouring of genuine remorse; the chance to show he understood it clearly now and how he'd do better in future. But there was no future, not anymore. He had lied to and betrayed her for the very last time and it had killed her. *He* had killed her.

'Accidental drowning' had been the official cause of death. Her parents hadn't even contacted him to say she was gone. He'd heard it through their friends. How despised he must be. He doubted it could compare to how much he hated himself for all that he was and all he had done - terrible things that could never be undone.

He slumped on the barstool and faced his pitiful reflection in the cheap mirror behind the bar. The warped image mocked him with its accuracy. How could he have screwed up his life so badly? He drained his bourbon glass and waved for another. The bartender delivered the drink silently and with an overstretched arm, as though wanting to avoid the toxic space he occupied. There was satisfaction in it. He deserved to be rejected by humanity. To add to his punishment he retrieved the faded photograph of her from his wallet and forced himself to face his victim. She was smiling, long hair like golden wheat blowing about her face. Her eyes brimmed with secrets and excitement and her lips were a big, red bow. She looked like she was on the verge of… something indescribable and amazing. Whatever it was, it was the promise of something magical.

He had never deserved her. He'd always known it. She had loved him honestly and completely and it had been a foreign feeling to him, a gift he did not know how to receive. Deep down he believed she would come to her senses one day and see that he wasn't good enough for her. One day she would leave him. So, he had played the field in anticipation of that day. It had given him a sense of control and a chance to be with women he felt he measured up to. It had been six months since she'd caught him out for the last time. He had sat mute in panicked horror as she confronted him with his sins. Then when her anger had ebbed to reveal the raw pain beneath, he had died inside. As he'd watched the light go out in her eyes and her crumpled form as she'd walked away, his prophecy had come to fruition.

That was the last time he had ever seen her. He was left with the photo of who she once was in his hand and the crushing guilt of what he had turned her into, branded on his heart. Desperate for redemption, he reached for her from the prison of his mind. *I'm so sorry. I was never worthy of someone as incredible as you, but I loved you. I loved you more than I was ever capable of showing you. I'm a fool and I'm sorry. If you could hear me, it would take me a lifetime to make you understand how much I wish you had stayed.*

The dream was beginning to fade around the edges. The sorrow in his heart pressed down on my own. He scrubbed the tears from his face with both hands and hung his head over the photo. My body jolted with the shock of what I saw. Instead of the girl with golden hair, it was very clearly Lilly's face in the photo. Same pose, same facial expression, but the other girl had been replaced. "Lilly? Lilly!" I yelled as confusion and fear took over, wracking my body in convulsive waves. An explosion of light blinded me and there was an almighty crack like thunder. I was terrified. "Lilly!"

My stomach dropped as the rest of my body felt as though it had been launched off a slingshot. Then my shivering form mashed into something that felt like cold steel, skidded across its slippery surface and connected with something warm and familiar. I cracked open an eye. "Lilly?"

## Lilly

I was bent over, clutching at my melting butter knees and trying to steady my breathing when the unthinkable happened. Jay catapulted out of empty space in the middle of the corridor and was spat towards me, face down, arms and legs splayed, his whole body shaking in terror. He skidded to a stop at my feet and my knees gave out altogether.

"Lilly," he gasped, trying to lift himself upright.

My hands grabbed his shoulders and my eyes frantically swept the hall. There was no one about. Nobody had seen. "Jay, what's wrong?" I demanded. "You can't be here. We talked about this." My voice was shaking.

"I'm sorry. I was asleep and I had a crazy dream and next thing… I don't know what happened. It wasn't intentional." Glazed eyes the size of saucers fixed on me.

"A dream?" So I wasn't the only one having strange dreams. "Can you stand? We have to get out of here right now. No one can see you." I wasn't sure if I could stand myself but I scooped Jay's shaking body from the floor and threw his arm around my shoulder for support. "Come on. Let's go. My car isn't far."

I steered him down the long, marble corridor, past classrooms brimming with students. *This was a disaster! What was I going to do if I saw someone I knew?* Jay was moving in slow motion. I could have sworn he was drunk.

"God, this building is incredible! Where am I exactly?" He was almost shouting like a child overwhelmed and bedazzled by too many gifts.

"This is where I go to school," I replied in a demonstrably hushed tone, "but this is no time for a sight-seeing tour Jay. We have to hurry."

By the time we reached the campus lawn, he'd just about given himself whiplash. Then he saw the great tree with its colossal trunk and heavy branches and fell into awed silence, stopping cold in front of it. The ancient one stood as a silent witness.

"Jay, please! We have to get out of here. Hurry!" I pleaded.

"How old is that tree? My God, it's incredible! What species is it? I've never seen anything like it!"

"Please, Jay, we cannot stay here!" I was dragging at his arm. I felt like thief who had become overly greedy and now couldn't shift their prize. Reaching the car and slamming the door, I pressed my hands and forehead to the wheel, breathing hard.

Jay reached carefully toward me and placed his hand on my shoulder. "Lilly, are you okay?"

"No, I'm not," I shook my head. "It was incredibly lucky that no-one saw you."

"Okay, but I'm sure we would have figured

something out if they had. It wouldn't have been the end of the world, would it?"

I slowly raised my head from the wheel and turned to him with an incredulous look. I felt beyond tired. "And how do you know that, Jay? Maybe it would have been. We don't know what the consequences are for what we're doing." All the comfort I had taken from yesterday's conversation with him had fled me. All the certainty I had felt while telling Sky about us was gone.

Jay reached for my hand. "Hey, it's okay. Nobody saw us. But we need to go before somebody does. Do you want me to drive?"

"No, I'm fine." I started the car and drove. We both stayed silent for a good while before Jay spoke again. "So, I know I gave you a scare back there, but it wasn't intentional, Lilly. I promise."

"I know that. It just couldn't have happened in a worse place, that's all," I said, trying to fob it off and hoping for the silence to continue. I needed some thinking time.

"Are you sure you're all right?" he pressed. "You don't seem to be yourself at the moment. You seem... well..."

"Stressed?" It sprang from my lips like a slap and I didn't even pause long enough to register his shocked expression. "I'm pretty sure that if our roles had been reversed, you'd be stressed too!" I kept my eyes locked on the road.

His passive aggressive retort returned the slap

I'd delivered. "Well, *my* friends have already met you and they like you a lot, by the way, so..."

*Ah, so that's what this was about for him: the fact that I hadn't introduced him to my friends. Was he serious?* I couldn't believe it! "How am I supposed to explain you to my friends, Jay? You shouldn't even be here. You don't belong in my world." My voice was clipped, strange, and it occurred to me that I sounded... *angry.*

It was as though someone held back time for a little while, breaking whatever spell I'd been under just seconds ago. He fell silent and I could see that I'd hurt him. I paused to collect myself and reached across to touch his tense forearm. "I'm so sorry. I didn't mean it like that," I whispered. "I meant you don't belong on Panacea. Ah, this entire situation is so complicated." Yesterday I had been walking on air and today I was falling from the sky. Foreign feelings of anxiousness and irritability were insinuating themselves into my usually clear mind. This entire day had been a nerve-wracking nightmare and I couldn't seem to steady myself. All I had wanted to do was go home and clear my head and get to the bottom of whatever this was. Jay was right. I definitely wasn't myself. I was reacting to things that seemed to be out of my control and hurting him in the process. This was *not* the go-lite way. We did not act rashly or emotionally to the detriment of others. I knew better.

Whatever past life karma lay between us, whatever unfinished business, it needed to be resolved and I knew the dreams held the key. This wasn't the first time we had been taken over by the energetic remnants of our past relationship. It had happened before when Jay and I had spoken to one another like two completely different people, having a conversation that only they understood. It was time to share my suspicions with him and I could only hope that his heart and mind were open enough to deal with it.

"I truly am sorry Jay. You're right. I'm not myself. You said you had a dream that brought you here? Well, so did I - a past life dream and I think it's the reason I'm acting strangely. So we'll go somewhere quiet and figure it out, okay?"

He sucked in a deep breath and suppressed his hurt. "All right. Where are we going?"

# TWENTY-THREE

## Lilly

Until that moment, I'd just been driving on auto-pilot. All I knew was that I had to get us out of town, far away from curious eyes and questions I could not answer. It turned out that I was literally heading for the hills. Mount Glorious was painted on the horizon in a wash of purples and blues. The entire area was a nature reserve. No houses or people for miles - perfect.

"Somewhere quiet," I smiled, pointing ahead of us. An eagle drew lazy spirals on the golden air. As we travelled closer, we could see a wreath of living colour encircling the foot of the mountain.

"Oh my God, I've never seen wildflowers like that," Jay pointed. "What are they?"

"You'll see," I smiled.

The mountain was living up to her name. She was encircled with every colour of the rainbow like tributes laid at her feet. Busy insects buzzed and flitted as we picked our way through the slender blades and blooming stems. Tissue paper petals fell like confetti along our path - pink, red, yellow, purple. Jay walked slowly as though in a dream, his arms outstretched to feel the wind and the sun and the birdsong. I walked three paces behind and watched the rise and fall of his shoulders as he breathed everything in.

He turned back to me and his face was dazzling. His eyes, his smile, his aura, reflecting the beauty all around us. I beamed back at him as he moved towards me and reached for my hands. The energy of him shot through my palms and filled me up in an instant. He was warm and electric. The breeze carried his scent of sandalwood, salt and rainclouds as he bowed down and placed a soft kiss on my lips. His lids closed over the two green worlds of his eyes. His eyelashes caught the sunlight turning them to gold. I closed my eyes and swam in the warmth of his lips in this long, sweet and tender kiss. There was something so utterly familiar about the way our lips melted together like lost puzzle pieces that could finally join and settle into place.

Time slowed and the world disappeared into a haze of rapturous sensation. Every movement was heightened. Every caress, sheer ecstasy. We sank to our knees in the blooming meadow and he drew me into his arms and into his heart. Breathless and dizzy, I felt the blades of grass tickling against my skin as he lowered me down on a bed of petals. I opened my eyes to the sky and saw him above me, wreathed in sunlight like an angel aglow. My heart took flight on a hummingbird's wings to see him so filled with love and joy. The angel's face wafted closer and the touch of his lips to my cheeks and along my neck was intoxicating. My vision swirled with the tender green of swaying grass and the blinding gold of fractured sunlight. His hands brushed over my shoulders and down my arms and slid over the shape of my hips. Heat licked through my thighs and I felt an uncontrolled urge to feel the weight of his body pressed against me. My hands raked urgently at his back and I yanked him down towards me, our foreheads bumping together with a dull thud.

"Ouch," he laughed.

The shock of pain pierced through the love dazed fog. The spell I'd been under dissolved and scattered like the petals falling around us. "Sorry," I mumbled and blinked my eyes hard, scrunching up my face. When I opened them again, he was poised above me with patient concern. "Are you okay?"

"Fine," I breathed out while squriming from underneath him and sitting up.

"Are you sure?" he checked while rubbing his thumb over my forehead.

"Yes," I assured him. I was feeling fragmented and a bit off balance. Like I'd just woken up from a dream.

*Oh no!* It had just happened again - that

magnetic pull between us that was all-consuming. It was overwhelmingly powerful and I had a real sense now of the danger in it. If *I* couldn't manage to hold onto who I was while I was with Jay, I wondered how intoxicated *he* must be by the energy between us. Did he even recognise what was happening? How much of what we felt belonged to us, and how much belonged to the couple who had loved each other such a long time ago? So, I took a deep breath and began.

"It's just… I need to talk to you about something… the dream I had."

I watched him school his expression of disappointment into one of reluctant interest. "Um, okay then. I'm all ears." He planted his palms behind him and rested his weight on bronzed arms.

"Well, it was about a past life on Earth," I began slowly. He flinched ever so slightly and his two green worlds grew a bit bigger. I paused for a second and continued. "I was alone on a beach but I didn't feel lonely. I was in my favourite place. A place I felt calm and peaceful and at home. I went into the sea and I never came back out. I was a strong swimmer but a freak wave pushed me under and I drowned. I couldn't have been more than twenty-five years old."

Jay sat bolt upright, the crease in his forehead became deeper. "Were you a girl or a boy?"

"I was a girl. I know it's not much to go on but it's my feeling that you and I are not meeting for the first time." I waited while he digested the enormity of what I'd just said. He seemed deep in thought and was staring past me, into what, I did not know.

"What did you look like? Could you see yourself?" he asked mechanically.

"Yes. I... she was quite tall and lanky. Long, straight hair, blonde, well, golden really. Fine and pale gold. She had a kind and simple face. She looked... honest. There was a lightness about her. Full lips and big round eyes." Jay just stared at me. He wasn't moving at all. It was as though he'd been encapsulated in ice. "Are you okay? I know this is a lot to take in." More staring. I could almost hear the cogs turning in his brain and then a range of expressions flashed across his face in quick succession like someone had sped up a movie - shock, disbelief, uncertainty, anger, pain. I waited silently while he turned it about in his mind and eventually he spoke.

"So you think this dream is a past life memory?"

"Yes, I'm quite sure. I also had a vision of myself drowning straight after I met you. I believe I knew you in a past life. I am almost certain that we were in love and my drowning put an abrupt end to the life we had dreamed of sharing together. I was so young, Jay. My whole life was ahead of me. We never got to have the love story we dreamt of." The whole story spurted out of me like a gush of water. He remained in the ice. Waiting for him to say something was like waiting for it to melt. "I'm sorry if this is difficult to hear," I said softly.

"It is," he nodded his head solemnly. "But not for the reason you think."

## Jay

I didn't know how to tell her. I could barely wrap my head around it, let alone explain my dream and what I had seen. I told myself that it was a coincidence. That Lilly's description of the girl could have been anybody. What I could not argue was the intense sense that this was all true and that our souls had been reunited despite being worlds apart. If these dreams were past lives, how could I tell her what a worthless, lying sack of shit I had been? How do you explain to the soul of your dead ex-girlfriend that you're sorry? How could I sit here now and tell her it wasn't a beautiful romance cut tragically short? It was a devastating nightmare that had caused her to drown herself because I had broken her heart.

I scrubbed my hands over my face, maybe in an attempt to erase who I was, who I had been. Anger swelled in my gut. I was going to lose her again. Once she knew the truth, it would be over. *What was the point of all this? Was it God playing some kind of sick joke?* My stomach was a ball of fire and for the first time in a very long time I wanted to hit something, smash it to a pulp. Panic, guilt, anger, all swirled in a toxic cocktail that raged through me like poison. I felt sick. I prised my hands away from my clammy face and made myself look at her.

Her expression was gentle and her eyes held

me steadily, not wanting to let me fall. God, she was so beautiful. It was almost painful to look at her. She reached out to me then. Wordlessly and softly, she wrapped herself around my numb body and I tried to not let her feel the sobs welling in my chest and fighting to escape. We stayed there for the longest time, silent and still amongst the paper petals blowing in the wind.

## Lilly

The afternoon sun was biting at my skin as I stirred. I sat up, squinting into the harsh light. The gold orb was hovering above the mountain's peak, making her look like a queen wearing a glowing crown. It must have been around four in the afternoon. Jay and I had been asleep for hours. The amount of time I spent sleeping these days was becoming ridiculous! Was it the energy drain from these past life personalities taking over? Maybe it was exhausting to maintain a physical connection with Jay. Or was I just laden down with far too much going on in my life? I was trying to hold it all together but I was starting to doubt that I could. I wasn't Christian. I wasn't my father. I looked down at Jay. He was counting on me. I could only hope that I was enough.

A sheen of sweat clung to his forehead and pasted his hair in tawny twists. He looked so serene it was a shame to wake him. I had not pressed him to talk about it any further. It was clear he was distressed and needed time to get over the shock. I knew he would talk to me when he was ready, but I couldn't help but wonder if he had already guessed at the larger conversation we were yet to have: about the importance of those past life dreams and what they meant. If we kept slipping into the personalities of who we once were, how could we be free to love each other in the present?

As I gazed at his face, an enormous dragonfly appeared and darted above him. Its wings were a blur of flashing green and silver. It zipped and hovered in an erratic pattern before alighting on his hair. I watched in fascination as it planted its feet with bold confidence and ceased all movement. The light played tricks on its frozen wings. Were they green or silver or purple? An uneasy feeling came over me as I read the symbolism of the dragonfly's presence. They were messengers of mystery, illusion and self-deception. Was Jay deluding himself about something? Before I had time to ponder it further, he stirred and the dragonfly flitted away to a place my eyes could not follow.

"Jay." I touched his cheek with my fingertips and brushed the tawny twists from his forehead. He took in a dazed breath and forced his eyes open. "We fell asleep. It's getting late," I stroked his cheek.

He sat up and yawned, stretching his stiff limbs. "God, I don't even remember lying down. I didn't mean to fall asleep."

"I think you needed it," I smiled, "Besides, I only just woke up myself but now we have to get you home and I'm not exactly sure how to make that happen. Any clues?"

"Ah… not really, no." His face contorted as he realised the predicament we were in. "Maybe you're just stuck with me now," he shrugged. The sleep seemed to have revived him and he was light and happy again.

I wished I could say the same. I felt more tired now than before we'd fallen asleep."I believe you have a life to get back to with obligations and people who care about you," I countered. "Besides, we agreed you wouldn't 'visit' here until we figure out if it's safe."

"I know, I know. Wishful thinking. Well, maybe it's as simple as thinking about it in reverse. If I can blip here by concentrating my thoughts on you…"

"Blip?" I laughed.

"Yeah, blip, appear, whatever. You're not helping."

"I know, sorry. Please, continue with your theory on 'blipping'," I snickered.

He ignored me and carried on. "I'm thinking that if I concentrate on home, I'll *blip* there. And hey, maybe if I say, 'there's no place like home, there's no place like home' and click my heels together three times, it will work." An expectant grin lit up his face.

I stared at him blankly. "Um, I don't know what you're talking about. Are you serious? And why are you grinning at me like something is funny?"

"The Wizard of Oz? The movie?" he prompted.

"Sorry, I'm not up with movies." I shook my head.

"Hmm, doesn't matter," he said sighing, "I'm going to give it a try anyway… minus the Wizard of Oz bit, obviously."

Another twenty minutes passed and we were no further advanced. "Jay, I've been thinking, if your heart connection to me is what brings you here, maybe you have to disconnect from those feelings to get home."

A pang of pain ran across his face. "How would I or *could* I do that? You make it sound like my feelings for you are a plug that I can just disconnect from a socket."

His feelings were hurt but I needed to somehow teach him that he had the power to choose his feelings instead of letting his feelings choose him. I took his hand and smiled. "Just listen, okay? I know our feelings for each other are not wires wrapped in plastic, but you *do* control the switch to your mind. Just close your eyes. He did without question and I settled opposite him and held his hands. I drew conscious breaths into my heart. "Imagine that your breath is filling your heart and then flowing through your entire body," I told him. Our hands were sweaty as though the sun was trying to melt them together and a dewy sheen sparkled off Jay's arms. I drew energy from above and below and funnelled it into him. I could feel his attention shift its attachment from me to what was building inside him. "What you are feeling is life force," I told him, "now see if you can feel it without my help." I gently released his hands.

The energy swirled through him, making him

larger somehow. Peace and contentment washed over his features smoothing away the lines of concentration. He was so full, he glowed. "This is what you make with your breath - life force. It's yours. It was generated by you and it is for you. You choose how to use it."

Jay sat serenely in a glowing field of energy. He was strong and beautiful and magnificent, his face radiating peace and love. It was several minutes before he spoke. "I didn't learn *that* in meditation class," he smiled.

"How do you feel?" I asked quietly.

"Different... peaceful, calm and light."

I could see the calm focus in his eyes, hear the clarity in his voice and his facial expression was completely serene and open. I was looking at the real Jay - free of suffering, the person I knew he could be and he was glorious. Warmth rose in my chest and my heart became louder. He plucked a nearby wildflower and handed it to me. My heart was pulsing wildly. His fingers brushed mine and I noticed that the electricity that usually sparked between us whenever we touched was replaced by an all-pervading warmth, so soft, yet so strong and enduring. He leaned toward me, his breath touched my skin and his warm hands held my face between them. I was breathing heavily, just like the day I'd thought there was something wrong with my heart - the day I had seen a brilliant coil of light spring from its centre. I started to close my eyes to look inside and see if it was there again, but Jay moved my head between his hands to keep my attention on him.

His sea-green eyes were calm and glittering. He wanted me to see something; he wanted me to see *him*.

"I love you, Lilly." It was almost a whisper. Then he kissed me. It felt completely different from the hazy, emotional fog that had consumed us before. This kiss was clear and heightened, like a chime struck from atop a silent, solitary peak, a single, pealing note travelling across light and shadow to resound in my heart.

He drew away. "Thank you." His words blurred with his vanishing form. He shimmered and was gone.

A wave of dizziness made my body slump and I touched my fingertips to my lips. I sat alone as the bright sun abandoned the meadow, leeching the vibrancy from her colours and making the mountain a dark shadow. I looked down at Jay's parting gift. The translucent white petals were already falling to the ground.

# TWENTY-FOUR

## Jay

I was back on my couch. The room was dark and the stars were winking through the lounge room window. My sketchpad lay open on the floor and I wondered if I'd just woken from a dream. *Did all of that actually happen?* I was giddy. The waves of love that still ran through me and made me feel light and peaceful, told me it had. The feeling was incredible and disorienting all at once. My whole body hummed. It was as though all the sharp edges had been removed from the world. There was nothing left to scratch, snare or cut and from here, it looked like there never had been. Everything felt soft and embracing. My mind was clear and quiet in a way I had never experienced before and I had a sense that a wiser version of myself was standing behind me, just watching it all unfold; ready to place a steadying hand on my shoulder when needed. I also had the distinct sense that this feeling had come solely from me. I had followed Lilly's instructions and had actively looked for it inside myself. Although I couldn't recall ever feeling like this, it was at the same time, warm and familiar. Something old and forgotten just waiting to be rediscovered.

I floated into the shower and couldn't help but marvel at the water as it hit my skin. Time seemed to have slowed down and the hot spray running down my body in rivers, the rainbow light caught in the water droplets, my muscles surrendering to the feeling of it, was like magic. I stood with my eyes closed and let the water pour onto the top of my head and cascade down my body. I didn't want the feeling to end. I was at peace... content. Then Lilly's face came into my mind. It must have been the water rushing over my head that triggered my memory of her past life dream and the tragic drowning of a girl who had her whole life ahead of her.

Lilly's smiling face blurred and transformed into the girl with pale gold hair and I felt my stomach drop and my heart clench. My mind immediately jumped back into gear and time sped up again as I relived the panic I'd felt when the dream was recounted to me. The floating feeling turned to sinking and I could no longer see anything magical about the water at all. I wanted to get out of here.

I angrily screwed off the taps and fumbled for my towel. My head was firing thoughts like a machine gun. Each one had me climbing another step up, into a state of panic. It was like my building was on fire but I was running up the stairs toward the flames instead of moving to the exit in an orderly fashion. Every worried and desperate thought only added more fuel to the fire. It was a vicious cycle. The higher the flames grew, the more inflammatory and dangerous my thinking became. I didn't know what to do. I didn't want to lie to Lilly and keep my dream from her but I felt sure that this was a deal breaker. It didn't matter how loving, open or wise she was. I had messed up my past life badly, this one was a pretty decent mess too and it all amounted to me just not being good enough for someone like her – plain and simple.

I finished drying off and threw the towel to the floor. It landed in a limp pile along with my self-worth. I stared at my reflection in the misty bathroom mirror bracing myself against the sink. A stranger stared back at me. Not because I looked any different to what I had yesterday, but because I realised I barely knew myself at all. I felt like I was right back at square one. Like I had never seen Dr. Ferguson or made any progress with myself.

Jessica's face entered my head for the first time in a long time. She was laughing the way she had when she'd thought something was ridiculous. It made me want to punch the mirror. I pushed her image out of my head. Who was I kidding? Lilly was completely out of my league! I had stupidly thought I could heal and grow and become the man she deserves. But I was still so broken. I still had so much work to do. What did she even see in someone like me? I turned from the mirror in disgust and charged into my bedroom.

Throwing myself down on the unmade bed, I wondered if this was all just a part if it. Maybe I was so broken that the 'powers that be' had decided I needed extra help and had sent Lilly to me. I sat on that thought and examined it. It felt comfortable and true in an obvious sort of way. It was the most plausible explanation for everything that had happened. I laughed as the bitter pill slid down my throat and hit the pit of my knotted stomach. It was an ugly, defeated sound. But really, what had I expected? *I'm just as big a fool as I've always been.* As I lay on the creased, musty sheets, blinking into the dark, there was only one conclusion I could draw. It felt like razor blades in my heart to admit it but I couldn't keep lying to myself. No, Lilly and I weren't destined to be together. She was only present in my life to help me heal from all the terrible mistakes I had made. This entire whirlwind adventure, this impossible romance, had been nothing but a delusional dream. It was ironic that it had taken another dream for me to wake up and see it.

## Lilly

As I approached the front door of Elder Tunes' home, a swarm of butterflies took flight in my stomach. I didn't really know what I hoped to learn about my situation with Jay, only that there had been a nagging urge to follow up on my promise to show him Great-grandad's manuscript. I hadn't managed to find any answers in its pages for myself and now I was wondering how I could ask for his help without revealing the truth. It made me feel like a human spy on a covert mission.

The house was constructed from gigantic blocks of rough-hewn stone the colour of oyster shells. The sprawling, two-storey structure had been designed to fit in with the existing landscape, so instead of being rectangular, it was curved. Viewed from the air, it would look like a chalky smile carved into the landscape. Multiple panes of clear glass, set into pointed arches, repeated a pattern across the front wall. Each one was bordered by a line of small glass circles, as though the windows wore lustrous strings of pearls.

The book was heavy in my hands as I reached the top step, the sweat from my palms soaking into the parched leather. The imposing double doors were wide open and there didn't appear to be a door knocker or bell. I had the feeling the doors were rarely closed, negating the need. A capacious alabaster hallway stretched before me, two stories high and just as wide, making me feel like a tiny porcelain figurine. It travelled through to the back of the house and ended its journey, seemingly where it began, at an identical set of doors to the ones in front of me. They opened onto an ivory terrace that hugged the river bank where I could see emeralds winking on the water. A stiff breeze blew in, ballooning the sheer curtains up to the ceiling and then sucking them back down in white twists and flutters.

"Hello? Elder Tunes, it's Lilly Flights." My voice volleyed off the dove grey stone before being carried away on the wind. Teetering on the threshold, I could see slices of spacious rooms with soaring ceilings. The walls were the same blanched stone as the exterior and the floors were smooth, silver pearl limestone. Then a sweep of moving colour rounded an archway and flew straight towards me. It was a magnificent eagle, its enormous wings stretched, displaying its dappled plumage. They were every shade of sienna and cinnamon, combed with streaks of white. My breath caught at the sheer magnificence of her flight. She glided to a graceful stop, alighting on a twisted driftwood perch by the door and eyed me alertly. After taking my measure, she voiced a few short screeching noises and lifted her wings, gliding back the way she had come.

I obeyed the impulse to follow and found myself in a sparsely furnished, bone-white room where Elder Tunes sat in meditation. Three feet of empty air separated him from the meditation cushion on the floor. He floated peacefully, his short stubby legs folded and his rotund body looking like a lotus bud about to unfurl. His snowy hair stood up in unruly wisps, at odds with his tranquil expression. He appeared to be slightly transparent like a projection or a photograph that had been over-exposed. As I took a curious step closer, and then another, he looked not so much like flesh and blood, but luminous and translucent.

Elder Tunes was an Ascender; he had the gift

of using Source energy to lighten his corporeal form in order to levitate. I'd not seen this gift used often and never this close. It was as though he wasn't really there at all. Before I could act on my child-like urge to stick out my hand and see if I could wave it through him, he took in a full, deep breath and opened his eyes. They were as still and serene as the blue ice of a glacier; those deep, ancient layers that have witnessed the passing of a thousand years and in their stillness, have endured.

As he exhaled, he drifted back down onto his cushion, full colour flooding back to his body and he appeared solid once more. "Miss Flights, how good of you to come. I'm so pleased to see you again." A resplendent smile flooded his face and flowed into the joyous crinkles around his shining eyes. "I see the beautiful Aquila showed you in."

High above us, the eagle clutched onto a swing suspended from the ceiling. She beat her powerful wings and her leathery talons tightened on the perch to balance their immense weight.

"Hi, Elder Tunes. It's lovely to see you too." His elation lifted me like the strong sweep of Aquila's wings and I glanced up to admire her. Her watchful amber eyes traced my movements. "She's so beautiful," I said. "Does Aquila live here with you?"

"She came to me over twenty-five years ago," he said. "I hadn't thought our journey together would be such a long one, but she's still here, and so am I, for now.

When one departs, so will the other."

I knew of the spirit animals that accompanied the Elders. I had never met one though because they were usually invisible to all but their bonded Elder. They were said to stay by their sides in spirit form to lend strength and guidance and as reminders of the lessons they had mastered in this lifetime. Once a spirit animal appeared in corporeal form, it was a sign that this particular life was coming to an end and the Elder would soon transition to Utopia - the next world in a Soul's evolutionary cycle. Although, Elder Tunes seemed altogether too spritely for one approaching the end of a life.

"You have brought your Great-grandfather's manuscript! How wonderful! It's such a glorious day I thought we could have tea outdoors on the terrace, if you are agreeable."

"That sounds fantastic!" I beamed. Because it did. It could have been raining outside and I still would have agreed. Elder Tunes would have found the perfection in it. His joy was like a magnifying glass. He felt and saw the beauty and perfection in every tiny thing and displayed it for those who couldn't see it for themselves.

"It's this way," he said, straightening his waistcoat and pottering out into the colossal hall. Now I understood the need for so much space. Aquila's wing span was wider than my outstretched arms. She followed us onto the terrace, and working her mighty wings, soared skyward and disappeared into the glare of the sun.

Before us, the Ponderence River curved into the shape of a deep fish hook. Elder Tunes' home hugged the outermost bank and across the water, the Butterfly Gardens spilled onto the circular piece of land looking like a giant, floating centre piece in a lavish table setting. Reaching branches were laden with blossoms of fiery red and royal plum, interspersed with sprays of flourishing green. High laughter drifted across the water as children played together and couples strolled hand in hand along the rambling pathways, and sometimes, stole a few moments in a hidden leafy corner.

"Have a seat my dear," he gestured, pulling a heavy driftwood chair out from a matching table.

I sat on the bleached seat and laid the book on the smooth, silvery tabletop.

"May I?" he asked without preamble, looking at the manuscript.

"Of course." I slid it toward him and I thought he was going to levitate again with sheer delight.

"How marvellous," he sighed, running his chubby fingers over the cover and peeling it back to leaf through the brittle pages. He had produced a pair of warped, wire-framed spectacles that he sat crookedly on the end of his nose. He peered intently through the strong lenses as his eyes drank in page after page of flourishing script and intricate diagrams. "How much of this have you read, my dear?"

"About a third."

"And have you found what you were looking for?"

There was something in the directness of his question and the way his serene gaze went right through me that invited complete honesty. "No, I haven't." My reply bubbled up easily like water from a mountain spring.

He sat back in his chair and returned his attention to the manuscript. He didn't ask for an explanation and I didn't feel pressed to give one but my heart was beating a little faster as I silently watched him turn page after page. His face filled with excitement one moment and concentration the next. "You know," he began with an impish grin, "your Great-grandfather and my father were the best of friends."

"No, I didn't know that," I said with genuine surprise.

"Oh yes," he nodded smiling. "In fact, I have a journal that belonged to my father and it mentions Grayson Flights often and the progress of his extraordinary work. Although, I think the word *extraordinary* might be somewhat lacking considering what he managed to achieve."

His comment hinted at more than my Great-grandfather's academic contributions. "I'm not sure I understand you Elder Tunes."

"As you well know my dear, understanding is all a matter of changing one's perception so that what was once invisible, can now be seen." He picked up the manuscript and gently placed it before me, tapping his finger on the page he was just reading. "Now, what do you see?" he asked with twinkling eyes.

# TWENTY-FIVE

## Lilly

I stared down at the page and carefully read the words on the brittle parchment. It was much further into the book than I had managed to read. I completed the page and looked up at Elder Tunes expectantly. "I still don't understand," I said.

"That's because you are only seeing the words and trying to assign meaning to them. Words are just pointers to what's really going on in the background. See past the words to the true meaning."

I frowned and bent my head back to the task.

"You're trying too hard," he giggled. "Read this book like you would read a patient. Feel and see the content energetically, not intellectually," he instructed. "Feel the meaning with your heart. Don't try to read it with your head."

My facial expression softened and I opened my

heart connection as I would to examine someone. Warm energy flowed through me and as I watched the page through the eyes of love, faint marks began to come into view. Between the lines of flourishing script, more writing was materialising in deep green ink. I gasped as more and more words appeared on the page and Elder Tunes chuckled in delight.

"There!" he exclaimed triumphantly. "The truth can only be found through the eyes of love. Well done young Acolyte."

"But... what is this?" I stammered. "And how did you know this was here?"

"If you had been unable to see the script, I would be unable to answer that question, my dear. As it is though, you have passed with flying colours and now, I have quite a story to tell you. So, I think the time has come for a restorative cup of tea to recover yourself before I begin."

He bustled away inside and left me gaping at the manuscript. I began leafing through every page to see if there were more hidden passages. By the time Elder Tunes returned with a gleaming silver tea service, I had managed to only find three pages with the deep green script. He placed the tray down with an excited clatter and poured some steaming ruby red liquid into delicate china cups. It smelt like roses. "Here you are," he said, offering me the cup and saucer. It rattled slightly as I took it from him.

"Elder Tunes, what does this all mean?"

"Well Miss Flights, as I have told you, Grayson and my father, Thomas were the best of friends. They had grown up together and held each other in love and confidence and the highest regard. They shared everything as great friends do. Grayson was passionately devoted to his work and didn't marry until much later in life."

I picked up the feather light cup of gleaming ruby tea. A lone velvet red rose petal spiralled on the surface. "Yes, my Great-grandmother's name was Aurora. She was foreign, from Escartes, I believe."

Elder Tunes just smiled quietly and continued his story. "Yes well, until he met Aurora, Grayson was a very solitary man and Thomas had often worried that his friend would bury himself in his work and never find his true love. It was only after he married Aurora at sixty-four years of age that he confided the truth to Thomas." He sat back and seemed to look deeply into me before continuing. A tiny smile twitched at his lips as he took in a deep breath and said, "You see Lilly, Aurora was from Earth. She was human." He sighed and fixed upon me with his glacial blue eyes, measuring my response.

My teacup clattered onto the saucer and my hands flew to my cheeks with a gasp. "What? How can that be?"

"Apparently, Grayson had known who his true love was all along because he had met her when he was just eighteen years old. He was still in training as a Soul Guardian and was drawn to Aurora to assist her. A whirlwind romance ensued. His life's work was really about discovering a way for them to be together." He smiled at me expectantly but I could feel the blood draining from my face and dizziness washing over me in waves. "My dearest girl, I know this is shocking news but there is really no need for alarm. Besides, if you continue to swoon, I'm not sure this frail old body would have the strength to pick you up should you collapse," he chuckled. Although he was trying to make light of my shock, there was compassion in his expression. It said that he remembered the roller coaster of emotions that chases youth; the twists and loops that make the inexperienced dizzy.

"I, I don't know what to say," I stammered. "Does my family know about this?"

"From what I have read in Thomas' journal, I believe only Grayson, Aurora and Thomas knew the truth."

I felt like a swarm of butterflies had invaded my body and were beating their wings against my insides in a terrified frenzy, trying to get out. I tried to comprehend the enormity of what I'd just heard. When I finally spoke, my voice came out in a strangled croak. "Are you telling me that Aurora could see Grayson when he was called to her as a Soul Guardian?"

"Presumably, yes," he affirmed. "It's unlikely that they fell in love without ever meeting, wouldn't you say?" He was thoroughly amused by my shocked state and smiled broadly at me while he waited for my mind to catch up.

My head was reeling. *Could this really be true? Could my Great-grandfather have walked the same path that I was walking now with Jay? And had he found a way to be united with his love?* I was completely stunned. Did Elder Tunes somehow guess at my situation, or worse still, did he know? How in the world could he know? I'd only met him recently at the ball and he'd been so interested in seeing the manuscript. Perhaps it was just innocent curiosity. He had, after all, inherited Thomas' journal and knew that my Great-grandfather had brought Aurora here from Earth. Perhaps he just wanted to see if the manuscript held the secret to how. "So why are you telling me, Elder Tunes?"

"An intuitive hunch," he winked. "Had you not needed to know this information, I don't believe Grayson's instructions would have been revealed to you. We are always given what we need at the time we need it."

*'At the time we need it.'* So he did know! But how? In that moment, I wanted to tell him the truth about Jay. I wanted to free all the hysterical butterflies beating inside my head and my heart. I wanted him to tell me that it was all going to be okay, that I wasn't doing anything wrong, that this was my destined path. Instead, I fought down the impulse. "Is that what the green script is? Instructions?" I asked bewildered.

Elder Tunes nodded. "At a glance, it seems your Great-grandfather has documented the process for bringing a Soul from one dimension into another. Fascinating and utterly brilliant!" he hooted.

I was dumbfounded and Elder Tunes was elated. At this point I couldn't have been more shocked and confused. I resisted the urge to slap myself across the face or dunk my head in the Ponderence River. "But Elder Tunes, doesn't this defy some spiritual law? Or at the very least, break the Guardian's Code?" I asked shaking my head.

He looked at me thoughtfully whilst still grinning. He leaned his rotund body forward, propped his stubby elbows on the table and steepled his fingers to his lips, as though he were about to pray. "Which spiritual law might that be, Miss Flights?" He sat perfectly still and waited for my reply.

"I don't know," I answered, still shaking my head. "A Soul cannot reincarnate to Panacea until they heal themselves of all their wounds, forgive and gain true compassion."

"You're absolutely right of course," he agreed and said nothing more. He just looked into me with those glacial eyes. They were clear and glistening on the surface, but if you looked deeply enough, you could see layer upon layer of remembering. Of adventures had, beauty beheld, secrets kept, all preserved in the still, quiet place within his memory. They held such love and compassion that it felt as though a key had been placed in a lock to my own mind and slowly turned with a satisfying click. Just being in his presence opened all the places inside where I'd felt scared and unsure. The unconditional love that flowed from him began to soothe away my tension and weariness, seeping into my being in a flood of warmth and softness.

I surrendered to it and allowed the impassable mountains within, with their sharp rocks and treacherous footholds, to smooth into endless, open plains. I felt a strength return to me that I hadn't known was missing. It began to dawn on me; a new perspective that made me spring from my chair and throw my arms around his neck, giving back as much love as I could. "Thank you Elder Tunes," I whispered as I buried my face in his warm shoulder.

"All right now, there, there," he chuckled and patted my back. "It seems you have a bit of reading to do in light of this discovery." I drew back from him and he took both my hands in his and gave a reassuring squeeze. "May all that you are and all that you do, be light and love my dear." Then he dazzled me with his beautiful smile as a small tear of joy rolled down his rosy cheek.

As Elder Tunes had waved goodbye from the doorway of his alabaster house, he'd looked liked a firecracker in a snow tunnel. I was bursting with excitement as well. Everything he'd shared with me was settling into my bones and becoming real. If he had guessed at the truth of my situation, he hadn't pressed me and didn't seem to share any of my trepidation. I hadn't realised what a tight reign I'd kept on my feelings until he had shown me a ray of hope. For the first time, I allowed myself to really let go and imagine what a life with Jay would look like. What it would mean to him to live in my world of love and beauty and peace. What it would feel like to walk down the street, hand in hand; to feel his arms around me at night; to become lost in his beautiful eyes whenever I wanted. I was bright and full with imagining.

I lay on my bed and hugged the manuscript to my heart, it's worn leather soft and smooth beneath my fingertips, its musty scent signalling comfort and purpose. It held the secrets that would make dreams possible. My eyes glistened with gratitude for all the moments that had led me to this one. For the moments that had inspired my Great-grandfather to hold on to his faith. His enduring love and devotion would be my beacon. My unwavering, guiding light. I would decipher his instructions and learn the way to bring Jay to Panacea.

All that remained was for Jay to grow into the truth that he was discovering more and more each day. I had witnessed him bloom in the harshest conditions and open himself in spite of the pain he'd endured. He was strong and beautiful and he would heal. I thought of him in the meadow, radiating love and light; a glimpse of who he would become. There was no doubt in my mind now that this was our destiny. We were meant to find each other. Our connection was an unbreakable bond that conquered time, space and even death. I would wait for him to chase away the remaining shadows that prevented his light from shining as brilliantly as it could. I would hold his heart and he would hold mine until he learnt that when nothing exists inside of you but love, the whole universe can't help but reflect it back.

# DISCOVER WHERE IT ALL BEGAN...

# GET THE FIRST BOOK FOR FREE

Visit www.gabriellea-author.com to receive your **FREE** copy of *The Guardian's Soul*, book zero in *The Lost Souls series*, plus your very own full colour illustrated copy of The Soul Guardian's Code, plus a replica of the original monograph indexing all known go-lite powers. Get everything you need to dive into Lilly's world and discover what happened 15 years ago when memories of Jay and Lilly's previous life together were still fresh in her mind... that is, until a powerful spell changed everything.

# LIKE THIS BOOK?
# YOU CAN MAKE A BIG DIFFERENCE

Plucking up the courage to publish my book after procrastinating for ten years, (yes, I'm serious) has been a terrifying and life-changing experience, and one that is only just beginning. So, I wanted to thank you for reading my debut novel and tell you that it literally means the world to me because I'm working very hard to make full-time writing my world.

You can support me on my journey, and all the other authors and artists you love, by posting honest reviews. We depend on reviews for our work to be validated by the retailers and noticed by others who might like what we have to offer. So, if you want to spread some love today, take a few minutes to leave a star rating wherever you purchased this book. I will be sending you a big smile and much gratitude if you do.

If I've learnt nothing else in life, I know that we all have a duty to listen to our heart's desires and create the life and world that we want. When we're happy and doing what we love, we shine light into the world. I hope this book has brought a little light into yours.

Gabriel x
www.gabriellea-author.com

**1.** I accept Soul Guardianship as a blessed gift of service. I offer my dreamscape as a place of healing and support to all Souls.

**2.** I will offer strength and support in times of struggle and remain a compassionate and impartial observer.

**3.** I respect every Soul's destiny, the experiences they have created and the lessons they have chosen to learn.

**4.** I see only light in the heart of every Soul and help them to remember, recognise and bring forth that light.

**5.** Healing is a choice that each Soul must make. I will only guide those who ask for my guidance and honour the free will of all Souls.

**6.** I honour the precious life of each and every Soul in my care and place none above another.

**7.** I perform my duty without judgement. Every Soul must tread their own path to knowing in their own time.

**8.** I vow to fulfil my purpose to help other Souls evolve, just as I was once helped to evolve.

**9.** May love guide me and light keep me as I continue the quest that my ancient ancestors began.

**10.** This I vow: No Soul will ever be alone. No voice will go unheard. I am a Guardian of Souls, a light in the darkness, and I will watch over them.